Truth To Tell

Mavis Cheek was born and grew up in Wimbledon. She failed her eleven plus twice and was put in the B stream of a secondary modern school, where she tried, completely unsuccessfully, to learn to become a good and dutiful clerk/typist. She left school at sixteen with no academic qualifications and began her working life as a receptionist for the contemporary art publishers, Editions Alecto. London was buzzing in the mid sixties and Mavis graduated to their gallery in Albemarle Street, where she worked with such contemporary artists as David Hockney, Allen Jones, Patrick Caulfield, Gillian Ayres and Bridget Riley.

After twelve years at Editions Alecto, Mavis decided to take a degree. She went to Hillcroft College for Women where she graduated in Arts with distinction. Shortly after this her daughter Bella was born and she began her writing career in earnest. Journalism and travel writing at first, then short stories, and eventually, in 1988, her novel *Pause Between Acts* was published by Bodley Head and won the *She/John Menzies* First Novel Prize.

Mavis Cheek now lives and works in Wiltshire.

Truth To Tell

MAVIS CHEEK

arrow books

Published by Arrow Books 2011

2 4 6 8 10 9 7 5 3 1

First published in Great Britain in 2010 by Hutchinson

Arrow Books
Random House, 20 Vauxhall Bridge Road,
London SW1V 2SA

www.randomhouse.co.uk

Addresses for companies within The Random House Group Limited can be
found at: www.randomhouse.co.uk/offices.htm

The Random House Group Limited Reg. No. 954009

A CIP catalogue record for this book
is available from the British Library

ISBN 9780099547525

The Random House Group Limited supports The Forest Stewardship
Council (FSC), the leading international forest certification organisation.
All our titles that are printed on Greenpeace approved FSC certified paper
carry the FSC logo. Our paper procurement policy can be found at:
www.randoomhouse.co.uk/environment

Typeset by SX Composing DTP, Rayleigh, Essex
Printed and bound in Great Britain by
CPI Bookmarque Ltd, Croydon, CR0 4TD

For Vee and our own Venetian *passeggiata*

So absolutely good is truth, truth never hurts
The teller.

Browning

It is not fair to thrust Truth upon people when they don't
expect it. Only the very generous are ready for Truth
Impromptu.

Christopher Morley

One

TIPPING POINTS ARE peculiar things. One minute the
thought or the desire is not on your radar, the next it is not
only on your radar, it is looming so large it blots out almost
everything else. And a tipping point, as Malcolm Gladwell
says in his book, helpfully entitled *The Tipping Point*, is
irresistible. I'm not sure if you can strictly have a tipping
point for one, and certain it is that I was more or less alone
in my conviction that something must be done, but hearts
and minds did follow – eventually. Much as some people
are quietly trotting down the road towards Damascus,
perfectly happy to tell those Christians a thing or two, and
they suddenly get God. I got the next best thing. A bomb
blast called Truth. When did that go from our lives?

* * *

Robert was fulminating in front of the television. Again.
When we first met, of course, both of us wore anti-
apartheid badges, got knocked on the head by a passing
policeman in Grosvenor Square and some of our best
friends were vegans. But marriage, children, a nice house in
a nice area and the settled ease of middle-class life reduced
the political passions. It didn't mean we weren't still
committed to good, liberal beliefs, it just meant that we

1

weren't going to chain ourselves to the railings for them. The ballot box was sufficient. But it was the ballot box that let us down – the ballot box that was, indirectly, to blame for my personal tipping point. And faith in the democratic process would never be the same again. Nor, probably, would I. If you consider marriage, or its unendorsed equivalent, as a microcosm of the world it might help to understand why the application of Truth could be so devastating. Try it. Go on, I dare you. Try being truthful to your nearest and dearest for just one week. It will be what the Chinese so delicately call *interesting*.

Back to Robert and me. We were both supporters of the Labour Party. As it segued into being New Labour we tacitly accepted the change and went on voting the same way. One day the proper voice would be heard. Then came Blair and Iraq and everything changed. Especially for Robert, who suddenly, in his middle years, re-engaged with his persona of a scarf-flinging, radical Essex student. I didn't know whether to join in or stand by with an ice pack. And though I felt a certain amount of pride in my beloved husband's resumed passionate stance, I also felt a certain amount of alarm; politicians and their deceits – *his* politicians – created a dynamic that was quite enough to give him a coronary. 'These are the dangerous years,' my mother told me lugubriously, 'for blocked arteries.' For which piece of helpful information I naturally thanked her effusively.

'Liar, liar, pants on fire . . .' Robert shouted at the earnest face of the then prime minister. 'Smug bastard.' Then he started stabbing at the air, saying, 'Tell the truth, tell the truth, tell the truth.' From what I could make out, this particular rant was with regard to the lying, scheming snake of a twisted politician who had, it seemed, signed up for abortion rights when in power and then converted to Catholicism when out of it. Added to the Bastard's assertions about weapons of mass destruction and saying children should be educated in state schools while sending his own to a select establishment, this new outrage of political hypocrisy – otherwise known as telling lies – consigned him to further bouts of Robert's new-found wrath.

This evening Robert's ear tips were pinker than I had ever seen them. For a moment I stood behind him, fascinated, then I said very loudly, 'Red or white?' and he stopped jerking about and said 'Red. Thanks. What are we having?' Normal service was resumed and we sat down opposite each other in the kitchen for pasta and salad. We do not have a television in the kitchen. We did, once, have a television in the kitchen but since it reduced both of us to something akin to Bacon's screaming popes – it was banned. Our children, properly reductive members of the family, in their late and bumptious teens, begged to have the thing restored on the grounds that we now expected them to talk. This seemed symptomatic of the middle-class, well-brought-up child; the idea that they think they are at the centre of the universe. 'We don't have the telly because it makes your father and I argue,' I told them firmly. 'You certainly don't have to talk if you don't want to.' And then, with that blinding moment of fear that comes from too many programmes on the radio about child psychology, I scuppered my ascendant position by adding, 'But of course we'd love it if you did . . .' And looking from daughter to son very earnestly. You do wonder how they learn to roll their eyes in that particular way.

Fortunately tonight it was only the ex-prime minister of England who had suggested that when he said black he really meant white, and Robert's response would be containable. If he had been followed by the outgoing president of the United States, one George Dubya Bush, coming to the screen with one of many pronouncements things might have got nasty in the coronary department. Things having hotted up considerably on both the political and financial home front over the last few months gave Robert a new zest for rage. We survived much of the monetary catastrophe most probably because both our children were finished with university and off to pastures new for a few months. They were expanding their experiences, going peacefully, and travelling where they might learn to be good citizens of the world. In other words, they had been dispatched afar to give their long-suffering, middle-class, never-say-boo-to-a-goose-or-a son-or-a-daughter parents a break. Educational costs were over. With one bound we were free.

Which nicely left a gap for Robert's sudden renewed passion for the outing of hypocrisy and the denunciation of lies which had arrived very suddenly and not quite exited stage left and chased by a bear. Thus we were on best behaviour. With each other, with ourselves and our psyches. We did not want to waste a minute of our precious freedom. A row between us would be foolish. So I, naturally enough, shut up. One of us had to. Blessed are the peacemakers. Years of marriage allows you to put yourself somewhere on the baby-slopes of the Mount along with Blessed are the Meek.

But at least, as the pasta and wine went down, Robert's fascinating ear tips slowly returned to their usual pale hue. This was the cooling-off period, similar to what happens in a gym after a workout. After a quarter of a century of marriage you know about such things. Just as a deep-sea diver needs to reorient his system before returning to life above the waves, so did Robert need a period of gentle relocation before normal service was resumed and this certainly happened much more quickly now that our delightful children were not around. They enjoyed winding their father up mercilessly. When our departing prime minister gave his Sedgefield farewell speech the wind-up register tightened; the very words 'I did so out of belief' were enough to bring on a hernia, repeated as they were with lip-smacking gusto, and often, by both Tassie and Johnno. For the next few days, if ever they were party to criticism, they would fold their hands as if in prayer and say, 'I did so out of belief . . .' Given that and its cheering result, what they would now do with the world in financial turmoil and bankers' words (we can't be blamed for others' greed) was best not contemplated. At least now, without them here, I could control the temperature. Though there was – looking back – already at that point a creeping sense of resentment for this service to harmony. Blessed are the peacemakers, for sure, but do they always have to be the women? Yes, according to Robert and a good number of other thinking people, Tony Blair was a liar – I was sure of it – but I couldn't, really, see the point of allowing it to bring on an aneurism. Politicians lied, was all I thought, and the public pretty well universally put them, along with journalists, at the bottom of the honesty heap. Now bankers and hedge-funders, the Allen Stanfords and Bernard Madoffs, joined them as the lowest of the low. QED. But we all lied, didn't we? That was the little seed of a pea of a thought that lodged itself in the rational part of my mind during these trying months without my knowing where it would eventually lead me. We lied. We all lied. Didn't we?

That evening I risked a joke. 'What do you have to do to make a little fortune nowadays?' Robert looked at me, and then softened. 'What?' I smiled, it was working. 'Start with a big one,' I said joyfully. The result was reasonable. He countered with the joke about Blair and Bush and we talked about the bottom of the heapers and their lies in a calm way until the subject gradually moved on to the Griffiths' new dog. A small, yapping, white thing of which, on the rare occasions the yapping ceased, it was hard to say which end was which. It was always good for a conversation. United, we, in distaste. Lies and liars were forgotten and it would probably have been just another evening in for the Porters of Wimbledon if Hugo Gibson hadn't rung while I was still feeling slightly raw about blessed are the peacemakers. A fulminating husband who may or may not have blocked arteries is a disturbing presence and I had – in the beautiful fading April light – hoped for an evening of domestic harmony. Quiet and unexpectant I sat on at the table and sipped my wine and thought about the summer ahead and what it would be like for just the two of us. Nice, I thought – it *will* be nice. Then Robert picked up the phone and mouthed, 'It's Hugo . . .' And everything changed.

I don't know why. Maybe the bottle of Chianti was to blame for being strong and delicious. Maybe it was the Zen Moment of Rightness when everything turns. Or maybe – maybe – I was just plain fed up with my husband's holier-than-them attitude towards honesty. I'd seen him stuff drachmas into slot machines and get off speeding points with the aid of a good solicitor. I knew.

Every year Hugo, the chairman, took his cream of team at International IT Systems (UK division) on a bonding jaunt. This year, despite the apparent total collapse of absolutely everything mercantile, was to be no different. This was, it seems, because ITS (UK) held most of its contracts with governments. Personally, looking at governments, it didn't feel like they were any safer than any other outfit, but it seemed that they were. Well, not Iceland, obviously, but India and China and some of the EU. So the bonding exercise was still on. And every year the wives went too.

We wives scarcely saw each other apart from this week-long event, so it was, as our friends across the pond would have it (and ITS (UK) was an American subsidiary), a nice chance to meet up and bond, too. For a whole week we stayed in some magical, exotic place while our menfolk did unspeakable things with jet skis and golf balls and the like. Thank heaven the days of Iron John were over – the brief flirtation with the Arizona Desert and the mythopoetical male's search for modern initiation ritual was appalling, including, as it did, quite a lot of headbutting, little laughter and manly unshaven chins. Now we had reverted to the usual gender pattern. We women starved ourselves before we left home, sank holes in the family finances in order to dress ourselves creatively, and then drank and ate too much while away. We avoided talking about whose husband was earning the most points (oh yes, there were points) and we soaked up the killer sun by the pool lushed out on disgusting drinks. It was hell on earth and I had never, in all ten years of Robert's being Hugo's deputy, managed to enjoy it or get out of it. It was just a bright smile, wear that saffron floaty thing and your gold sandals and drink your cocktails for the duration. In the weeks running up to our going I was, like the others, on a strict diet, and in the weeks after our going, just like the others, I was also on a strict diet. Now, as Robert began to talk with false good cheer to Hugo, I looked down at my plate. I had left nothing at all for Miss Manners except a slight covering of sauce – and we were due to fly in twelve days. Yup. I was still eating tagliatelle. Slathered in cream and mushrooms. It was intolerable. But even more intolerable – as I cocked my ear to listen – Robert was lying. He was on the telephone to his immediate superior, and he was telling very, very big porkies. Blair-sized porkies, I thought.

Robert was not what one might call a man's man – though he did like motor racing, which gave him an honourable status among the true sports-loving blokes without enticing him into the sportier realms of actually knocking a ball around, of whatever size, or, when the back muscles went, spread betting on Indian cricket matches at two in the morning. Thus, although he was by no means a fully subscribing male in terms of team-building machismo, he could dredge up enough of it to convince his peers. Bravely, he always managed to overcome this macho-inadequacy and enact the team spirit with considerable aplomb. I both did and did not admire him for this, but mostly I was grateful. His gung-ho enthusiasm for the horrible, team-building experience meant that his job was assured and that our children could afford to go travelling in safety while we continued to live well. The good life based entirely on deceit. 'You're a great team player, Robbie,' Hugo would pronounce as we parted each year at the airport, and Robbie (no one else was allowed to call him this) and he would do a high five (whatever happened to slapping each other heartily on the back?) and walk off proudly with their pumpingly masculine arms around their wives' expanded waistlines.

It was shameful, really, when you put it alongside the radical Nina and Robert of yesteryear. But this, of course, is what being an adult means. First you sow your wild oats and later they become prunes and All-Bran. To us, the middle classes, growing up and taking your place in the

8

world meant becoming the comfortable bastion against anarchy. I had long come to terms with this. I reckoned that since I had worked in government and paid taxes, worked tirelessly in the home, produced and reared two perfectly decent – pause to consider Johnno, move on quickly – citizens of our nation who would one day be producers of national wealth – pause, consider Johnno again, move on even more quickly – while helping out at the local school and all the other stuff that the middle-class mum is heiress to, I had earned my place in the world. Robert and I remained married largely because – like women through the ages – I had given him the false belief that he ran things, and because – well – better to say it as not – we could afford to be comfortable. And although the world was now in financial and fiscal turmoil, the Porters of Wimbledon were unlikely to find themselves struggling. A little wing-clipping here and there probably, but nothing major. And it would, could, all have continued like that, had that tiny pea of a seed of uncertainty not begun to grow into a tipping point.

As usual, I heard Robert say in his best breezy tone, 'Hugo. All set?' and obviously Hugo said that he was, so Robert added with absolute conviction and toe-curling bonhomie, 'Yup – really looking forward to it too. No, no, never been to Florida – strange to say – fantastic, absolutely fantastic. Oh, absolutely. Home of our fathers. It'll be good to see where the whole operation began. Really good.' I thought, squirming, that he did not have to be quite so apparently thrilled. And then Hugo must have said that he had been to Florida and that it *was* fabulous because Robert said again, 'Well – we're both really looking forward to the trip. Really.' Then he listened, making little grunting noises of agreement, and I could picture him nodding before saying, in a much more serious tone now, 'Oh sure, sure –

given the present climate – it probably does seem a bit profligate. But on the other hand it does what it's supposed to do and we get a lot of mileage out of it –' He listened again. Grunted again. And then finished with great good cheer. 'How's Lorna? Good, good. Yes – Nina is fine. She can't wait either. Loves it. Just loves it.' And then he put down the phone and groaned.

'Liar, liar, pants on fire,' I said quietly. But Robert did not so much as laugh, dammit, which goes to show just how queasy the whole situation really was.

'What was Hugo saying?'

'We may have to tone it all down in future. Given the state of things generally. He thinks it looks a bit self-indulgent for the company.'

'Well, at least that's something,' I said. 'Florida! Jesus H Christ. I don't know how you stopped yourself laughing. Liar, liar.'

He did not look at all amused. He merely picked up his newspaper and finished his glass of wine.

At least for the rest of the evening and during the ten o'clock news, Robert remained subdued and somewhat under rather than atop his high horse. He was obviously irritated by what I had said, but aware of the truth of it. This is a confounding position to put your partner in. On the one hand you have dealt out personal criticism, on the other you have allowed them no room for manoeuvre. Similarly, although I understood, I was irritated myself. I couldn't quite get the contradiction out of my mind. The problem was, it seemed, that like nicking the office pencils and not calling it theft, truth was a matter of degree. I was just as guilty of this application of truthfulness as Robert, as most people, really. And how could you expect a politician, journalist or banker to be truthful, when you were just as much a liar in your day-to-day life? Not much of a journey from there to a grey-haired political grandee assuring the House that his expenses were all in order and that to continue his awfully important political work he needed the rest and relaxation of a visit to a lap-dancing club from time to time.

I went to bed that night with the seed of a pea even more increased in size and I pondered upon this ambiguity, little thinking how the radical Nina of yesteryear would surface as a result of the experience. I saw the innocence of my youth in which I could firmly adhere to all that agitprop because I didn't actually have to do anything about it. Elbert Hubbard's 'Live truth instead of professing it' recurred and recurred during the night. Beside me Robert slept, easy breathing, still and at peace. I so wanted to be like him but at three o'clock I was still churning. Elbert Hubbard is better known for his other, more famous apophthegm: 'Life is just one damn thing after another.' A slick saying which I just added to the pile as I searched for the comfort of sleep. Sometimes you can know too many such quotes. I have a very good memory for them. My employer and friend, Brian Donnolly, inappropriately nick-named Brando, once asked me to find where the latter quotation came from and I'd waded through quite a number of Elbert's sayings to get to it. The one about truth lodged and stayed. And kept me thinking, even in my fitful dreams, for most of that night.

Two

Fletcherise: to chew thoroughly.

Mitford Mathew's *Dictionary of Americanisms*, 1956

NOT A GREAT deal has changed over the centuries, alas. One of the great benefits of the secure middle-class life is that it is still, usually, though not always, the husband who brings home the bacon, which leaves the secure middle-class wife free to work at what she chooses. She might be a barrister, she might be a teacher – or she might – as in my case – be a researcher. Middle-class wives tend not to work as cleaners or food packers or shop assistants (unless it's in a friend's boutique) and when governments urge wives and mothers to get off benefits and go back to work even though they have small children, generally speaking they are not offering them jobs like mine but jobs like – well – cleaners, food packers and shop assistants. Bad enough that one cleans the lavatory in one's own home but tipping up for work every day and cleaning someone else's? Who, given the choice, would select that as a job option? I pinched myself nearly every day that I was blessed with both the good life and a friend who wrote books and was lazy and was prepared to pay me. And if you think this is about to be a story concerning the loss of my comfort zone and a denouement in which I end up cleaning toilets and Robert lies around drinking himself into an unemployed stupor and watching daytime TV, forget it. This did not happen. It seldom, in the real world, does. In the real world all that happens is that those very far down the pit get pushed down further, while those of us who are up somewhere near the daylight merely have to switch allegiance from Waitrose to Netto and possibly get rid of the second BMW.

Brando had made a fortune out of a book on quirky words and their origins. It was one of those Christmas loo books that sold phenomenally well and got taken up by America, then the rest of the world. Generally it was thought that many people owned it and few had read it. Brando did not mind in the least. Millions of copies were sold worldwide and the fortune he made was well invested. If the credit crunch affected him, it too was likely to be uncomfortable rather than devastating. As a man who had been to a minor public school, become a minor actor and starred in a minor television soap, he could not have been more delighted to live out his days in a major self-indulgent pastime. He was lucky. The book came about while he idled and jotted away time on the set of the soap. He produced, with my help, one or two follow-ups, which did quite well, and cheerfully dilettanted his way through life. And although he was approached by the publisher of *Catchy Words and Quirky Phrases* to produce another gold-spinner, he never did. He wanted to indulge himself in something altogether darker and more adult. He chose to devote his entire working life (something of a misnomer considering plumbers and farmers and firepersons) to a series of gazetteers on the seamier side of tourisms' most revered shrines. We were currently working on a really good one, which was, of course, Venice.

One of the joys about Robert's job was that it left me enough free time to do what I liked best, which was to poke my nose into anything, anything at all – I just loved rushing about and looking things up and hunting things down and cracking it. I worked as a parliamentary researcher before the children and that is a real challenge – when someone stands up in the House and declares that black is most definitely black, you then have to speed off and find something that proves – conclusively – that it is – largely – white. And if it does give you a slightly cynical view of the veracity of facts, it is a great way to earn a living. Already my radicalism must have been on the wane, for politics then were more a matter of expediency than truth and I rose to the challenge of finding a way. My mother, on hearing of my appointment, just said that I was bound to be good at it as I always was a nosy parker in need of winning an argument.

After marriage and during children, Brando had used me occasionally and it was nice to get out and about. Now, with more free time and less to do, Brando's gazetteer scheme was perfect. We did a bit of preliminary selection – I mean, there was no point, really, in looking for horrible things to write about in Zurich or Bonn, whereas Istanbul or Berlin were rich in all those lovely things that make you shudder and be so glad that you live now . . . Once the preliminary stuff was complete, we began. There was no payroll exactly – I gave him a list of my expenses once in a while, an approximate number of hours I thought I'd spent, and he would settle it more or less accurately. I can say, quite truthfully, that I never fiddled anything. I'd always supposed that this was because I had more than enough to live on – but since our own dear political expenses scandal, I realised that it was because I was not greedy. I was many things that I would rather not be but that made up for some of them. To know that you are not greedy is a very wonderful thing. In my moments of bleakness, when I sit in a heap and think how horrible I am, that is what I cling to.

Pathetic, I know, but we all need a spar on the water. The sporadic nature of Brando's payments to me meant that it was never going to be a full-time job, which was perfect. Robert was rather impressed with the amount I was paid per hour, and mighty impressed with the efficient look of my office upstairs. Apart from that he never asked any questions. Just as I never asked him any questions about IT. With the obvious difference that I know nothing of it and could frame not one.

Brando's plan was that I would do a bit of research, find out something interesting – the seamier or more grisly the better – and then he would go off to discover more about it. There was nothing new under the sun about any of these places – Rome to Lisbon, Athens to Paris – such dirt as existed had been dished times aplenty – but putting it all together was a good idea and would probably do well. It kept Brando busy and on the move and we liked each other's company. And if I occasionally wished that it was me who caught the plane and flew off to see the results of my research for myself, I never gave it more than a fleeting thought. Brando took a few photographs, wrote notes about what he saw, indulged in a bit of high life, before coming back to his overstuffed house in Kensington and handing it all over to me to turn into reasonable prose. After setting up each place we agreed that Venice was by far the most rewarding of all the seamy sites we'd chosen. There never was such a city, historically, for laying clean satin sheeting over mouldering filth.

The day after the Hugo phone call Brando and I were in our favourite restaurant for lunch. Had I so wished I could have had lunch in style most days and called it work, but you soon learn that a long and large midday meal leads to crying when stepping onto the bathroom scales. A very good lesson about the value of riches – one which Venetians, certainly, never learned despite all their sumptuary laws and bracelet burning – is that everything does, indeed, pall. If there was a downside to Brando's way of life it was that he could have anything – well, nearly – that his heart desired, which took away that delicious condiment of life – delayed gratification. True, Robert and I had a life that was a little dulled by comfort – but not enough to make us want to do anything about it.

So, to keep its sparkle I agreed to lunch with Brando rarely and any other meetings happened at my home. After these meetings I brought forth the occasional piece of order out of chaos, but I think we both knew that the travel series would probably never be finished. It was all far too cosy, far too much fun for either of us to wish it. And just in case you might misconstrue any of this, Brando is indefatigably gay. And I do mean indefatigably. And when I say gay I do not mean cheery. Most gay men like to have one close female friend and I was his. We had been in each other's lives for a long time and we knew each other very well. We met when I was waitressing and at university. He was ten years my senior, resting and able to keep one cup of coffee going for an entire afternoon. He liked to look out of the window at the passing possibilities, as he put it, and he made me laugh a lot. He was beautiful then but something of a picture in the attic now. Robert tolerated him and Brando tolerated Robert, they seldom met, and that kept everything smooth.

Brando poured me a glass of very pale greenish wine, the scent of which was instant and betokened a very nice bottle of whatever it was. Some kind of Soave, I guessed, but I didn't embark on that conversation – which would have been a long one – as there were other things I wanted to talk about. As we sipped and waited for our food I told him about the anomaly of truth in our household and how it was like a bit of grit working away inside me. What had begun fairly flippantly was becoming much more serious. 'You see, I've started to think about truth and how we all lie – and once you start thinking about anything in a compulsive manner, it just gets worse.'

'Yes,' he said, 'I do know what you mean.' He looked around searchingly.

'I do not mean sex, Brando, I mean little things that go circling in your head and buzz away like a needy wasp until you do something to settle them.'

'Isn't life hard enough?' he said. He held up his glass and squinted through it. 'Why make problems for yourself? Truth? What's that? I taste this wine as one thing, you taste it as another. Truth, as dear Byron said as he sat on the banks of the Grand Canal, truth is stranger than fiction.' He sipped and winked through the glass again. 'And anyway – as you say – none of us is wholly truthful.' He looked over the rim of his glass now, wide-eyed with pretended innocence. 'Not even me with you. And I have absolutely nothing to lose.'

'Yes you do.'

'What?'

'People finding out that you wear a toupee . . .'

The surprise on his face was, for once, genuine. 'You know that?'

'Of course.'

'And you never said you knew. How very dishonest of you. And anyway, it's called a hairpiece.'

'Brando! I was being discreet. That's unfair.'

'No it isn't. Anyway – I thank you for your – discretion. We'll call it that. Which, I opine, is even more dishonest.'

'Sensitive, actually. But – since we're on the subject – I've always wanted to know how you manage when – you know –'

'No,' he said, even more guilelessly, 'I do *not* know – and neither – ever – given our predilections – will you.' He leaned forward and chinked his glass to mine. Our calves' liver, pink and juicy with blood, arrived and we began to eat.

'Why aren't we having it *à la veneziana*?' I asked.

'Onions,' he said, smiling at someone over my shoulder, 'are not pleasant accompaniments to the finer things in life. Those Venetians were – are – an unrefined lot – quite prepared to get down and dirty in the cause of their city – including smelling of cooked onions in an embrace. Oh, what a feast we will find when we dig even deeper. Theirs is probably the least truthful and the most grubbily interesting of all those city states. Wonderfully dreadful.' He went on smiling over my shoulder.

'You hope,' I said. 'I've always loved the place and never thought of it as grubby before. Splendidly seamy, perhaps. Gorgeously gross. But not plain grubby. Robert and I had some very nice times there before the children –'

'*Nice?*'

'Well, maybe a little bit more than nice. She's sexy, she's the serenely, satinate Serenissima – the grand deceiver.'

'Absolutely. So, my dear Nina Fauntleroy, immersing ourselves in Venice is rather like living within one big lie, yes? And you'll enjoy that in your new-found revelatory mode. She lies, she cheats, she enchants – the perfect courtesan. Can you take her on if you're feeling so pious?'

'I wish you'd stop addressing me as if I were a nun.' I poured more wine into my glass. 'I suppose there are deep and dark bits – of course there are – but I've always thought of her mostly as a beautiful place, absolutely romantic. But sexy, too.'

'Hmm,' he said, giving the passing waiter – a young man with a square jaw and stubble – the eye. 'Exactly. The Great Seducer. We shall have some fun with her.' He smiled over my shoulder. 'As you should with all the best whores.' The waiter turned, Brando smiled, the waiter smiled back nervously. Brando raised his voice a little. 'She is so divinely spellbinding that you'd forgive her anything.' Impossible to say of whom this was addressed – La Serenissima or the rapidly retreating young man. Brando turned back to me a little reluctantly.

'Not for you,' I said.

'What do you know,' he said, in mock contempt, 'about putting yourself about?'

'One day I might shock you and have a go myself.'

'You? Mrs Purity? Don't make me laugh . . .'

Fauntleroy? Purity? He certainly knew how to make cosy goodness seem a barb of inadequacy.

'Florida,' I said later, gazing mournfully at the empty wine bottle. '*Florida* . . . I just can't bear the thought of it.' I ate the last piece of cheese with a flourish of disdain.

'You must do your wifely duty, Mrs Porter.'

'But Florida, Brando. And Robert just lied to Hugo down the phone, smooth as butter, and said how much we – *we* – were looking forward to it. One minute he was jumping up and down at the iniquity of our beloved ex-prime minister and the next he was telling Hugo we actually wanted to go to the bloody place.'

'Ever been?'

'Well – no.'

'Well then.'

'I've never been hit over the head with a mallet but I know it would hurt. And now, with all this financial meltdown and cheating banking liars and whatnot –'

'What a delicate way you have with your description of the complete collapse of capitalism and its most nourishing hotbed.'

'Well, I can't think that anywhere in the States is going to be very jolly at the moment. Anyway, it's not the place, or the people necessarily. It's the silliness, the falseness of the whole set-up. Robert and Hugo and all that lot acting like a boyhood of Peter Pans. If that's business then you can keep it. Business is buying and selling and making a profit on goods, not selling yourself with the deal.'

'Or it was once,' Brando said. He indicated to the sommelier that another bottle of wine was required.

'And probably will be again. Bankers and cockroaches. The two species that will survive Armageddon.'

I looked around the restaurant. Hard to tell that the world was in the grip of a new kind of all-out slump. Not everyone was suffering, or would one day. This place was much as it always was. A cool place – cool art on the walls, minimal decor, black-and-white-checked floor. Almost like a Dutch interior so posed did it appear. You could easily imagine a blue silk frock sitting with golden ringlets dangling over the virginals and not be very surprised. The customers, too, looked posed, with besuited young men, eager, earnest, watchful, conducting business with other besuited young men, and young women in slightly sexier suits, with the de rigueur white shirt and neat little earrings beneath well-ordered hair, looking groomed and poised and doing the same as the young men in a slightly less obvious way. The men in grey or black, the women in navy blue. I remembered my mother's favourite piece of fashion advice: 'Get yourself a nice navy two-piece and it'll never go out of fashion.' To which I'd said that as far as I was concerned, nice and navy was an oxymoron, and she looked despairing. Brando and I were probably the only non-business types eating there. We were certainly the only true splashes of colour. It's a wonder they let Brando in at all with his tomato-coloured jeans and pink bow tie.

'How are you going to manage with your investments?'

He waved his hand and looked contemptuous, and said, 'Oh, I shall manage perfectly well with even the most reduced of incomes – as it is I make far more than I can spend and much goes to the taxman – and I rather regret that it then goes back to the banks. I don't mind all this at all. In fact, I quite like the way it's shaking everyone up . . . stopping their profligate ways.' The wine arrived. Brando waved the waiter away without bothering to taste it.

'You're a fine one to talk.'

'Oh, I shall never cease but it seems to have curtailed our company brethren.'

'But not enough,' I said gloomily. 'I'm still going to Florida.'

He leaned back, wiping his mouth. 'Don't go then,' he said.

'What?'

'Just say No.'

'What – and invent a lie – my granny's dying or something?'

'No – tell the truth.'

'What?!'

His smile was quite as evil as it was when he was politely declining his publisher's various offers about *Catchy Words* Mk II. Quite as evil. He was in control, his favourite position. 'You heard,' he said, with a Mephisthophelean leer. 'Just say No. If you want to Get Truth – then get it. Put up or shut up, darling. Now, my dear Nina, more wine?'

Usually I drank only one glass at lunchtime. The days of

the two-bottles-and-still-standing lunches had long gone, along with my innocence regarding abused liver function. Though I did find those fools who go out to lunch and then drink water, saying to the waiter, 'Yup – a drop of sparkling Perrier, or Ashbourne, or even a jug of tap, would just hit the spot,' made me want to reach for a passing sommelier. But this particular lunchtime it was different. Given the effect that Brando's words had on me – producing a kind of quivering excitement hitherto only found in Victorian heroines – I held out my glass and his eyes gleamed as he refilled it. I gazed at the glowing wine. I sipped. I sipped again. I could, I thought. I could do it. I could just say to Robert – I'm not going – I hate going – that's it – going is not on the map – I am not going ever, ever again. Rather than lie. I could. I *could*. I drank deep of the wine. It was certainly a thought.

'Now,' said Brando, 'while you chew that over we have a book to get on with. What about those lions' mouths? The secret denunciation boxes? How many still exist?'

'A few,' I said. 'They're called *Bocca del Leone* but they're not all lions. The one in the Doge's Palace is a human grotesque.'

'But they don't use them any more?' He looked hopeful.

'Might be a good idea if they did. They've started to use pastiches of them here in motorway service stations. Fun for all the family. The Venetian version of truth, dare, love or promise.'

'Proles.'

'Snob.'

'I may be a snob but I am not a liar.'

He gave me another of those triumphant looks. 'I'll go and take a look. Book me into the Gritti for a couple of weeks and I shall seek them out and ruminate upon them.

You can mark up a map for me. And we'll do a bit on Casanova and the Bridge of Sighs.' He picked up the menu and ordered himself a tiramisu and then continued. 'Something on all the tortures, the ways to get at the truth.' He raised an amused eyebrow. 'There must be a few blood-chilling instruments lying in a dank cellar somewhere there. And some bordellos – there must be some outrageous bordellos, or stories about them. That sort of thing.' He smiled again, knowing he wasn't helping. 'Truth. Ah, that wriggly little item. I wonder how much of that came out of those dungeons? Or lay in those iniquitous beds. The embrace of that seductive Iron Maiden . . . the turn of the screw . . . They'll have museums, archives, that sort of thing, won't they?'

Sometimes I wondered if I were supporting a psychopath, though Brando insisted that it was all to do with *Schadenfreude*, which was why he thought the book would be such a great success.

'It's quite likely those canny Venetians threw all the evidence of their evil ways into the Grand Canal when life there moved on. Not many civilisations want to leave the proof of their corruption behind. Especially if it was its iniquities that made them rich.'

'But surely, if they did it with God on their side,' he said, tucking into the pudding, 'they'll have taken pride in it.'

'Possibly.'

'Well – do your best. Speculation will do. Find a learned Venetian professor to do some speculating. A little more about all that, please, the darker the better. That's if you have time, given all your other pressing pursuits.'

He leaned forward in his chair, dropping the *poseur*, and looked earnest. 'Don't go to Florida, Nina. Stay and uphold the glory of truth and the teeth-rattling charm of

Schadenfreude. There's plenty of lovely dark stuff for you to be getting your nose into back here. Why not just tell Robert to shove it? You've been the good wife for far too long.'

'Just about as long as he's been the good husband, actually,' I said hotly.

Brando raised an unconvinced eyebrow.

Why is it so many gay men friends want to see your life unravel? Perhaps it is their innately unhappy state. I looked at Brando. He didn't look innately unhappy. Indeed, he looked positively delighted with life and with himself. He was eyeing everything male and under seventy with cheerful gusto while relishing the food and wine.

'Did you ever want to settle down?' I asked.

'Never,' he said. 'Particularly if it would mean I'd end up as hypocritical and smug as you and Robert.'

'Those who come to mock, Brando, sometimes stay to pray.' I had a sudden rush of sentimentality. Of course I had to go with Robert. Of course I did. 'My marriage is very nice, thank you. And I don't want to mess it up. Florida *mon amour.*' I was absolutely resigned to it. Absolutely. 'To Florida I shall go.'

And out came my hand again with its – surprisingly – empty glass.

Three

Spleenful: angry, peevish, fretful, melancholy.

Samuel Johnson's *Dictionary*, 1755

ROBERT DID NOT speak to me all the way to the airport. To drive him there seemed the least I could do. Stony silence was not his usual way and I apologised whenever we stopped at a set of lights. As we came closer to the car park I turned to him and said, again, 'I'm sorry, Robert, but I just – well – I've got to do it. If I don't take a stand now I shall end up as one of those people who lives their life the way others want them to live it. I can't justify pointing the finger at others for dishonesty if I'm dishonest myself.' Somewhere in the ether I heard Brando's sardonic tones saying smug, smug, smug. Robert merely set his jaw.

It crept up on me, beginning after the lunch with Brando and my rather well-oiled attempt to buy the kind of clothes I needed for the Home of Disney. It seemed shockingly wasteful, especially in the light of global fiscal suffering, to buy flame-coloured floaty things that I would never wear again and little silver sandals with false jewels sprinkled all over them. That wasn't me. In my be-Soaved state I thought that it couldn't, really, be anybody – they were gross, in design, colour and price – and disgracefully perfect for what was required. I left them where they were and walked out into the day feeling a huge sense of moral certainty.

And so it began. Despite the huge sense of moral certainty collapsing, that night I said as much to Robert. 'Robert,' I said, 'it's just too decadent.' He, with irritating absent-mindedness as he turned the pages of *Big Computers* or some such, said, 'Oh, well . . . Never mind. Just grit your teeth and get on with it like I do.' But as the days wore on I did mind, I minded more and more – indeed, I kept hearing Brando mocking me as a sham little Lady Fauntleroy and seeing Robert's unruffled inattention. Of course she will go, this latter seemed to say, of course she will, she's a good supportive wife who knows which side her bread is buttered on. She'll go, she'll lie, and she'll wear a flame-coloured floaty thing and agonisingly silly sandals.

Which was when the Bomb of Truth on the Road to Damascus, detonated. So I just said No. And once I had said No, I stuck to it. Robert scarcely noticed at first. So I said it louder. 'I am not going,' I said. It does not feel right.'

Robert looked up. He looked puzzled. 'Not going where?'

'Florida.'

'Don't be daft,' he said, with irritating good humour, 'I can't go on my own.'

'Well, I'm not coming. Definitely.' And I meant it.

The days went by. I remained determined. I began to feel quite pleased with my resilience. Robert said I was behaving like a prat. I said he was behaving like a prat. Robert said I'd be foot-stamping next. I said he'd be throwing his toys out of the pram. He asked if I was on something. I said I was stone-cold sober. And so it went on. I dug my heels in and he was furious. Instead of convincing my radical, idealistic husband that we should unite in our fight for truth, I merely appeared to be selfish and silly. I could read his mind then, as I could read his mind now. Ungrateful. That is what he said before clamping up entirely. 'This may be the last one. Why can't you suspend your bloody epiphanies for a few

more weeks? Most of the wives in the world would give
their eye teeth for a freebie with their husbands to somewhere warm and glamorous. If they understood what love
and loyalty were all about.' He eyed me coldly. 'You could
show a bit of gratitude.'

It was such a patronising statement that I ignored it. Nor
would I rise at the obvious gibe of 'If you loved me you
would . . .' Bringing up two children gives you insight into
the vagaries of manipulation. Instead I rose to the other,
more absurd idea.

'Warm and glamorous? You are joking?' It was the last
straw so far as Robert was concerned.

Once upon a time he would have seen the humour of it,
and laughed, but not now. I knew he was worried about
the future but I just couldn't stop, we had the possibility
to make a stand, to speak the truth. Too much was at
stake.

'Perhaps you've gone off me?'

'Well, I can't say you're my favourite person at the
moment.'

'Or maybe you've had it too easy, Nina. Perhaps you've
been spoiled.'

'By whom?'

He said nothing but his irritating little shrug suggested
the phrase, If the cap fits.

'By you? How disgustingly unliberated. If ever I might
have been persuaded to go to bloody Florida I shall
certainly not go now.' That night I slept in Tassie's room
and words, apart from the odd practical request or comment, had not been exchanged since. Been spoiled, indeed.
'That is unworthy,' I said. And that was that.

Eventually, as we pulled into the car park he turned to
me and said, 'I suppose that's what you think of me? As

someone who will continue to live at other people's beck and call?' He looked angrier than I had seen him for years. In fact, he had never looked that angrily at me before. I'd wounded him somewhere very deep. I had a fleeting thought that this was the prelude to a midlife crisis – and I had caused it – before thinking, righteously, that all I was doing was telling the truth and already my marriage was under threat.

'No, I don't think of you like that at all,' I said. 'It's different for you – it's your job, your workplace –'

'Our mortgage, our lifestyle, our heating, our lighting, our telephone and our bloody polenta –'

'All that,' I said. This was no moment to remind him that I did, actually, contribute some funds to the family pot. 'It feeds into what you want to be. But I'm your wife. It hardly matters if I fit into the world of corporate IT or not – it's your job. And anyway, I don't jump up and down and demand absolute truth from politicians while telling lies myself –'

'You lie all the time. We all do. It's how we survive.'

'How you survive, maybe. But no, not any more. Just for once I'm going to do things right.'

Then he got really angry. He brought the flat of both hands down on the dashboard like a demented driving instructor heralding an emergency stop – and I jumped. 'Do you really think I wanted to spend my life doing stuff with computers for other people? Do you? No. I spend vast chunks of my life doing the job I do so that I can spend the rest of my life the way I want to spend it with you. And the children.'

'Oh, Robert,' I said. 'Then don't go either.'

We stared into each other's eyes. And I knew that he was lying. He was feeling sorry for himself, he had nearly convinced himself, but he was lying. He really did want to spend lots of his life doing what he was proud to be good at. He liked it. Only fools are dismissive of their skills. *Big Computers* was his pornography. He was a happy man, as much as anyone can be happy in this mortal coil, and I had belittled him so he lied. 'I have to go,' he said, and got out of the car before I had the chance to tell him that I knew he loved what he did and I thought it was great, fine, wonderful – I loved him for loving it even if to me it was as interesting as yesterday's gravy. Before he closed the car door he looked at me very hard, as if he were a schoolteacher and I was his wayward pupil. 'Think about what you've done,' he said, 'while I'm away.'

'Will you ring me?'

'And say what? I'll only be gone a week. You'll survive without hearing from me. After all, it's Florida and not your sort of place.' And then he slammed the door.

While he dragged his case out of the boot I sat there and stared glumly ahead. Stop now, I thought. Be the silly wife. Say it's a hot flush. Anything. But I just couldn't. I got out of the car. Robert was walking away with that huffy stride that I'd seen occasionally but never, quite, so pronounced. I hurried after him and pulled on his arm.

'I love you,' I said.

'Do you?' His eyes were flinty. Then soft. Then flinty again.

'Yes.'

We squared up to each other. I waited. Nothing.

'You've got a very funny way of showing it.'

'Do you love me?'

His eyes remained flinty. In a minute, I thought, he'll be the old Robert and say that of course he loves me and –

And then a very familiar voice rang out, bathetically cheerful, and it was all too late.

It was Hugo. 'Nina? What are you doing here? Are you coming after all?'

And then it was Lorna's turn. 'Oh, Nina. Thank goodness for that. We'd be miserable without you.'

We both turned. There were the two of them, crisp and bright as a pair of new fivers, with matching luggage and perfectly folded Burberrys (linings turned outwards) over their arms, coming towards us at a keen pace.

'Nina,' said Lorna again, reaching out to touch my arm, 'you do look very pale. Shouldn't you be in bed?'

'I should?'

'Or at least in the warm.'

From beside me my husband let out a long groan.

'Robert?' said Hugo anxiously. 'Don't tell me you're going down with it, too.'

'Oh, don't be so silly, Hugo,' said Lorna. 'It's an ear infection. Ear infections are not contagious. That's why the poor thing can't fly. Or are you better now?'

She gave me a look of deep and rare and beautiful sympathy. I could no longer look her in the eye. So I looked at Robert instead. Robert was staring at me with such ghastly horror on his face – such a message of Oh Please Keep Your Mouth Shut – that I could not do it. I backed away looking sad (nothing in this Truth idea about facial expressions, after all) and said, 'I'm going straight to the doctor's now. I just wanted to see Robert off properly . . .'

They nodded, sweetly friendly in their agreement. Robert gave me a glassy smile, quite horrible to behold, and raised his eyebrow enough to say 'Gotcha'. As far as he was concerned I had just told a lie for him, and against my will, and he was delighted. So now my husband, my dear, familiar partner of so many years, whose mixture of strength and weakness reflected my own – all that – was behaving like an alien. How could something that meant so much to me have caused such a change in him? I had never seen him this cold, or confrontational. Nor had I remained so impassive. Maybe, in all these years, we had never been tested. For all I knew we could be on our way to divorce over this. When he got back from Florida – or perhaps, I thought crazily, he never would come back. Despite his current flinty grimace, he was a good-looking man and certainly desirable. The more so to me now as I thought of letting him go. Robert Redford without quite so many lines and freckles, I fondly thought. Well, nearly.

'Ahhh,' said Lorna. 'But we'll take him under our wing from here. Poor Robert. Now, off you go and see that doctor.'

As I drove out of the parking bay I saw my husband, Poor Robert, look over his shoulder at me with an expression of both gratitude and – almost certainly – triumph. White-lipped triumph. He not only thought he had made me tell a lie, he was delighted by it. The bastard. I was beginning to see a side of this man I had no idea existed. Perhaps this was why he was so successful? It was an uncomfortable thought. You think you know someone and then . . . Well, you needn't be quite so triumphant about my lapse into lying, I thought, because I really am going to go to the doctor's. It was the day of our doctor's first come, first served Well Woman Clinic at the surgery. It was about time someone probed my female parts again and so – quite truthfully – to the doctor's I would go.

I waved at the trio one more time and they waved back. I hoped I'd put a certain air of Brave Little Woman into the gesture, just to add authenticity. I watched them until they were out of sight, and then I thought, when Robert got home I would kill him. If he didn't kill me first. If he ever came home. And who cared if he did or he didn't? How dare he lie on my behalf? I suppose he dared because he was, in fact, lying on his own. How dare he look so pleased with himself? An ear infection, indeed. But it was clever. Very clever. The perfect lie. What could be more irretrievable than an ear infection for an eight-hour-plus flight? I wished him to hell. But mostly I really loved him. Not that he deserved it. I loathed him. I loved him. Well, one or the other.

Four

Jejuneness: barrenness, particularly want of interesting matter, a deficiency of matter that can engage the attention.

Noah Webster's *American Dictionary of the English Language*, 1828

I HAVE ALWAYS found our doctor's waiting room a haven. Almost certainly this is because I have never been seriously ill. The worst that has befallen me is raised blood pressure in pregnancy and the occasional need for antibiotics. The waiting room is a place into which you can take a newspaper, leave plenty time for waiting, and just get on with it. No mobile telephones to disturb, no yelling yobs, just warmth and peace and quiet. Reading the newspaper there is a perfectly justifiable pastime no matter what time of day. At home I am always aware of the million things that need doing domestically in the garden or house, or in my office I am always aware of what needs doing for Brando. Cafes are bustling, noisy places with people hunched over their laptops or shouting into their BlackBerries. But in the doctor's waiting room all is serene. There are no distractions . . . None at all . . . Especially no mobiles. Just the occasional ring of a telephone that will be answered, the laughter of a child, and the sporadic calling of a patient's name. That is all. Unless – well – you find yourself the victim of people who wish to confide. Or compare symptoms. Or just chat about the colour of nothing. Or even the colour of something. Like skin.

Oh, it begins in a friendly enough manner, with a little smile, and a little suggestion that if the seat next to you is unoccupied they may as well take it – and then it progresses. Given the location, you are not entirely unlikely to sit next to, or opposite, someone who needs to talk about their ailment. You know them before they utter. You feel their twitchiness as they arrive, you sense their hungry searching of the vacant chairs to find the one nearest to someone of weak and sympathetic sinew, and you can almost inhale their desire to get your eyes off the *Guardian* and on to their face. They may bump you and then apologise and then, in that split second of eye engagement, when you say, 'Oh no – really – that's fine,' they will pounce. 'Clumsy of me,' they'll say. 'Don't know what's got into me today,' they'll say. 'It's only since I got this . . .' And they'll be off. Pretty soon they will start talking about how very ill they are or they were – or they might be or they have never been – and after that you will be fair game for whatever they wish to say. It will range from illness to the weather and will, almost certainly, end up pottering around the margins of immigration.

It is so difficult to decide whether to go with the devil you know and sit between two people who appear – at the time of your arrival anyway – to be reasonably sane and without either serious illness or racist intent, or to strike out for emptier shores and sit away from the throng. The danger of this latter is that it actually leaves room for the verbose fascist to sit next to you, and then there is always room for communication.

Today I chose to sit slightly away from everyone. I owed it to my bruised and battered self to spread my newspaper wide and get a good arm's width without having to apologise. I wanted to immerse myself in the news, however depressing, rather than think about Robert and that expression on his face. So I did and there it was, page after page of it: financial meltdown, honour's meltdown, greedy bankers, greedy politicians, greedy all of us, lying yobs, lying police, lying all of us – the death by a thousand cuts of our collective, civilised humanity. But I was right, the world's iniquities certainly took my mind off my own paltry difficulties. Given the number of women waiting I would be a good hour before being seen – and likely to get through most of the paper. And I could always ask the doctor for Valium if the effect became too depressing. Think positive. It was going to be a better day than it seemed when it began. Including the victory of under- mining Robert's lie. Here I was, I thought happily, at the doctor's. Honour intact. I would never be able to tell him, of course, for it just wouldn't be wise to meet him off the plane in a week's time in triumphalist mode, but at least *I* knew. And then the chilling thought returned. I might never meet him off the plane, triumphalist or not. He might not want me to. It might all be over. I buried my nose back into the relentlessly awful news and thought, with cheering savagery, that if anyone tried it on with me today they'd get very short shrift.

All was serene in the vacant chairs either side of me. And then – about twenty minutes into the delights of silent, public reading – it happened. A man and a woman, both in well-worn, drab-coloured mackintoshes which had certainly never even hung close to a Burberry, sat on either side of me. They were together – I separated them by my presence – and they would be denied nothing. They proceeded to have a conversation around the back of my newspaper. I stood up and turned to the man and said, 'I'll move for you.' He smiled up at me like a grateful – if hungry – puppy and they were off.

If he'd had a pound for every time someone had been kind and thoughtful in this place, he wouldn't, it seemed, be a very rich man. 'She's the ill one,' he said. 'My wife.' I looked at his wife. She had a porridge-coloured face and a smile of determined satisfaction which she now bestowed upon me. 'She's been back and forth I don't know how many times.' Ranulph Fiennes's mother could not have sounded prouder. It was not too late, I told myself silently. I slid into my new place with just the slightest of smiles at him as he shuffled into my old one and I proceeded to flick my newspaper as my father used to flick his so dismissively all those years ago. It had worked for him. It did not work for me.

'We're waiting for the test results.'

I turned the page with firm intent and said, not looking away from World News and the death of banking, 'Yes.' It was the best I could manage and should have warned anyone with half a brain that this person was not for inclusion. And if I were to follow my new-found integrity, I would sooner or later have to say, at the very least, 'Leave me alone.'

He began to speak again. 'Test results,' he said with satisfaction. 'Dr Granger. Nice young lady. You can understand everything she's saying – if you know what I mean.' I did know. And we had got there without benefit of even a nod at the warm weather for the time of year. And then he stopped. A voice from behind our chairs said to his wife, 'Mrs Foster? Do you want to slip in now? I've got a bit of a space.' It was that nice young Dr Granger and her perfect enunciation, smiling and extending a hand of invitation. I

nearly hugged her. With ease of conscience, as the two of
them creaked up off their chairs and proceeded to follow
her into the surgery, I said with a big, beaming smile, 'Good
luck!' And they smiled with equal warmth and said, 'Thank
you.' Dr Granger smiled at me too. It was going to be all
right. They had gone. I'd been saved. And even though I
could not forget Robert's pale and angry face or Brando's
smug and cynical one, I had found a little sunshiny ray of
justice. I had not compromised truth. So far so good. Had
they not moved away I was poised to ask them – politely –
to allow me to continue reading and not to talk. But Fate
had taken the cup from me.

When the elderly couple came out of the surgery they
caught my eye as if seeking me out. I quickly looked away.
She looked bright about the eyes and the porridge was now
slightly pink at the edges. He looked brave. To my horror,
they came towards me and sat down. Oh please, no, I said
to myself and resolutely went on reading the article about
global warming. But the gods of veracity were not disposed
to be kind.

'It's the worst scenario,' he said. 'An operation. We're
waiting for our son to collect us.'

'Oh,' I said, thinking that truth had to take a back seat
over the worst scenario.

'Groin area,' he whispered.

'I'm so sorry,' I said, which was truthful. Oh God, I
thought, something serious in the groin area. 'But you're in
good hands here.' I didn't stop to think.

'Well – you say that – but –' he said, looking about him,
his gaze settling on one of the practice nurses who was at
the desk checking notes. It was Louise whose parents came
from Gujarat. Louise herself, she once told me when she
was taking my blood, was born in East Sheen.

The elderly man opened his mouth to say more and I was ready for him. Or was I? I mean – what right did I have to champion Just Cause with someone whose wife might possibly be dying from her groin area? 'Oh well,' I said, lamely, feeling my good self dissolve in a mist of cowardice.

'I only hope the surgeon's white,' said his wife loudly, and she gave the unknowing Louise a significant stare.

There it was. Right out there. Several elephants sitting around in a very confined space at our feet.

'Or I won't understand a thing he's saying.'

'Might be a she,' I said gaily. 'The surgeon.'

Mrs Foster blinked. Do not play games with her, I admonished myself, that is not kind.

'Well,' she said, 'I wouldn't mind so much if it was a she . . . probably.' She was obviously weighing this up against the other, even more dastardly possibility.

'Why would it make a difference?' I asked timidly. 'I mean – as long as they're good surgeons it really doesn't matter what colour or sex they are –'

'You say that,' said the man, 'You say that but one slip and –' He looked over at Louise again, who saw, and smiled. He quickly averted his eyes.

I added, bravely but lamely, 'And anyway – you'll be under anaesthetic so you won't need to have a conversation. They'll know exactly what they're doing no matter how they speak or where they come from.' That told them. I flicked my newspaper very firmly. There – it was over.

But then his wife said, 'I'm having local anaesthetic. So I'll be awake.'

Dwelling momentarily on the cheering thought that it was amazing what they could do nowadays, I mean, full-blown surgery with just a local anaesthetic, I smiled. 'Much better for you,' I said. 'I had no idea they could use locals for major surgery.'

She nodded and looked very proud. 'Yes,' she said. 'It is amazing. Femoral hernia they call it.' She nodded in a satisfied way. 'Femoral.' She gave a little pointing jab with her finger in the direction of her groin area before slipping on her gloves. And then they both stood up. 'There's Alan,' they said. 'Nice talking to you. Not often you meet someone like-minded.' And off they went.

A hernia, femoral. I had slewed my truthfulness for a hernia. I should have stood up and defended the very tenets of my political being, I should have waved the flag for social decency, I should have – I should have – and I didn't. I took a vow. Never again. Never would I be compromised by social mores again. In the name of honour I would henceforth do battle. It had increased my resolve. And, unfortunately, my rage.

'Good heavens,' said Dr Crewe, looking up. 'Are you all right?'

Which I thought was a bit rum coming from a doctor.

Well, the whole exercise was pointless. We began by taking my blood pressure which was so high that the doctor looked suspiciously at her instrument. 'Hmm,' she said, peering at the reading. 'You're usually spot on. Anything out of the ordinary happened?'

'It's been a pretty difficult day so far,' I said.

'So I see. Care to talk about it?' She's a good doctor, one of the best. How many doctors would volunteer to hear their patient's emotional woes with a busy surgery out front?

'No,' I said, perfectly truthfully. 'But thank you for asking. I think I'll just go home and have a cup of tea and come to the next clinic. Shall I?'

'Good idea,' she said. 'I'd like to take another reading just to be sure.'

I left the surgery feeling very limp and very stupid. The femoral hernia and her husband were gone but the others all stared as I walked past. They were like a sea of souls who wanted something from me. I kept my eyes focused straight ahead and left the building feeling a complete failure. I had been *nice* for God's sake. To a pair of racists. And all because of a hernia. I needed something to take away the heavy feeling that hung around my heart. It was not an auspicious start. First my husband and now this. Being an honest person is not as easy as you think, I told myself. Maybe at home there would be a message from Robert. Lunchtime flight. He'd have boarded by now. But he might – just – have rung beforehand. He might – just – have been overwhelmed with a flood of marital warmth and want to put things right. He might have been on his knees with husbandly regret. He might.

Five

Swacker: something huge; figuratively a great lie.

Reverend Robert Forby's *Vocabulary of East Anglia*, 1830

I DROVE HOME thinking about Gandhi – which was quite a surprise but probably sparked by Louise's family origins. Gujarat was where the blessed Mahatma was born. She had told me that, too. When she was a teenager her parents took her back to meet her family there and she said she felt touched by the place, that it was all Peace and Love and flowers. She went out a stroppy teenager and came back a thoughtful young woman with her mind made up to become a nurse. I remembered university days when we sat around drinking cheap beer in pubs and discussing things like Truth and citing everyone from Confucius to Camus and Huxley to Hesse in the last dregs of the years when we students really thought we could change the world. Before Baader–Meinhof poisoned the well and made us all feel far less solid and right-thinking. Gandhi had a maxim that might bring me a little comfort now. He reckoned that it was the little things you did to chip away at the one big lie that moved the mountain of the world's deceit; although enraging one's husband and showing cowardice in the face of racism didn't exactly feel like I was making great philosophical progress, I would continue to try. It was my personal path and I could not, would not, shake it off. If I could get through this first week, I thought, I might manage to be truthful for the rest of my life. And if not, well, nothing is wasted. Even one week of honesty might bring down a pebble or two from the big mountain. Cars are great things for making you feel in charge of your bit of the world. Cars are territorial. The question was, would I feel quite so in control of my life once I'd parked and got out?

Comforting as it was to drive home with Gandhi's words shoring up my virtue, I was also reminded that the chipping away to bring down a mountain model was the same one we used for gender equality once. Keep chipping away and the foundations of male dominance will crumble. But had it happened? On the board of Robert's international company there were three women out of hundreds of board members worldwide. And the *Guardian* that very day had told me that young married or partnered women, mostly but not exclusively with children, were becoming the highest growth area for stress and mental problems. They'd made it to the job market but hadn't found anyone to take on the other jobs attaching to them as women. They therefore remained the mainstays of the home and children – with the result that more women between the ages of twenty-five and forty registered with depression, and were on sick benefit for same, than at any other time in our history.

Contemplating this lot I felt even worse about Robert. He was a good partner and a man of integrity who had never raised barriers to anything I wanted to do – not even those subconscious little put-you-downs. As much as a man in his kind of business and at the level he was could be liberated, he was. If I wanted any more it was there for the taking. True, paternity leave was more difficult the higher you climbed up the employment ladder but when the children were born he had managed to be at home for a week –

which was quite unusual then – and my mother has had stars in her eyes about him ever since. If I believed her, my father never so much as changed a nappy. Yet I would not have given up my time at home with the children for anything on earth, that was the truth. Yes I was a feminist, but what that meant to me was that we should live in a world where we both had the same choices, where nothing was forbidden or compromised by being female, not that I should want to be a man. Robert, and men like him, I reminded myself, were working in the real world and dealing with it how it is, not how we would like it to be. I – with my enjoyably useless research and jolly lunches with Brando – was not. Gandhi's chipping away was as true for a change of balance as for anything else. At least our children had grown up seeing their father iron a shirt and rinse out milk bottles as well as leave the house in suit and tie with a briefcase under his arm. He could also be infuriatingly bossy when I was driving the car, of course, but no amount of shared feminist principle would get rid of that behaviour. It was as integral to masculine life as pretty lace on underwear was to the feminine. It'd take removal of the entire Alps to sort that one out.

Gloria Steinem, still beautiful, still speaking out at seventy-five, famously said that the Truth will set you free – but it will piss you off first. Truth-telling, truth embracing, not only pissed me off, it apparently pissed everyone else in the room off, too. Gloria Steinem had a wonderful wit. And honesty. When she was asked if being a stunning woman helped her career she said that it certainly did at first, but later – when she wanted to be taken seriously – she was still thought of as just a chick. Oh, how I missed those glory days of women's liberation when, despite the current souring of its history, we *did* have a lot of laughs and we *did* discover that women's humour was just as funny as men's – only different. We knew we were held back by the glass ceiling and sticky floor and we were honourably set to change it. Nobody got depressed, there was no time to reflect, we were in the thick of the war. Now it's the uneasy peace and the glass ceiling is still in place and the sticky floor is less a sign of women's desire to rise than women's inability to manage everything they have to do and keep the kitchen floor clean too. Robert, along with the shirts and milk bottles, had always been good at cleaning the floor. I'd watch him do it with that extraordinary focus and dedication that is one hundred per cent male and enviable and not a little infuriating. But when he'd finished it was shining. And he never went down on his knees to do it, he always stood. A good lesson. He was also – still is – good at cleaning windows – with the same ferocious dedication – and always did it looking up.

I turned the corner and there were those very windows now. Gleaming in the April sun. Opening onto silent rooms and empty chairs. The mental muscle from the journey diminished rapidly as I walked up the path, opened the door, entered my totally silent house and felt totally empty myself. But there was hope. Two messages winked at me from our ancient answerphone. I pressed the button and listened eagerly, like a girl who's just been on a date and hopes he'll ring. (Where's the emancipation in that? Who cares? It's what happens.) Neither message was from Robert. The first was from Brando asking me to ring him back. The second was from my best friend Toni. Now there was a can of worms to be opened if ever there was one. I took the coward's way out and rang Brando first. The thought of speaking to Toni, with my new undertaking for truth, did nothing for my blood pressure. It also brought out the very possible latent alcoholic in me. In 'The Fall' –

aptly named given my present predicament – Camus said that sincerity could hardly be considered a condition of friendship because truth was a destructive passion. The wisdom of the thinking French. If I was going to call Toni back, it could only be done with a large glass of wine to hand, and it was too soon for that.

I thought Brando's call had been made remarkably early until I realised that Italy was an hour ahead of us. He, most certainly, would have a large glass of something to hand as he sat on the Gritti terrace, raised his glass to the health of Salute (or she to him more appropriately, given that she is its embodiment) and gazed on La Serenissima. How very much I wanted to be there with him, or anywhere, really, that did not involve returning a call to my oldest friend. Toni and I had met at university and our friendship largely survived because of lack of truthfulness. As most friendships survive. And now I must include her in my pledge. If I had never been truthful with Toni on a regular basis – as, I was sure, she had never been with me – I had been particularly untruthful in the last four years. Since she began her affair with the horrible Bob. Nearly thirty years of good, solid, looking-the-other-way friendship between us and all likely to wash straight down the plughole once I made that call. It just didn't seem fair. Piss you off, indeed, Gloria. Piss you off, indeed.

I made myself a cup of coffee, settled down at the kitchen table and tapped in Brando's number. He answered immediately and I could hear the sounds of Venice bustling all about him. If I couldn't quite detect the slap of water on stone, I felt that I could.

'How's the truth drug going?' he asked affably.

'Predictably,' I said.

'Still convinced?'

'Pass.'

He laughed.

'Is that why you rang? To see how little Lady Fauntleroy was doing?'

'Don't be peevish. I rang because those letter boxes – the lions' mouths, or gargoyles, or whatever they were –'

'Mostly lions' heads but sometimes human grotesques. Not gargoyles, Brando – gargoyles have the added attraction of spouting water. They went under the collective name of *Bocca del Leone*, and were dotted about the place in the name of public vigilance. You just slipped in your written secret denunciation and let the rest take its course. Think of them as truth boxes, if you like.'

'Or untruth boxes?'

'Indeed. It got so corrupt at one point that the authorities banned them unless you put your name to the accusation. After that they became more meticulous.'

'Well, we need some case histories or something. A touch of the spine-chilling. Otherwise they're hardly news.'

'I told you that.'

'My, you are snappish today. So find out some dirty deeds to dish. They were sometimes used to check on adultery, weren't they? There must be records of real women who were tested – and failed.'

'Or real men?'

'Unlikely they'd do a truth test on a man, surely? But anyone will do. What happened to the women who failed? There must be something appalling recorded somewhere.'

'Maybe. I'm not sure if the meticulousness of process stretched to accused women. Unlikely.'

'And some are still there?'

'There are a few. There's a good one on the riva degli Schiavoni, hidden but intact. And one in the Doge's Palace.

So you won't be sending the punters off to look at a blank space – even if we don't have a record of a particular punishment. I'll see what I can find out,' I said wearily.

'You can make something up if you like.' He laughed, not very nicely, and then added with relish, 'Oh, no. You don't do that any more, do you?'

'Not very funny, Brando.'

'You do sound fed up.'

'The score is,' I said, 'that you have only been there for a day and a half and already you are twitching and poking at me and I have just seen my husband off to Florida – where he may well decide to take up with a nubile young Disney enthusiast on the grounds that his wife has deserted him for some old singleton called Truth and it's all too much.'

'Male or female?'

'Truth is always female.'

'I didn't mean that. I meant the nubile young thing in Florida.'

'I'll ring you back this afternoon,' I said. 'I've got to ring Toni now.'

'And speak truth?'

'And speak truth.'

'Now that is a conversation I wish I could listen in on. Are you going to stick to your principles?'

'Of course.'

'And you'll call me back?'

'Once I've found out what you want.'

'Juicy now. I want them to be juicy. And –'

'Yes?' I snapped.

'Is Robert really going to Disney?'

'Unlikely, but you never know.'

'Good Lord,' he said. 'Thank God I'm not corporate.'

*

I went upstairs to make our bed – just to delay things a little. I tried to remind myself that women who worried that their husbands would stray were insecure. I quite liked it if I saw Robert across a crowded room and he was chatting to a woman or two. Mine, I used to think comfortably, all mine. Now it felt wrong pulling up the duvet on that empty expanse. You don't think about the marital bed and all that it symbolises until you think you might lose it. If I remembered rightly the beds in America were huge. Robert would feel lost. He always needed to cuddle right up. Or maybe he really would find someone to cuddle up to? I tugged the duvet back sharply. That was quite enough wallowing. To hell with coffee – I'd take the burgundy. And then I'd ring Toni. Perhaps conscience, like truth, doth make cowards of us all. I certainly did not feel brave.

Our room. The bed was smooth. The dressing table was empty of his things and he had not taken his robe. Of course he hadn't – hardly because he planned to frolic naked – they supplied them in hotels, didn't they? There were a couple of empty hangers on the floor, which I picked up and hung back on his side of the wardrobe. They looked empty and accusing as they swung there along with the other empty hangers. He had even taken his black jeans, and his black leather jacket. The children laughed at him when he bought it and he wore it rarely. I never laughed at him in it and I wasn't laughing now. Those black jeans and that leather jacket meeting up with a gorgeous woman of a certain age on the prowl certainly wouldn't make her laugh either. I slammed the wardrobe door shut. And went to the telephone to try Robert's mobile. Nothing. I didn't know whether it was better or worse to make the call to Toni in this frame of mind. But at least I could now overcome my worries about having a drink. It was noon at last.

Antonia and Georgina. We sounded like heroines out of a Barbara Pym novel and – in our contrasts – we were not far off. At university we were known, with cheerful affection, as chalk and cheese. How to explain the yawning physical gap between us? With deep envy, is how. Toni was very small – only about five foot one – and very dark – hair almost blue it was so black and eyes so large and lustrous in their perfect, pale, oval face that they were two seductive inky pools. And seduce they did. Should I go on? Should I explain how it felt to be five foot seven and feel like a giantess? How in the summer Toni's skin turned a gleaming *café crème* while mine looked like someone had been flicking marmalade at a canvas? How she had a way of moving that was the slide of a cat to my castanet knees? And how – for all this – we were mates? You have to like someone very much to overcome such terrible barriers as size four shoes and Degas hands. I was brainier. That was the only – very small – compensation. Then it scarcely mattered to me. But now – now – if I were being truthful and not quasi-mature – it also did not seem a great compensation.

Fortunately we did not share the same taste in men. I wanted someone tall and solid who would make me feel dainty, and who had a radical view of the world and a Pythonesque sense of humour. Toni said that anyone over five foot eight gave her a crick in the neck, that anyone with a strong political bias was boring, and that what she really liked so far as humour was concerned were the two Ronnies. Perfect. She married Arturo, a wonderfully romantic Italian, five feet eight inches tall, mama's pasta around his girth, a strong footballing bias, no politics except the usual Italian view of the world that whoever was in power needed removing, and who laughed at nearly everything. Arturo was adorable, if a bit diddy, and wrote a European sports column for his Rome-based newspaper. Toni was a legal secretary. She intended to become a solicitor but got pregnant while training and that – *plus ça change* – was that. She did not mind. They were both delighted at the time and married straight away – and they were happy.

And then, years later, two children on, somewhere along the way, she met Bob. Bob was six foot two, had been a Tory candidate of the hang 'em and flog 'em school, was unreconstructed and seemed to find no-one very funny except himself. Bob was very fond of his own opinions and the starry-eyed Toni was fond of his own opinions, too. Robert couldn't stand him and I couldn't stand him and, it seemed, even his own wife couldn't stand him. He had never had children – out of choice – which was not surprising – they would take too much attention – and Toni would sit and gaze at him as he spoke as if he were Socrates to her Aristotle. I bore it – as most of us do with our friends' totally appalling choices – because I was Toni's best pal – and because I was a coward and because I could lie through my teeth. When she said to me tearfully that she could not imagine living without him, I did not say what I wanted to which was: well, bloody well *try*.

Dear husband Robert – who told Bob pretty sharply that he was never, ever called Bob himself – said that someone should tell Arturo what was going on. I suggested he volunteer. No one told Arturo. Robert blinked at the situation and we all just sat in a heap and watched in stupefaction as

Bob and Toni became more and more intertwined and Arturo became more and more unsettled but unsuspecting. One thing about being brought up by an adoring mama with pasta, it seemed it made him immune to ideas of rejection. When he became really anxious and confided his anxieties to his sister she told him it was probably to do with Toni's age – women started to act strangely after their fortieth birthday – and Arturo decided this must be so. We all breathed a sigh of relief. With luck the ill-matched adulterers would fizzle away and Arturo need never know. Some hope.

The affair became more and more magnetic for Toni as well as more and more painful. Bob did logistics. He went to the Middle East and did them. He went to Romania and did them. He went anywhere and everywhere to logistics people's troubles away. And while he was doing so, Toni stayed at home and mourned. About the only piece of truth I ever dished out to her was that I was certain, absolutely certain, that Bob never had foreign affairs. He was far too unadventurous for that. I never quite understood how the two of them became an item except that they met when Toni's practice was dealing with some matter of international law and she fell off a chair into his arms. I imagine the sight of my lovely friend standing on a chair fixing the light or something and then tumbling like a featherweight into his manly chest was too much even for Bob's cold blood. I never asked. Nor did I ever ask why they did not run off together. I did not have to. Right from the world go he told Toni that it was out of the question. The wife. Bob's wife was the money behind the business. Divorce her, divorce his beloved trucks. Clever. At a stroke he made himself desirably unavailable. Toni was completely hooked.

*

Truth was not an option. It was perfectly and crazily dreadful and I was Toni's listening ear. Not once, in all this time, had I told her what I really thought of Bob. Somehow I'd managed to fudge it when she went all dewy-eyed and showed me the roses that he had sent from Perth or Peru, or told me touching tales of his loving kindnesses as performed in a motorway Travelodge. Arturo continued to be sweetly baffled by his wife's changing moods and absences but accepted them. It made me wince and it broke my heart. But up until now it was Mates United – I could not, would not, say anything that might break our bond. Well, it was no good avoiding the issue any longer. Toni had rung, Toni had left a message, at some point I must ring her back. That point was now. Maybe the god of little truths would take pity and show me a way. Maybe Toni just wanted to see me for my own sake and not for my listening ear. And maybe pre-bacon material was suddenly available in an airborne position.

I rang. While it was ringing I looked longingly at the glass of wine. I resisted. Not yet. I had to be very, very clear-headed for as long as I could. The nearest I had ever got to telling Toni what I really felt about the whole situation, and what I really felt about logistical Bobby, was to buy her a copy of Sylvia Plath's *Ariel* poems – they seemed appropriate – and, predictably, she loved them, moons and yew trees and all. Now the words 'A ring of gold with the sun in it? / Lies. Lies and a grief. Lies and a grief . . .' floated round in my head, and the forlorn anthem 'Love, love, my season' was about right. 'Love is a shadow. / How you lie and cry after it . . .' I mouthed, as I waited for her to answer. Would it be the glooms or would it be the joys? I prepared myself for either and was therefore shocked into confusion by her opening question.

'Georgina, have you and Robert had a row? A serious one?'

'No,' I said.

'Then what have you been getting up to?'

'What?' What had *I* been getting up to?

'I know all about it.'

'All about what? And hello, Toni – Antonia – and just how are you?'

She ignored this. 'Well, I heard from Sally that you've refused to go away with Robert. So . . .?' Sally was one of our mutual friends. Local to me, she was a hearty woman with several dogs and bright red walker's cheeks. I couldn't imagine how she knew – and then I remembered that Alec her husband and Robert sometimes shared the Tube to work. If that were so then things were even worse than I thought – Robert, in that masculine tradition, was not usually one to divulge the personal unless someone was threatening to pull out his fingernails.

'Toni, I can't talk now –'

'Why – is there someone there? Someone, perhaps, who shouldn't be there?'

This beggared belief.

'No, it's just that I've got to go out to the British Library and get some stuff that Brando wants. He's in Venice at the moment. Are you OK? Just give me the headlines.'

'I'm OK. I'm more worried about you.'

'Don't be.'

'Is it – ?'

'What?' I said sharply.

'Well – can you have lunch tomorrow?'

'Difficult.'

'Why?'

Well, what could I say? Difficult had been perfectly truthful but that was as far as it went. She knew Robert was away and she knew Brando was away and she knew Tassie and Johnno were away. She also knew that my mother was hale as a horse so I couldn't even summon up a ministering visit to her. Anyway, lying – even in the name of a friendship – was, of course, out.

'Yes, then,' I said. 'But late.'

We agreed to meet at a busy pasta place. Somehow I thought it might help to be somewhere bustling and noisy and slightly rushed. Toni had wanted to go to Anya's which was discreet and perfect for conversation. This boded ill.

'Ask,' I said.

'Ask what?'

'I mean, let's meet at Ask. Two o'clock. Got to go now. Bye.'

I set off for the British Library feeling very low. This truth thing was supposed to make me feel better, wasn't it? And while on the subject of truth there were those utterly fallible *Bocca del Leone* to consider. It wasn't hard once I started researching them to find juicy ones. They were all juicy. In fact, it seemed that right up until the end of the eighteenth century popping a little note into that ever-open mouth, and denouncing your fellow Venetian with the biggest lie you could get away with, was the favoured sport of the tribe. Annoyingly, but unsurprisingly, Brando was right. Men were never called on to take the lie-detector test in matters of infidelity. Only women. Predictable. The lady was required to put her hand into the mouth of the lion and if it was hurt or damaged on retrieval, or couldn't be freed, the lady was guilty. Imagine a nervous young woman, innocent or not, knowing her life depended on an unsullied hand.

You'd shake, wouldn't you? And the thin opening of the rough stone would scrape away at your delicate, white flesh. Oh, it didn't bear thinking about. Mind you, in matters of politics, men did not escape the mouth test. Notes of denunciation were almost always used against men in matters of trade and state. 'Twas ever thus. The domestic, trivial stuff stays down among the women, the world stage belongs to men.

The *Bocca del Leone* I wanted Brando to see on the riva degli Schiavoni was connected to a nice combination of those two spheres, domestic and political, by a noblewoman, Eleanora de Monti. She used the box to denounce her husband for plotting against the Doge. This, apparently, came as a surprise to him as, indeed, did his removal to a particularly unpleasant part of the dungeons by the secret police. It came as quite a surprise to Eleanora de Monti, too, when, later, locked in the arms of her young and handsome and impoverished lover, she found that foreplay included being handcuffed a little more roughly than she would have liked and also being hauled off to the Doge's dungeons. Her young and handsome lover was suddenly no longer impoverished. It seemed that the state felt that the de Monti possessions were really far too abundant and that, without a husband to contain her, Eleanora might well go out of control. Better all round to dispatch both of them and make their considerable fortune a ward of La Serenissima. The lover took a happy trifle for his trouble. Herein, I added as a postscript for Brando, lies the proof that honesty is the best policy and marital infidelity a foolish and dangerous path.

I suppose it was inevitable that these boxes were remembered more for their iniquity than their useful truthfulness. In principle it seemed an excellent idea to have safe places for people who wished to remain anonymous to post information without fear. But in a city that based its very existence on insecurity and brutal justice, it was hardly likely to be ignored by those with a mendacious agenda of their own. Truth had little place in Venice, I wrote in my notes to Brando, power and money – with virtue as its hostage – held all. Go to it, Brando, go to it, while I stay at home and mourn.

Brando was enchanted with my text about all this. Probably because, somewhere deep within, he was still the schoolboy from the far-off barbarian days of his minor public school watching another schoolboy being beaten and giving private thanks that he wasn't the one bending over the chair. I suppose there is just something about Venice that brings you close to decadence, to the sinister within, to the dark side of the soul. But if he wanted more, he would have to wait. Womankind can only take so much evil. There would be more about *Bocca del Leone* when I was feeling up to it. I had a heavy emotional prospect lined up for tomorrow: a truthful conversation with Toni.

On the few occasions that Robert is away I always relish having the whole bed to myself. That night was quite the opposite. I felt lonely and I felt stupid. Robert hadn't rung and I didn't know where he was. I could have found out but not without putting my hand up and shouting that I was gossip-worthy. In the old days I would just have rung his secretary and said something like: Oh, I must have written the number of the hotel down wrong – can you confirm it? But now that was out of the question. Truth popped out and wagged her finger. I should say here that for anyone having doubts about the good sense of remaining married after a length of time, it is quite a good, if painful, idea to go through something like this. It concentrates the mind perfectly. Suddenly, lying there in the dark, I imagined Robert never returning and myself back in the swim of the world, single. It was a very unpleasant thought – nice little fantasy when you know it isn't going to happen, nasty little fear when you think it might.

Nevertheless, I am my father's daughter in matters of conviction. Some might say stubbornness. He went to his grave (too early) a convinced Conservative who said, most memorably, on seeing John Major with his soapbox, 'That's done it. We'll never win now.' And when they did, instead of being overjoyed, he remarked, 'I was wrong. But we don't deserve the victory.' Which I thought even then was impressively honest. Truth was important and I wasn't about to give in. I couldn't, anyway, as I had no one to give in to. By now Robert was locked in the warmth of Florida with, it was to be hoped a bad case of jet lag, and not – as my closed eyes showed in visions – a leggy blonde or two hanging around him, all cleavage and overstocked white teeth, smiling wetly as he placed his chips on the roulette table. Late at night, alone in bed, and feeling mournful, the image of American women took on extraordinarily desirable proportions. Banish the daytime reality show of the supersize me obesity problem and the sensible under-standing that ordinary American women look like ordinary British women. Not at night and alone they don't. And banished were those terrifying hockey moms from the reality zone, too. At night, in bed, without my husband, American women became Venus personified. At night, with my husband on the loose, American women become sleek, dangerous and very, very sexy.

Six

Truphane: a deceiver, apparently from Old French *truffant*
or medieval Latin *truffans*, a fraud.

Mairi Robinson's *Concise Scots Dictionary*, 1985

YOU DRESS WITH care when you are preparing for a date
that might render you best-friendless. You dress even more
carefully when you think you might also look like a wraith
from Hell. It had been a very bad night. And as I dressed the
next morning I wondered what message I wanted to give
with what I wore. This was bad. I'd never in all my life
worried about what to wear when meeting up with a woman
friend. But then, I'd never met up with a woman friend
before having undertaken to speak the truth, the whole truth
and nothing but the truth. So, what did I want to say with
what I wore? That this was an unremarkable event, two pals
having pasta, nothing more, and if the ordure hit the
rotational mechanism, I could not be accused of plotting.
Such is the convoluted madness the truth part of the brain is
heiress to when brought out of retirement. I wore a dark red
jumper (the better to hide the blood, perhaps), knee-length
black skirt and flat shoes. Less unremarkable than downright boring and nothing to excite the senses. I also wore the
vintage garnet and pearl necklace Toni had bought me for
my fortieth. Not only would it stand as a bond of friendship
but its droplet stone would match my eyeballs. I really had
slept very badly. I checked the answerphone, and my mobile,
before leaving the house. Nothing.

One thing I had learned, I thought, as I sat in the restaurant and waited, was that it was not only an uneasy conscience that kept you awake at night – it was the prospect of having an easy one, too. This might be the proof of Hamlet's acuity about conscience. I was almost ready to admit defeat – and then I saw Toni – all shadows under her eyes, her spare frame even thinner than usual – wearing the daft and vulgar gold necklace that Bob brought her back from Lahore, and which I had to say, in the presence of Arturo (who looked gratifyingly surprised), that I had given her, and dressed in black. This was not my friend any more – well, not in any useful sense – and I prepared myself for the worst. But she spoke first and – despite the circles beneath them – her eyes sparkled with a strange new light.

'Come on,' she said as she sat down, 'what are you up to?'

'I'm up to absolutely nothing.'

'Don't give me that. You refuse to go away with Robert and you haven't had a row?'

'Not in any accepted sense, no.'

'Meaning?'

'It's a disagreement about truth, that's all.'

'Truth? What do you mean, about truth?'

The waitress hovered. I studied the menu. 'Shall we order?' I tried to sound nonchalant but the damnable thing about friends is that you are never nonchalant with them, so when you attempt it, they know something is up. Nonchalance is left for acquaintances and post-embarrassing incidents with strangers (as in I really meant to trip over that step).

The waitress began tapping her pen. We ordered.

She was still scrutinising me with that bullshit-detector

look. 'How are things?' I asked. I had not meant to say anything like that. This was not supposed to be an occasion on which to give her any chance to confront my truth-telling.

'So?' she said.

'What – so-so or – what?'

'I mean you and Robert.'

'So – nothing. I've just asserted myself a little and done what I want to do instead of what other people want me to do – and Robert doesn't like it. I'm just re-establishing the basis of our marriage. Redrawing the boundaries.'

'That doesn't sound like marriage to me,' she said doubtfully. Pretty rich coming from her. Perhaps we all wear hypocrisy as discreetly as our underclothes. Toni once said that because of her secret life with Bob she was perfectly happy to agree with Arturo on everything – thus making their marriage a very happy one – because it no longer mattered. Only of course, it didn't make the marriage happy. Once she started saying Yes to everything, Arturo got very, very anxious. It's the myth of the Stepford Wives – the forever male fantasy of the obedient home-maker, mother and whore – which thus produces boredom. We all need to fight for things a little bit.

'It will pass,' I said.

'Well, what's this truth thing all about?'

That was safe. I told her all about Robert and the politician on television and how I'd just decided to do something about my own petty lies.

'You,' she said, picking at her pasta, 'are one of the most truthful people I have ever met.'

A little prawn, as shocked as I was, slithered back down from my fork to my plate. That was not what I wanted to hear. That was dangerous ground. 'So you see,' I said, rushing on as cheerfully as I could, 'since I really didn't want to go to Florida and go through all that corporate stuff again, it seemed like the perfect time to attempt a bit of honesty.'

'And what did Robert say?'

'He didn't. He's not talking to me. He didn't even kiss me goodbye at the airport. In fact, he's furious.'

She gave a little shudder and put down her fork. 'Arturo would be like that.' Then she sighed. I knew what was coming but short of tipping my red wine everywhere there was no way to stop it.

As I expected, Toni gave me her usual little apologetic look and plunged in. 'But I'd so like a bit of honesty back in my life. I hate all this pretence. Sometimes I just think I'll sit him down and tell him the truth and then move in with Bob and that would be that . . . But of course, Bob couldn't leave his wife because the business would collapse without her money and . . .'

I'd heard this so many times. It was as if by saying it Toni got the guilt off her chest for a while. But then, oh then, it happened. She picked up her fork again and pointed it at me. 'You don't think I should tell him, do you, Nina? Not really?'

'Well, yes,' I said, 'as a matter of fact, I do.'

Stasis. Apart from the plop of falling prawns. Then she waved her fork about a bit and said with that false cheeriness I recognised so well, 'I know – in theory – but in practice it's impossible, of course. Arturo would be miserable, Bob would be without his home or his business, and how would the children be about it all? I'd feel terrible doing all that.'

'But you're living one big, fat lie.'

'Don't,' she groaned. 'You know I hate it.'

It occurred to me that she hated it the way Thomas à Becket hated his hair shirt. With relish.

'I don't think you could feel any worse. Could you? I mean, it's been four years and he's still not committed himself and you're just living in a day-to-day cocoon of deceit. And you look ill.'

'Thanks.'

'You usually look so fabulous, I mean. This is wearing you out.'

'Well, it's not easy at the moment because Bob's away.'

'He should leave his wife – bugger the business – and you should leave Arturo, if it's what you really want – kinder, eventually, on him and kinder, eventually, on the children. And then you'd feel better about yourself – and be well again. You really do look like shit.'

Silence ensued. Neither of us was eating but we were looking at our plates. Then she said in a very low voice, 'So – what do you think I should do to bring about this great change?'

'I think you should sit him down and say that you are not going to go on with the affair and that you want him to come clean with his wife so that you can come clean with Arturo. And if he won't, you should turn your back on him.'

'I couldn't do that.'

'You could.'

'But I love him. And he loves me.'

And then, of course, I flipped. The moment was here and the moment would not remove itself. 'No he doesn't,' I said. 'Or if he does, it's a bloody warped version of it. That's not love. It's called having your cake – it really, really isn't –'

'Oh – and you would know?' She fingered the horrible necklace and gave a horribly sentimental leer. 'He gives me lovely things and remembers my birthday and – he shows me in a hundred different ways.'

'Except the one that matters. Words aren't actions, Toni. And why wouldn't he go on buying you nice things and remembering your birthday and all that stuff – those stolen nights of passion somewhere off the M40, those moments of ecstasy as he fumbles with you in the car, the secret telephone calls? He obviously loves all that intrigue and sex and titillation.' This, I thought, is pushing it. Bob, to be fair, had never struck me as the kind of man who would recognise titillation if it got up and bonked him. But it suddenly occurred to me that maybe Toni did just that. One of them had to like it. It also, disloyally, occurred to me that I would probably love it as well. Some years ago Edna O'Brien said to the Archbishop of Canterbury that everyone needs a little adultery in their lives now and then . . . He, being of the Church of England, laughed politely. You have to wonder how the Inquisition would ever have got off the ground if it had been run by the C of E. 'Warm up the tea urn, Mrs Brown, we're coming in . . .' I'd always thought the excitement of adultery was a truth and something that the less brave of us peek at over the marital stone wall. But loving its thrills – if indeed she did – quite clearly wasn't keeping my friend from suffering. Putting aside the fleeting irritation I felt that she was, at least, losing weight, and that I, despite everything, was not, I battled on. 'No, Antonia. What he doesn't want is commitment – worrying over the gas bills, remembering to put out the rubbish, remembering to wipe the ring off the bath – he just wants the glamour and you get left with the dregs.'

This was hardly fair on Arturo and the children.

'I mean the dregs of having to live your life in one big lie. Bob has no children, Bob is scarcely ever at home – he doesn't know what you go through and he doesn't want to know what you go through, and you don't tell him. You just pitch up when he's ready for you and run yourself ragged with pain the rest of the time. He's not going to change his ways now. And that includes leaving his missus. Why would he? But for you it's no life and he's – quite frankly – a shit.' Another deep breath. In for a penny, in for a pound. 'In fact, he's a first-class shit. Don't shoot the messenger, Toni, but actually, if you want to know the truth, all your friends think that.'

The very dreadful thing about telling a truth that you have kept hidden for so long is that the guilt of not doing it soon gives it a momentum and it just rolls along once you get going. I should have stopped before this. As the gunsmoke cleared her face was like a piece of stone, staring at me. Suddenly I really, really wished I was in the Venice of five hundred years ago and had a handy *Bocca del Leone* to fall back on.'

'Oh God,' I said. 'I'm sorry. I've gone too far.'

She stood up. Her eyes were amazing, like liquid fire. There was colour in what had been parchment cheeks. She put a twenty-pound note on the table and spoke through her teeth. 'You,' she said, 'and your little, perfect life. One perfect son, one perfect daughter, one perfect husband, one perfect house and your perfectly equable eyes on the low horizon. Whereas I – at least I have lived.'

And then, inexcusably, I laughed. '*Toni!* How could you say that? Particularly about my house.'

But even though she looked just a little discomfited by what she had said and realised there was something fundamentally wrong with it – my house had never been perfect and hers, by comparison, was – nor indeed had life always been easy with either Johnno or Tassie – Toni's children were far easier which was not saying a lot – she still took the high ground. 'Very amusing. So you all think that, do you? All my friends in their little covens, discussing me and my affair and knowing exactly what I should do but not saying anything. Why did you, my very best friend, and never mind all the others, why did you let it continue for all these years without ever saying what you truly thought?'

'Will you sit down?' I asked, as meekly as I could.

The waitress came and asked if everything was all right. Toni looked her coldly in the eye, straightened her back and gave a rather wonderfully commanding gesture with her little hand that had the poor waitress scuttling off as fast as she could. Toni was angry. Really angry. Which I suppose was marginally better than her usual twitchy misery. 'So? What stopped you? Why now?'

'I've been a coward,' I said. 'An untruthful coward. There should always be honesty between friends –'

But she did not wait to hear. And there was nothing I could say to stop her turning, keeping her head up, and walking steadfastly away from me and my friendship. She was absolutely right. We'd all lied and this was the consequence.

Beware, I thought, as I looked around the restaurant at all those placid lunchers, beware of cowardice in the face of the devil expediency. I paid the bill and left. That was that. Part of me wished, since there was no rescue, that I had told her I thought Bob was a prat and deeply, deeply unattractive – creepy even – and completely and utterly boring – but that was my anger. I was glad that I hadn't – it would only have hurt her and shriven me for a short while before regret twisted my throat. As I left the restaurant I remembered some lines from another Plath poem. It ended:

The lioness,
The shriek in the bath,
The cloak of holes.

Indeed.

As I walked back to the car I became angrier and angrier
and there was a haze about my eyes, from the gunsmoke
maybe. I am a martyr, I told myself. A martyr. The Emperor
Tiberius, living at the top of Capri, received messengers in
the open air, at the edge of the cliffs. If he didn't like what
they told him, over the edge they were tumbled into the
foaming rocks below. That was me. Thank goodness I
hadn't been standing anywhere near an oncoming bus. Why
should truth be so hard to take and lies so easy? We're all
grown-ups, I told myself, so why can't we all act like
grown-ups? By the time I got back to the Peugeot I was
thrumming with indignation. This was grossly unfair and I
had moral right on my side and who, just who, was she to
put me through the mincer when she, Antonia, the true
daughter of Tiberius if ever I'd met one, was –'
    I reached the car and pressed the electronic key. Nothing.
I tried again. Nothing. I swore and tried once more. Well,
that was all I needed – the battery in the electric key was
flat. The car was unopenable without my setting off the
alarm. And my friend had behaved *extremely* badly. Therefore, obviously, the car needed a kick. Well, something
needed a kick. So I kicked it, quite hard, on the tyre. It was
extremely satisfying and a great reliever of emotion for one
so usually tolerant and unaggressive. At university I
couldn't even manage the martial arts classes, seeing them
as brutal rather than about discipline and self-protection. It
was like scratching an itch I didn't know I had. I did it

again, kicked hard, also, this time, drumming my fist on the top of the car. The kick left a tiny mark. This made me, curiously, even crosser. Could one operate road rage at oneself? One more kick before I walked off to try to find someone who could sort this out. A garage. There must be one nearby. So, with joyful fury, I gave it one more lesson in how not to misbehave in front of its mistress with a neat little poke of my boot. And from behind me there came a furious shout of 'Hoi'.

Well, there are nightmare possibilities and there are nightmare possibilities. This was a good one. Bearing down on me was a nun. But not one of those sweet, dough-faced women in white wimples and floaty black gowns like those lovely beings painted by Van Gogh. Oh no. This was a modern nun. In a grey outfit more like a business suit, its skirt cut to the knee, its shoulders reminiscent of Margaret Thatcher. Only the headdress was nunnish. But the head inside the headdress was not sweetly doughy at all. It was bright pink and bore a pair of penetrating dark eyes behind flashing spectacles.

'Just what do you think you're doing?'

I'm not religious. Nor was I cruelly abused by nuns in my upbringing. Therefore I thought this was simple nose-poking.

'Well,' I said, 'better the car than a person.' And I gave it another bash with my fist for good measure. At which point the nun threw herself across the side of the thing as if protecting an infant.

'Stop it this minute,' she said, 'or I'll call the police.'

'Don't be so stupid,' I yelled back – yelling being equally satisfying I suddenly realised. 'Bugger off – it's my car and I can do what I like with it.' I kicked it again. We were all grown-ups, were we?

. . . I'll draw a veil. Or a wimple. Of course it was the wrong bloody Peugeot, wasn't it? Why wouldn't it be? And of course I had to bend the knee and genuflect a squillion times while trying to explain that I was not usually of a vandalistic nature. Nor an abuser of religious houses. This took a little while to be believed – with a nice, healthy crowd around us. 'Oh – look – she's attacked a *nun* . . .' Then I gave her my address, promised to pay for the damage, and walked off, head held high, to my own little silver car that did not so much as blink as I slid into it and beat my forehead on its sweet little steering wheel.

When I got home there was a message from Robert. It was icy. 'I thought you should have my contact details in case.' And he gave them. He also added, icily *and* sarcastically, 'And sorry to have made you break your little vow of truth. How *was* the doctor and your poor ear?' My hand reached out, I was ready to call, ready to spit, and then I stopped myself. Do not rise, I counselled. Peace and Love. Peace and Love. But only up to a point, Lord Copper.

It was the perfect antidote to my misery over Toni. Peace and Love left the room. I immediately rang the number he had left. I got the hotel – of course he would not be in his room – and I left a sturdy message of my own informing him that I had, indeed, gone to the doctor's after I left him at the airport, though not for my ear, and so honour was still mine. Then I put down the phone and fumed all evening, expecting him to call. He did not. War had truly been declared.

In this inflatededly justified frame of mind I wondered whether to call Toni and then decided that I had better not. I was too wound up and likely to say more unpleasant truths if she asked. I'd sleep on it. Let it simmer for a while, let the sand settle, and about six more comforting clichés before I was convinced. Part of me suffered from a creeping fear that she might act on my words and in her angry state declare all to Arturo. Which would be my fault and forever, I was sure, would it be laid at my interfering self-righteous door. Down on to those rocks I would tumble. What was it Mark Twain said? – 'Truth is the most valuable commodity – let us economise.'

At least that night I slept. Robert's reaction and my reaction to him was a touch more normal than all my imaginings about leggy blondes. He did not, as far as I could tell from the muffled message, sound like a man who had been playing James Bond in *Casino Royale*.

Seven

Carriwitchet: a hoax; a puzzling question not admitting to a satisfactory answer.

John Camden Hotten's *Slang Dictionary*, 1887

VENICE PROVED QUITE a comfort in these disturbing times and at least I had my researches. Things paled in comparison with the deceptions of La Serenissima. Even the idea of solid ground beneath one's feet is illusory there. The whole history of the place is steeped in deception and betrayal, and their good and holier-than-thou attitude was tempered by the much more seductive underpinning of profit. Our politicians now had nothing on their politicians then. The Venetian Council of Ten might tell the world that there were none more holy than themselves in existence. They might have been convincing enough to persuade the Army of Christian Nobility that their love and support was supreme. And in so doing cleverly win the said army's contract to provender and convey and make Venice the designated port of embarkation for the Crusades. But when the Crusaders arrived in Venice and wanted to set sail for the Holy Land, they found they were missing a caveat. Venice certainly supported them. But at a price. In the name of God we stand by you – yes – but only for cash will our merchants provide ships, men, stores, arms and everything else that you Crusaders asked for. Despite its being for God, and despite Venice being rich as Croesus, while the spirit is willing beyond price, we do actually have to sell you the goods to effect salvation.

The Holy Warriors were stuffed. But they were there now, no going back . . . The Venetians bowed low to them, said they believed wholeheartedly in their goal, agreed that their success would be good for the whole of Christendom, including their sinful selves. All that. But money on the table first, please. The Third Crusade, something of a disaster for Christendom since it left Saladin firmly in control of Jerusalem, raised twelfth-century Venice to the pinnacle of riches and mercantile influence and had them rubbing their hands together at the prospect of a Fourth Crusade where they did, indeed, present another large bill to be paid in advance. As I suggested to Brando, the Venetians were the true originators of that telling phrase: 'In God We Trust: All Others Cash.'

'I like it,' he said, and I could hear him scribbling away. Not for the first time I wondered why he was said to be writing the book and I was only said to be researching it. When – if – it were ever published – my name would not even signify. Was every situation that I held in my life holding untruth at its core? I completed what I had to do at the British Library that day and left. All these years of wishing I could spend as much time as I wanted in that quiet, helpful place, and now it felt wrong to be sitting there apparently calm. Apparently because I was not calm, I was agitated and not a little miserable. I couldn't settle, that was the truth of it. It continued to be exactly how I felt when I first met Robert and I used to wait painfully for him to call me, imagining all the while that he never would again because I had done something dreadful without knowing it or he had been scooped up by someone else. Now I really had done something dreadful – as far as he was concerned anyway – and for all I knew . . .

On the other hand, I thought, struggling on to the Tube, he was a first-class shit.

Back through the front door I came with a couple of useful books and a hopeful look at the answerphone. Nothing. Not surprising, really. My message to him had hardly been conciliatory. Fool, I told myself, flinging down the books, fool. One of the pages flopped open to reveal the picture of a woman in a scold's bridle. Chillingly appropriate.

Then Tassie rang. Just as I was settling myself down with a notebook and pen. I flung myself at the phone, eager as any teenager with a crush, feeling sure it was Robert and that everything was going to be all right.

'Hello,' I said with tremendous joy and laughter.

'Mum?' said an uncertain little voice. 'What are you doing there? I thought you were in Florida?'

My parents were terrible liars. Looking back I realised so many things they said were just not true. The first time I went away on a school trip, with tent, I anxiously asked if my parents would miss me and they said that they really wouldn't, not at all, that I wasn't to think it for a moment. Just go away and enjoy yourself, they said, as if it would be out of sight, out of mind for them, too. It was meant to cheer me up but instead I set off in the school coach feeling miserable and unloved. Especially as my abiding memory during that week away in the Welsh hills was the sight of my jolly-faced parents waving and smiling and looking for all the world as if they were intending to have a rip-roaring time while I was away. Later, much later, many years or more, when I remembered and told them how I felt, they were really shocked.

'Your mother cried all the way home in the car,' said my father, with a certain indulgent smile that always drove my mother mad.

'And your father was downstairs in his pyjamas at three in the morning for the first two nights you were away,' she rallied, 'checking with the Met Office.'

'If I'd known that,' I said, 'I'd have been so happy.'

Well – I'd been doing the same to Tassie. Saying we were fine, saying we hoped she was having a good time, not mentioning how dangerous some of the places were, nor that I had a pain like a hole in my heart for the first few weeks she was away. I'd go and sit on the end of her bed and look at the glassy eyes of her assorted teddy bears and her silly soft toys and dissolve into memories of holding her to my breast and singing her lullabies. It wasn't quite the same in Johnno's room. I missed him badly, too, but perhaps there is something extra in the connection with a firstborn. Robert was more robust but he missed both of them in smaller ways – like going out with Tass to get the Sunday papers and walking the long way round to come home. Neither he nor she would acknowledge that this was their regular bonding moment but that's what it was. Since she had been away he'd scarcely bothered to buy a paper on Sunday. And he missed Johnno's music so much that once or twice I'd found him sitting on the end of the bed, listening to a CD. I even suggested that we got a dog – or borrowed one – just so he had something to do, but he wisely pointed out that the one – and perhaps only – great benefit of our children having gone halfway across the world was that we were free to go anywhere we liked, too. A dog would tie us down. But as it was – apart from horrible Florida – we hadn't gone anywhere. Holidays had always been family events up until now, with the two of us taking the occasional two- or three-day break. I think that neither of us had the heart to go travelling until the two of them came back. Daft but true. Despite all this, to Tassie and Johnno we remained very cheerful. It was far less hard with Johnno because he so seldom rang home. But here was our daughter now, on the phone, about to ask a very direct question, and I had to answer her truthfully. Did I? I did.

'Mum?'

'Yes.'

'Why aren't you two in Florida?'

'Your dad is.'

'Why aren't you? Are you ill?'

'No, I'm fine. What did you ring for, if you thought we were in Florida?' As if our daughter would allow me to change course.

'I was just going to leave a message to send on some of my savings. I thought you'd be all mellow when you came back and Dad wouldn't go off on one. Why are you still there?'

'Oh – well – *Florida* –'

'Are you OK? I mean, is there anything wrong or –'

'No . . .'

'Mum?'

'Oh, your dad and I had a bit of a disagreement.'

'You had a row?'

'Not exactly.'

'What exactly?'

'A disagreement.'

'What about?'

'A matter of philosophy, actually.' My voice had taken on a defensive tone. And Tassie was too steeped in family nuances not to notice. 'So he went on his own.' I tried not to make this last sound pathetic. Possibly I failed.

'Oh for God's sake, Mum,' she said exasperatedly. 'Why not just get on a plane and go out there? Just go. Why not? You're obviously missing him.'

Babes and sucklings. Irritating items.

'Here's the truth of it. I'm not out there with him because I don't want to be there. I've about as much interest in being in Florida, wearing cruise wear and going to Disney World as you have in going to a Britten opera at the ENO.' That, at least, had the momentary effect of stopping our daughter in her tracks. She had, indeed, refused to come when we bought an extra ticket and she had, indeed, stressed very loudly and very firmly that it was her absolute right not to do things she did not want to do. There was a short silence, in which I could hear the cogs working in her devious little mind, and then she regrouped. 'Poor Dad,' she said, feelingly. 'Poor Dad.' To which, of course, there was no answer that did not sound uncaring or downright cruel, but I had a go.

'Why poor Dad? He's doing what he wants.'

'Yes, but not with who he wants. Well, I'm going to talk to him.'

'I don't think his mobile works over there.' That was a reasonable bit of equivocation.

'What's the name of the hotel he's staying in?'

'I don't know.' Also true. He had only left the phone and room numbers.

'Then I'll have to find out.' She paused and then continued in an enviably lofty tone. 'You know, it's the last thing someone like me wants when they are on their famously character-building travels – to find their parents acting like a couple of prats.'

You know so much when you are that age.

'I'm not acting like a prat, Tass, I'm doing what I believe in. And whatever you may think, and despite its causing ructions, I feel very good about it; I do not want to go on those jaunts any more and being truthful should be easy and good, and so far it's been quite the opposite. What does that tell you about society?'

'Nothing,' she said, 'that I didn't know already.'

In the end, I fondly believed, I persuaded her not to call her father on the grounds that he should have as carefree a time as possible. And with a dollop of common sense riding to the rescue, Tassie said she saw the point. Devious of me, but not untruthful. I promised to call her the moment he came home and was about to say 'I'm sure it will all blow over' before hanging up, when I realised that I didn't exactly feel it would. We'd been married long enough to know each other very well – this was no little blip, this had seriously rocked Robert – and me – and the picture of him coming through the door with a suntan, a bright smile and a nice bottle of my favourite perfume was not believable. Given the economics of a world in meltdown, it probably wasn't the right time to practise truth, but I was dug in now and short of dumping the principle and flying out to him and feeling (I knew myself well enough) a resentful martyr, *status* must remain in *quo*.

It was with an uncomfortable lump somewhere in my solar plexus that I went back to my screen and back to the comfort of Venice's seamy side. And much dirt there was. The Venetian and Augustinian theologian Paolo Sarpi, who took on the might of the Pope by starting a free church in Venice and removing the city state's allegiance to Roman Catholicism, said something I took to heart. 'I never tell a lie, but the truth not to everyone . . .' Which summed up pretty well the way, then and now, we all made our way in the world. If it was good enough for a friar and man of God, what hope for a twenty-first-century ordinary woman?

I found a sinister Goyaesque picture of a woman in late-eighteenth-century Venetian mask and dress, basket over her arm, reaching up to remove the teeth from a hanged man a-swinging on the gibbet. 'Apparently,' I told Brando, 'the best false teeth were made of real human teeth and worth a lot . . .' Even Brando had the grace to whimper. If he wanted it included I thought we would probably have to pay a reproduction fee. 'It's not unique to Venice, the practice of nicking teeth from the dead, but it's very Venetian to want to make a huge profit out of it.'

'We'll pay,' he said.

Usually I wouldn't have bothered asking, just gone ahead, but I suppose I needed to talk to someone and Brando, though many things that were not estimable, was wise. He was at the bar, Harry's of course, and moaning about how it had become so commercial and dull. He was on – it sounded to me – his third or fourth Bellini. It also sounded as if he had not been too successful in his particular brand of pursuing happiness. We talked for a bit about a few ideas he had and then he muttered something about this thing having hit me hard, to which I muttered that, well, yes it had. There was a moment's silence and then a sharp sigh and, 'Come over,' he said imperiously. 'Get on a plane and come over now. Spend a couple of nights here. You can get the juice at source. I insist.'

It was completely unexpected. And, when the identity of my next visitor was revealed, I could only wish he had made the offer a little sooner. I'd have been up and away before you could say coward.

Just after he uttered the words my doorbell rang out. It
has a penetrating ring. 'Christ – what's that?' he yelled
down the phone.

I peered around the blinds, half drawn, a sign of the way
I felt about my life. 'My mother,' I sighed. 'Goodbye, dear
Brando, and possibly forever.' Brace yourself, Georgina, I
told myself. Brace yourself. For I knew the line of those lips
intimately. They bespoke a rather dependable lack of
compliment from mother to daughter. Taking my own
counsel, I braced myself.

And then she was in.

Eight

Gleek: to joke, jibe or banter.

Nathaniel Bailey's *Etymological English Dictionary*, 1749

SINCE MY FATHER died my mother had developed an even greater fondness for Robert – she being one of those women most assuredly of the previous generation who liked to have a man in her life and to respect and cosset him. Until now this had not been a problem – certainly not for Robert – but not for me either. It is very nice to have a mother who approves wholeheartedly of one's marital choice even if she does not approve wholeheartedly of the daughter who married him – and Robert never turned it into anything sickening.

Under current circumstances, though, this bond was tricky. Her visit was hardly likely to be an ad hoc social call – my mother did not do things like that. After my father died she was very particular that she would not be a burden to either of her children. Since Laurie, my brother (whom I describe to people not in the know as the original confirmed bachelor), lives in Glasgow this was less of a struggle where he was concerned, whereas we only lived about five miles away. But she had stuck to her undertaking. Sometimes I had to practically go and yank her protesting carcass out of her house and into the car for a Sunday lunch. But not today. No – she had got on a bus to come over, she had not telephoned first, so something was definitely up. And although she sat on the sofa looking just like Mum, grey coiffed hair, minimal make-up, camel coat with matching scarf tucked in, nevertheless there was something about her that said this was only the outer shell. Inside she was a big cat.

'Tea?'

'No thank you.'

'Coffee?'

'No thank you.'

'Gin?'

This achieved not even a smile.

'Sit down, please, Georgina,' she said.

And in my own home, too.

I sat.

A little part of me was excited, pathetically, at the thought it might have been Robert who had alerted her to all not being well, but really I knew it was Tassie. If there was one strange thing that was happening in among all this moral struggle, it was the discovery that I really was frightened at the thought of losing Robert. I realised the enormity of what he saw – my breaking my loyalty. And let's face it, Nina, without loyalty what is love? Stand by your man is no different from stand by your woman. What would I feel if Robert had done this to me? If he had suddenly gone all po-faced and said that there were greater things in life than love and loyalty and refused to do something I desperately wanted him to do? I would have felt betrayed. No doubt about it. Well, too late now.

I stood up again. This was ridiculous. This was my own house and whatever had happened I was in charge here. I tried to help my stone-lipped mother off with her coat but she gave an impatient gesture with her hand and I sat down again. It seemed likely that she had rehearsed it all on the bus coming over and was not to be denied.

'Tassie rang.'

'I guessed that.'

'She told me that you'd refused to go away with Robert.'

'Yes, that's true.'

'To Florida.'

'That's also true.'

'Can I ask why?'

'You can.'

'I know it isn't really any business of mine.'

'No it isn't.' Well, it was the truth. Hang me for a flock of sheep as much as a single puny lamb.

She ignored this. She can be very wise and diplomatic, my mother.

'Why, then?'

'Because I didn't want to go and I was fed up with pretending that I did. I hate the whole thing, have always hated it apart from at the very beginning, and it seemed stupid to be my age and still telling lies about the way I feel. Robert doesn't like going very much either which is part of the reason. I wasn't prepared to lie about it any more, and he was. You should try it – watching the men make competitive twits of themselves while we women sit there wearing silly smiles and even sillier outfits. And anyway, I have work to do in Venice. For Brando. I have to fly out there. Tomorrow.'

At the mention of his name she closed her eyes momentarily. When she opened them again she looked at me with that unwavering pale blue stare. I'd seen that over the years as she dropped it on doctors, teachers, my father, Laurie (seldom) and me. Here it was, back on me again.

'Is there someone else?' she asked crisply. Then she looked around the room as if expecting a bank manager to fall out of the corner cupboard. 'You'd better say if there is and get it over with.'

'There is not,' I said. 'Never was, never will be.'

'Then what the blue blazes are you doing sending that poor man off on his own? He's simply doing his job as he has always done – and now he's surrounded by all those American women and far away and feeling miserable. Tassie says he's feeling very angry and very sad about it all.'

So she had ignored my advice and spoken. Viper. But I liked the use of the word sad. I tried to stifle the reminder about the other women and failed.

'What women?' I asked.

'American women,' she said, with a tone of voice and a look that intimated they were vagina dentata personified. You can take the girl out of the mother, but you can't take the mother out of the girl. We thought alike. No doubt American women, like any others, could be very sympathetic when they found a man being sad. In a black leather jacket and black jeans, I reminded myself. Wallow in Venice, wallow in self-pity, it's all the same.

'Well, he should try to understand.'

'Understand what?'

'That we should be more truthful in life. We can't expect the powers that be and the world around us to be honourable if we fib, lie and cheat all the time. And Robert had been going on and on so much about politicians and the rest not telling the truth that – well – I agreed.'

At least she blinked. I wasn't sure if I'd got my message across. She smoothed the empty seat next to her with her ageing hand. There was the wedding ring, thin and familiar beneath Dad's mother's solitaire. There were the perfectly shaped nails, free of varnish. Those were the hands that had been around me all my life, and usually – certainly since the advent of my children – they were on my side. Not now. The hand stopped its smoothing and hovered, fingers spread. 'Well,' she said sourly, 'I knew it was something stupid but I had no idea how stupid.' Upon which she slapped that hand back down on the cushion with a pumpff. 'You are just being wilful and silly.'

I will not rise to the word stupid, I thought. 'Great oaks out of small acorns do grow,' I said, primly. 'Someone has got to stop the rot. Remember – it only takes one good man to remain silent and –'

The hand made an irritated silencing gesture. 'Is it the menopause?' she said, lowering her voice and sliding a little way along the sofa to be nearer to my chair.

How nice it would have been to say – yes – yes it is – only hormones – nothing to worry about.

'No, Mum – it's the conscience. It's the fact that everywhere you turn people are lying, bending the truth, cheating – and I hate it. But I can't complain if I also *do* it.'

'Have you tried oil of evening primrose? It did wonders for me when –'

'It is NOT THE FUCKING MENOPAUSE.'

She slid very rapidly and in a very upright manner back along the sofa.

'Oh sorry. Oh God,' I babbled. 'Oh, sorry to swear. But it's making me feel miserable, too.'

'I think it will be something to do with the meno—'

I gave her a look. She had the good sense not to go on.

'I thought he'd understand.'

'Don't be such a silly baby, Nina. You'll lose him. He's a good-looking man. He's in his prime. And he's interesting. According to Tassie he's very hurt indeed. Doesn't understand any of it. And you are risking everything by doing this. Everything.'

I stared out of the window. A John Lewis van was delivering something to the house opposite. The elderly Mrs Parker was in her garden clipping her little hedge. A dog walker went by with three small dogs on leads. All very normal. All very desirably normal. Life going on. I looked back at my mother. Her lips were pinched, her eyes searching. She was silently saying, Well?

I wanted to say that it didn't say much for our marriage if he fell at the first hurdle of doubt. But I didn't – because I think I agreed with her. I was risking everything and it was unjust and I wished I had never started it. But I wasn't going to admit it. If that was questionable honesty, it was all right by me. 'Thank you, Mother.'

'Will you go? To Florida?'

'I can't.'

'Why not?'

'Because I'm going to Venice.'

'Then there is another man.'

'Only Brando. I promise.'

She leaned stiffly into the back of the sofa and blew out a sigh. 'That man. I knew him when he didn't have two ha'pennies to rub together. And now he wears those appalling leather trousers and minces around like a – like a –'

'Like a what?' (As a matter of fact, he has not worn them for several years – even old queens know when to hang up their bondage gear.)

I could see, suddenly, the shaft of reason penetrating those pale blue eyes. And it was this. If I, Nina's mother, go banging on about Brando and his sexual proclivities and vivid colour sense and his leather gear, and Nina is determined on this truth-telling business, she may well mention Laurence and I really do not want to admit the truth about *him*. As long as I don't know the truth then he might suddenly convert to being normal . . .

That is what I read there and that, I am sure, was right.

'Well, if you will, you will,' she said. 'Nothing's to be done with you once you get a bee in your bonnet. I should know. And I'm only trying to help.'

'Well, you're not. There's nothing you can tell me that I don't already know. And despite it all, it's good to feel I'm doing something honourable. Even if it does cock up my life. So please don't interfere any more.' I kept my back as straight as she kept hers. Who would blink first?

She looked hurt. Her mouth puckered again. I felt a little thrill of victory.

I smiled, nicely. It was over.

'I'll drive you home.'

'When do you go – to Italy?'

'First thing tomorrow. I want to be home in time for Robert. He gets back on Saturday.'

'You can bring me some of that fruit mustard I like. You get it on the Rialto.' Peace was declared.

She undid the buttons of her coat and pulled out the familiar Liberty scarf. Thirty years old, at least. I knew because I'd bought it.

'And I think I will have that gin before I go. You, Nina, are a fool. Worse, you are a stubborn one.'

I stood up. 'I'll join you.'

'Make yours a small one if you're taking me home.'

At the door I turned. 'Stubborn? Really? I wonder where I get that from?'

She had the grace to glimmer a smile.

Nine

Flahooler: a generous, big-hearted, good-natured person,
with a sense of gaiety.

Michael Traynor's *The English Dialect of Donegal*, 1953

HE WAS THERE, waving a very large saffron handkerchief,
as the motorboat came to rest on Dorsoduro.

'I haven't booked you into the same hotel as me,' he said,
'because . . .'

I looked with longing across the water to the Gritti Palace
and others. But I knew what the *because* was all about. He
wouldn't want to dent any possibility by appearing to have
a female in tow.

'That's fine,' I said. 'I'm surprised you've been organised
enough to book me into anywhere.'

'I haven't,' he said. 'Yet. I thought we could see what was
available. Do you know a reasonable hotel near here?'

'La Calcina, if they can fit me in.' I sighed as if
remembering. 'Oh yes, I know it of old.'

Brando ignored the sigh which I thought was most
unkind. 'Well – you can deal with my case.' We hopped
across the water and set off along the Zattere, zizzagging
our way through a smattering of extraordinarily dressed
tourists who seemed quite unaware of how gross they
looked in their holiday uniforms. I still wonder at the
peculiar mechanism of the brain that links the word
Holiday with Things You Wouldn't Be Seen Dead In
Usually. At least on this side of the Grand Canal there were

86

fewer tourists. Across the water at San Marco the place was thronging. Seldom does any category of human being look sensible and pleasing in a baseball cap. Possibly golfers. And players of baseball, obviously. It also says something about the wearer but I'm never sure what. Avoid me at all costs, perhaps? Beneath the baseball hats there were an amazing number of very large ladies in short shorts, fat men in tight T-shirts, thin men in very white trainers, short ladies in check golfing trousers and worse. I never got it right, either, until I watched what Venetians themselves wore and borrowed their white linen with black. I never quite dared go for their other great skill, the mixing of the colourful with the quiet. You see it in Venetian painting, simplicity and wild colour mixed in perfect fusion, and you see it being worn with exuberant elegance in the bars and restaurants on a summer's night. Today, looking back across the water, the indigenous Venetians stood out gloriously from these invaders as they wove their snooty way past the Doge's Palace and down the Schiavoni. You can come and spend your money here, they seemed to say, but you'll never be one of us. I sighed. With the spirit of Byzantium and the grandiosity of the baroque as their backdrop, the contrast between Venetian style and tourist absurdities was not even funny. At least Brando – despite his bright blue trousers and startling checked jacket – mostly navy and pink – looked eccentric rather than determinedly vulgar. I felt a rush of affection for him. 'It's good to see you,' I said, quite genuinely. He looked slightly embarrassed at my warmth.

'Sorry,' he said, 'about the hotel. I should have looked after you better.'

I nodded. 'Yes, you should.' He looked even more embarrassed and I was even more surprised. I'd never known Brando to be that unselfish, ever. And certainly not with me. 'Let's hope they've got a room. They should do. It's only April.'

I didn't enlighten him that I'd rather stay a good few vaporetti stops away from him. Besides, if it was good enough for Ruskin then it was good enough for me. I loved the Zattere.

Apart from a hall of mirrors in a fairground, Venice is the absolute doyenne of illusion. And full of clichés. La Salute still looked exactly like a cardboard cut-out against the April-blue sky, Tiepolo's colour. I stopped for a moment to look up at her; what a creation, what confidence, what superior pleading for succour against plague and pestilence was in those curls and scrolls. There was a lesson for the miserable somewhere in there – I may be down but I most emphatically am not out.

'We could have a Campari,' said Brando, also stopping, and not without longing. 'No rush, is there?' We both stood at the waterside, looked up again, and stared. Salute was almost shimmering in her whiteness. He nodded at the restless shape of her. 'Henry James said she was like some great lady waiting on the threshold of her salon, wearing a pompous crown. You can see what he meant.'

'And the Venetians call the side bits her *orecchioni* – big ears – which deflates the pomposity a bit. Does it look as if it's made out of cardboard to you? As if you could push it over?'

He eyed me slightly nervously. 'No-oo,' he said. 'It looks very solid and secure.'

See what I mean? Venice is all things to all people, including having big ears and forever changing her skirts. We set off again. For some reason I was now pulling my case over the cobbles, up and down the steps of the little bridges, along the narrow *callis* and feeling very happy to be there, albeit with the happiness underpinned with melancholy. The usual state of a visit to Venice as far as I'm concerned. Too much beauty, perhaps.

When we came here, Robert and I, we stayed in La Calcina – and we mostly ate at the cheaper restaurants lined up along the Zattere and stretched out over the water on their pontoons. Aldo's had been my favourite – they always managed to get the egg in a calzone – the most sensuous of pizzas – to be runny. But Aldo's had gone – others had taken his place, and the whole area looked posher than I remembered it. Happily, some of the facades of the buildings were still peeling and crumbling, making the contrast that is also Venice – Plath's 'old whore petticoats' worn beneath the watery city's perfect velvet and lace.

I was in luck. La Calcina had a room with a view. For a split second I thought Brando was going to suggest the cheaper option, of a single room without a view, and in my earlier incarnation I wouldn't have noticed, or commented. But I was probably giving off vibes – don't mess with me, not in the mood – because he paid the advance like a pussycat. In this city of secrets and winks and nods and waiters who blow kisses to each other to attract attention, he could hardly contain his excitement. It certainly beat cruising in Kensington Gardens.

'Happy?' he asked, oddly anxiously still.

'It's fine,' I said. And he left.

The *proprietaria* who signed me in was quite uninterested in me as a person but committed to me as a guest, which was exactly right. I wonder if there is another breed of people who are quite so good at judging the selling of services and goods. A Venetian will assess what you need before you know it yourself and without the side issue of morality. The buying and selling of commodities, any commodities, is above morals. I was once told by Toni's Bob – I winced to remember his existence – that the Japanese had this same skill with people as purchasers, but I couldn't judge. Both cultures use masks – maybe that's the link. In any case, I did not want to think about either of them. Not now. Toni and I must wait. I was here in Venice and I meant to enjoy it. The owner accompanied me up to my room. She showed me how to work the shower, how to open the shutters without damaging my nails, how to unplug one item in order to plug in another. Then she left me, and as she closed the door I felt both sad and excited at being so alone. Two days of being my own mistress entirely. It seemed that some things could compensate, just a little, for the bad stuff.

The simple room had long windows overlooking – sideways on – the Zattere and the Giudecca, and it was on the third floor so not too noisy or smelling of pizza – in fact, it was perfect. If I lay on the small white bed and turned my head, I could look out across the water to the line of little cafes and shops on the opposite shore. I lay there, twitching my toes, and wondering, suddenly miserable, why I had to be here alone. But there was also that faint and niggling sense of freedom. A very odd combination of responses for one who, until now, had been such a thoroughly married woman. The misery began to give way, just a little, to excitement.

The place certainly suited my mood. Every so often the canals and waterways of Venice are drained. For a time you can see the slimy foundations of the beautiful buildings and the sludge and foul detritus that sits at the bottom of those snaking pathways of water. Venice shows you her dark side, her secret filth, and then – when the cleansing and the dredging is complete – the snakes are refilled and the light shines down on them and you try to forget, for she does not want you to remember, the truth about her hidden nastiness. Perhaps it was the melancholy this thought caused, or the balmy breeze of the April afternoon, that sent me to sleep.

To be woken about two hours later by the telephone and Brando asking how I was getting on – he sounded waspish – irritable – and I guessed that whoever he'd had his eye on had not obliged.

'Very, very well,' I lied. And then I remembered. 'Actually,' I said, waiting for the storm to strike, 'I've been asleep.'

There was a swallowing sound, a hiccough that might or might not have been Brando about to strike, and then he replied with calm evenness, 'Good. So you'll be nice and ready to do a bit of research now. Have a bit of a wander. You can get a rover ticket.'

No water taxis for me, then. 'Yes – plenty to get on with.'

'Good. And you can join me for dinner.'

'Are you sure?' I teased.

'Sure about what?'

'Having dinner with me and not –'

'See you at seven, here,' he said, crisply. 'Or – no – wait – let's meet for a drink at Florian's. Outside. It's warm enough. Six thirty.'

'Ah yes, home of the kissing waiters.'

'Something like that.' He sounded even more waspish. 'Florian's,' he said, and put down the phone.

I took out my books and some old maps and a few other bits and pieces and laid them carefully on the table by the window. It looked extremely efficient. I then sat down and began to mark up places to visit, things to see, over the next couple of days. But really my mind was not on the task. Not at all. I loved being here. Just being here. And I longed to telephone Robert, really longed to; the view from the room made his absence all the more acute. Never mind the freedom, I could only think that we had been so happy here. But of course I didn't phone. What could I say if I did speak to him? 'I'm sorry'? But I wasn't. How much easier it was to tell a lie than an inconvenient truth. I began to have a tickle of sympathy for politicians after all. In the course of this procedure I'd managed to arrive this side of divorce from my perfectly acceptable husband, I had upset my daughter, alienated my mother (true this was not hard) and probably lost one of my closest women friends. Great. I could see myself ending up in a world in which my only ally was Brando.

I finished unpacking, showered and out came the white linen. Venetians notice everything you wear and can make you feel very inadequate – especially at a place like Florian's. They may take the money of the baseball-behatted crowd during the day, but in the evening it is back to good sense in matters of style, as if the entire population dresses for dinner. Of course, this is also fantasy, but that's the Venetian way – to give you fantasy at a price.

The early-evening air was warm. I would be about half an hour early for our meeting but I quite liked the idea of sitting alone and watching the world go by in the piazza. When Robert and I came here and visited Florian's, I watched a couple of interesting, elegant-looking single women – how much older they seemed to me then, the same age as me now – and thought how intriguing and sophisticated they looked – in an unselfconscious way – as if it meant nothing to them to be alone at their separate tables sipping their drinks in this most fashionable of places. This evening I thought I might do the same. Just sit and look about me and pretend to be fascinating – with a notebook and pen to hand in case some jotting of thoughts took my fancy. I was too late to go and see those lions' mouths this evening, anyway, and the archive would be closed. Tomorrow would do for both. There is nothing like wandering around a place like Venice if you have an object in mind – even if you never fulfil it. Those old lions had been in place for five or six hundred years – another day wouldn't worry them.

Even if they weren't used nowadays I could imagine it being cathartic to pop a vengeful note into the lips of the lion, despite its never being read. And they looked so decorative, so harmless. Some had the prettiest of lions' faces, with sweetly curling manes and not a tooth to be seen. Seductive and meretricious. Some were more honestly wrought with grimaces of rage or with sinister, curling mouths – but all with that same small but tempting opening of the lips, secret and perfect for a denunciation or two. Now, apart from the Doge's Palace, the rare ones that remained around the city were in various states of decay. Still, we only needed to look at one or two close by. I doubted if Brando would step further than he had to. The two remaining in the Doge's Palace would suit him, the best being in the Bussola Chamber where the face is still complete and sinister and you can easily imagine the moment when an ambitious politician or an angry spouse – a thought rather too near to home for comfort – dashed off a damning note with his quill and slipped it into that secret slit. Maybe they regretted it once done – but too late – like the Royal Mail, once inside the box it was the property of the state. Even in the benign sun of an April evening, I shivered. How many poor souls went to their tortured deaths through the heat of the moment and a rash deed? There is no reposeful balance in Venice, or very little. Mostly it stirs you up, the place, with its dynamic of movement and illusion. You can hardly call the baroque soothing. Perhaps it wasn't the best place to be when I was so stirred up already. Or perhaps it was. I hardly knew any more.

At least there was a table free in the piazza, and in the sun. Florian's band was playing Viennese waltzes – which was a relief from the tinkled up Beatles' numbers they were playing last time Robert and I were here. It made me smile, now, to remember how high-handed we were then. How we looked down our snooty, youthful noses at such wanton misuse of proper culture. Now I wouldn't have minded at all if they had burst into 'Yesterday' or 'Michelle' – I'd probably hum along. But this evening it was definitely Vienna. All in all I might have been sitting there in Napoleon's time, so fitting was the music, so correct were the cafe-goers. This is the time of evening in St Mark's when the tourist boats and the coaches parked by the station leave and the place becomes civilised and proper again. Now it was all elegance and serenity.

A waiter blew a kiss at another waiter and one was immediately by my side. I ordered Campari and soda – a very silly drink but pretty – and sat there idly looking and waiting – feeling slightly sad, slightly excited. Venice is never truly gay, she is too watchful, too much the merchant who has lost too much, not regained enough, has too many regrets to be careless enough for genuine jollity. The mood of her suited me. Truth was a hard thing to achieve.

Brando would be totally unsympathetic. He was not

bothered if I spoke truth or told him lies. He trusted me to
choose which for the good of whatever I wanted to do at the
time. Brando was sometimes entirely untruthful just for the
fun of it. But when asked, he never flinched from being
honest. How odd it was that he – most frivolous and
shrugaway of all my connections – should be the one with
whom truth sat so confidently. It would never occur to him
to worry about being hurtful. He would tell me that my
breath smelled of garlic as quickly as he would tell me that
what I had written made no sense. Oh the irony. When you
don't care a fig for the world and what they think, only then
can you be as truthful as you wish.

The drink arrived, I sipped it, and then I really was in
Italy. The brightness of the red, the deep flavour of the
bitterness, the hint of bubbles is a perfection found only if
taken in Italian sun. Anywhere else and it is very
unpleasant. You can soldier on with it back home but
eventually you'll abandon the attempt for a sensible gin and
tonic. And as I was thinking about this and smiling to
myself and remembering those cool- and collected-looking
women whom I admired as they once sat here just as I sat
now, something that I had not, for one moment, expected
to happen, occurred. A man came up, bowed slightly, and
asked if he might join me. A tall, lean man with
distinguished dark grey hair, elegant rimless spectacles, and
a slightly suntanned face. Not handsome but stylish and
confident. He was – at a guess – in his early sixties and wore
his black linen jacket open with a pale blue linen shirt
beneath. As the white is for the women, this is the
quintessential uniform of the casually dressed Italian male.

He carried an English *Times* folded under his arm, and
while he was not Marcello Mastroianni, nor was I Anita
Ekberg. And anyway, this was Venice, not Rome. I noticed,

as he smiled, that he had very good teeth. I was also aware, as I was about to tell the smiling lie that my husband would be along any moment, I couldn't. Not without rendering the whole exercise that had brought me here null and void. How useful lies are. How naked we are without them. I just stared up helplessly wondering what to do. He smiled again and gestured at the other, empty, chair.

'I'm not disturbing you?' He nodded at my notebook which was unopened on the table, the pen still clipped into place. 'It will be such a pleasure to speak in English. You don't mind?'

And he slipped comfortably into the vacant seat opposite me, put his paper down on the table, and smiled.

'No,' I said, 'I don't mind at all.' Which was, God help me, the truth.

Ten

Neezled: a little drunk or intoxicated.

Walter Skear's *North of England Words*, 1873

'YOU ARE ENGLISH as I hoped,' he said with satisfaction as he leaned back in his chair and looked straight into my eyes, most disconcertingly. I hoped it was only his spectacles that appeared to wink. 'I knew you were English.'

'How?'

He shrugged. 'There is something about you – an individual sense of style – a lack of arrogance – a politesse in the way you eye the waiters . . .' He shrugged again, most elegantly, as if apologising. 'You had to be English. I enjoy the company of English people.'

I looked about me. An individual sense of style? So much for the assumption that I blended effortlessly into the Venetian evening. I probably did look a bit pink compared to all those smooth, olive skins. And the lack of arrogance was just the passivity of the insecure Englishwoman abroad, the politesse of me and the waiters only a form of fear. It could probably all be summed up by saying that I looked every bit a Marks & Spencer's woman, and they, the rest, looked like Emporio Armani. But I did not rise. I merely smiled with my very English teeth and took another sip of my drink. At least a Campari was acceptable. Wasn't it? When I looked at the Armani signore, they all appeared to be drinking black coffee from tiny cups and what men there were appeared to be drinking either prosecco or whisky.

97

Nobody, but nobody, had a bright red glass of something on their table.

'Is this your first time in Venice, signora?'

That old line.

'Oh no – I've been here a couple of times before – with my husband.'

Smooth as the waters of the canal, he replied, 'But your husband is not here with you now?'

This is when I would normally have lied and said that he was at the hotel, or flying out later, or having a haircut, but now all I could do was concede. Alarming certainly, but also amusing. Well, at least it was *something*. I was English, as he had so pointedly made clear, and married, and we married Englishwomen are not inclined to be put on the spot by flirtations. Indeed, we Englishwomen tend to be running scared of seductive encounters of the flirtatious kind, especially if we have been married for a long time. But, I had been asked a question and if truth were the order of the day there was nothing else for it.

'No,' I said, as inscrutably as I could manage, 'he is not here.'

'Then I,' he said, turning to attract a waiter, 'must do his duties for him.'

I imagine my eyes gave away the thought process which was whether or not the double meaning was intended or otherwise. I think they may have sparkled. I very much hoped not.

'*Due Campari soda*,' he said, and then turned to me again with his sunny, inscrutable smile. 'This very fine weather.'

The correct approach for the English. I immediately fell into the conversational mode and agreed that it was.

'And is it also good in England at the moment?'

I agreed, again, that it was, yes, very sunny there, too.

Of the two of us, he was the more used to appearing to be friendly and bland.

'Now, why are you here alone?'

I picked up my glass, the better to savour the moment before replying, and found that it was empty. How on earth did that happen? I replaced it on the table and was very well aware that he was looking at me, and very politely.

'Another one comes,' he said, a tad too pointedly.

I decided to look him in the eyes but stopped somewhere near his nostrils – I couldn't. I don't know why, but I couldn't. So I ended up looking over at the colonnades on the far side of the square as if for the first time.

'I'm not,' I said. 'Alone.'

And then the waiter brought the drinks and I looked up at the waiter with gratitude while the waiter looked down his nose at me as if I were something brought in on a misplaced shoe. My companion did not speak so I looked at him, finally, and the eyes were questioning, quite pleasantly, and waiting, quite unconcernedly, for me to say more. So I did. Truthfully. 'I'm here with a friend. A man,' I said. 'He'll be here very soon. You must stay and meet him.' I thought this last was pretty clever, really, and expected him to make his excuses and leave. But he only leaned further towards me, raised one eyebrow, said, 'Oh, a man?' and touched his glass to mine. 'Thank you. That would be very nice. I always enjoy meeting the English. He is English, I take it?'

'Yes,' I said. Praying that Brando would not be wearing one of his more outlandish Versace jackets. There is something entirely recognisable in a fuchsia jacket with gold buttons, something that says this man is not, really, a woman's man. Brando might be any one of a number of ways when he arrived: he might be polite and civil in a fairly distant way; he might be outrageously flirtatious (though I thought my companion a tad too old and far too self-assured for him); he might play it straight, be very friendly and very interested and ask him to dinner with us; or he might be coolly polite and immediately take me off to the restaurant without a backward glance. But which tonight? The first or the last would be best from my point of view. When, however, did Brando ever do what was required of him?

We finished our drinks. My companion introduced himself as a Venetian born and bred – an archivist by profession and something to do with local politics. He also had curatorial duties at the museum – he pointed to the far end of the piazza. I said how interesting and that I was from London and that my name was Nina and he had pro-nounced it a charming name and said that he had a daughter whom he nicknamed Nana. He then said how much he liked London and which bit did I live in? And at the same time ordered another Campari which I said I did not want and which I decided to ignore when it was brought.

'You know London well?' I asked. Vienna had gone and the band was now playing 'Eleanor Rigby' – I tried not to think of Robert – and I found I was tapping my fingers on the side of the new glass. He noticed.

'You have lovely hands,' he said. At which I quickly whipped them off the table and out of sight. He gave a very amused little laugh. 'I forgot,' he said, 'An Englishwoman must never be seen to celebrate her good points. It is immodest.'

'That's all a bit old-fashioned,' I said.

He inclined his head. 'It's refreshing.'

I found myself smiling. And then I laughed a little, too. Nice hands, indeed.

'London?' I said.

'I lived near the British Museum for a while – nearly a year – when I was doing my doctorate.'

'Oh really? What was it on?'

'Late Roman and Byzantine trade routes. Alexandria, Haifa—'

'And the British Museum was the best place to be? I should have thought . . .' I gestured all around. 'Well, why not here?'

'You plundered your way through the world even better than we Venetians,' he said. And the way he said *plundered* gave me a very jellified feeling somewhere it shouldn't.

Then our eyes did meet.

'My ex-wife is still in London,' he said.

Clever. I tried to ignore the information. He was probably lying. He probably wasn't. He was certainly a very cool customer. Perhaps he was a crook? Perhaps he wasn't chatting me up. Perhaps he was just being friendly.

'My husband is in Florida,' I replied. Not meaning to at all. And for the first time I managed to get a reaction that was less than immaculate or planned.

'*Florida?*' he said, with some emotion. Then he returned to his cooler self. 'Is he a dealer in orange juice?'

Hard to say if it was a joke or not. 'No. Computers.' It sounded very boring and bland. Usually I'd have gone on to explain that Robert was at the top of his tree, really clever, a high-class consultant of the first order. But I didn't. I just left it as it was.

'Among the greatest mysteries of life,' he said. 'Computers.'

Unfortunately I warmed to him when he said that.

'Why Florida?'

I liked the way he could not keep his cool at the thought of the place.

So of course – of course – I told him all about it. I did not ignore the new drink. I used it for punctuation while I described the idea of truth and the trip I didn't take. The glass emptied. All around us were people having interesting conversations and I felt caught up in it all. The drawing room of Europe was abuzz and the evening sun softened the severe stone facades. This, I thought, was life. You see, Robert, you see – this is what happens if you behave unkindly towards me. This.

Our toes were practically touching beneath the table as we leaned in on each other and he told me that he had never been to America, never wished to go. And I told him more about the truth thing and he said, 'You know your poet William Blake? Your great visionary? You know what he said about truth?'

I shook my head. I did not mind at all not knowing. 'What did he say, then?'

'He said, "A truth that's told with bad intent beats all the lies you can invent." ' He laughed.

I was amazed. I was ecstatic. 'That's absolutely very bloody marvellous,' I said. And with a little careful negotiation managed to manoeuvre my chin onto my hand. 'Marvellous,' I said. 'Say it again.' And if I had then been asked if I felt it would be a good idea to make my escape before anything untoward happened, I would have answered, truthfully, 'No.'

Instead of repeating the line, he was looking over my head into the distance. 'Your friend,' he said, 'does he wear very bright clothing?' I nodded, wondering how he could possibly know. But I turned and followed his gaze. There was Brando – in ochre and pink – striding across the piazza, waving cheerfully while not taking his eyes off my new best friend while my new best friend, with elegance and apparent good cheer, stood to greet him as he summoned a waiter for another round of drinks.

Brando did not have a Campari. In the manner of a sulky child he ordered a beer. Such an inelegant drink for the piazza I found myself saying to him. 'So-o inelegant.'

'Really?' he said acidly. And sipped. 'And how did you get on with the research this afternoon?'

'Excellently,' I said. He wasn't really listening.

The Italian said, most charmingly, that he had taken me away from the work I was so diligently doing when he arrived. Then he admired Brando's ochre jacket. 'It is a rare Englishman who will be so bold.'

'It is a rare Italian signor who is not.'

Brando stared at the Venetian for a moment and the Venetian stared back at him – and then – as if an unspoken decision had been made – Brando beamed a smile at him. 'Indeed,' he said, and raised his glass. 'The jacket is, of course, Italian.' The Italian raised his glass also. 'I admire it very much. And you are right in your choice of drink,' he said carefully. 'How could you drink a red drink with that colour?' He said it very seriously. Brando gave him a look of questioning amusement – and then they both burst out laughing.

'Your friend is very naughty,' said Brando.

Signora Nina has been telling me why she is here,' said the Italian.

'Yes, she's very good at it really. And I am lazy. So I pay her to do it on my behalf. It works.'

He looked puzzled. 'You pay her – ?'

And then I went off into surprisingly wild – for me anyway – laughter – because he was obviously thinking about Truth with a capital T, and Brando was thinking about researching all things murky in Venice. So they both looked at me. And I, though slightly blurry, explained.

Good humour all round.

'Where do you stay?' asked the Italian.

'At the Gritti,' said Brando. 'Of course.'

The Italian bowed his head in agreement.

'But I'm staying at La Calcina,' I said, 'because that's all he'll afford for me.' I suddenly felt sad at being thought so little of.

'It is not that at all,' said Brando, signing for the waiter. 'It is that if Nina stays in the same hotel as me, people might get the wrong idea.'

The Italian raised his eyebrows.

'Yes,' said Brando, indicating another round of drinks to the waiter, 'quite the wrong idea. They might think I was a heterosexual.'

At which both men laughed loudly all over again. Brando was obviously relaxed and happy again because he ordered his favourite Negroni. The beer was removed. And I was now to be viewed as perfectly available.

I still found the timbre of the Italian's voice, even his laughter, very appealing. Brando had already asked him if he knew of any particular aspects of Venice that were not on the usual tourist route and were – well – not nice. He nodded. 'Venice, as you know,' he said, 'is full of such things. Even the body of St Mark, our revered patron saint, has a past.'

'A pickled past,' I laughed. My word, I could be witty. 'And he probably isn't in the basilica because the basilica burnt down sometime in the tenth century and his body was more than likely destroyed. But nobody actually admits he isn't there. Ha ha.' I tapped the side of my nose. Brando leaned back and looked unimpressed. 'That's hardly heinous stuff,' he said.

The Italian looked amused. 'Oh no, I agree – that is – well

– very Venetian – the art of equivocation. No – I was thinking more of how they smuggled the stolen corpse from Alexandria.'

I murmured 'pickled' again, which Brando ignored, nodding to the Italian to continue.

'The corpse was properly mummified – as indeed it should be being the body of a Christian saint – and to get it past the suspicious eyes of the Muslims they covered it in pickled pork. Lots and lots of the stuff.'

Brando clapped his hands. 'Now that is vile,' he said. 'Deliciously vile. Just the sort of thing. I wonder if they ate it afterwards?'

The Venetian laughed loudly and I felt a twinge of jealousy.

'But wouldn't the pickling stuff destroy the mummi-fication?' I asked.

Both men looked at me sadly and I knew that I had committed the same faux pas as giving the punchline to a joke before your husband begins to tell it . . . 'Sorry.' I, too, laughed. Also loudly. Rather more loudly than intended. 'Spoiling a good story.'

Brando said, half seriously, half playfully, 'Don't bring your quest for truth to the ball, dear Nina. That's not what my readers will want.'

'Our readers,' I said. And smiled at him sweetly.

He started to talk to the Italian about his first book and his luck. 'That's why I like Venice,' he said, 'because she understands wealth and approves of it.'

'Always,' said the Italian. 'Despite the little matter of the sumptuary laws and we managed to evade those largely. Venetians like a challenge.'

He looked directly at me. Being English, I immediately looked away and gazed about me as if the inference of his words were the last thing on my mind.

The piazza had never looked more delightful, bathed in the last golden glimmerings of evening sunlight and shadow, the water to my left flickering in the reflection, the basilica to my right glowing with mosaics and marble. Even the darkness of Giotto's tower looked elegant. The alcohol had given everything a halo, a gentle fuzziness, that was soothing to the eye. Mind you, I thought, as I let my eyes rove about while the two men talked of books and curiosities and the horrors of life under the doges, mind you, even this scene with St Mark's at its centre is unreal. No saint buried beneath the high altar. Nothing but ash. And the building itself – no monument of Christian values but everything about it – its marbles, its mosaics, its gold and jewels – as well as its saint – all ripped from somewhere else, all once worshipped by an alien world, all stolen and brought as trophies to Venice. I was almost in a doze and feeling very happy when the Italian tapped the back of my hand very lightly. 'Your kind friend has invited me to dine with you, and I have promised to share the secret of a little-known and very good place that Venetians keep to themselves.'

'Excellent,' I said. And I was very hungry. When I stood up my head felt light as goose fluff and just as unfocused. Brando put his hand under my elbow, as he sometimes did when we walked together, but with just a little more alacrity than usual. The Italian walked slightly behind the two of us as we exited the square, which I found disconcerting. I was much happier when he went in front to lead the way. In fact, I was very much happier watching his back moving so easily and confidently along the twists and turns of the route than I was being watched by him. I did not feel I was entirely elegant in my footsteps. Cobbles are the most difficult things sometimes and, in my bid to be elegant, I was wearing a pair of heeled sandals that were less sandal and more foot, if you know what I mean.

We walked unspeaking for a while, moving away from the busy little streets and alleys leading off from San Marco. I concentrated on staying upright and the others concentrated on moving out of the way of the oncoming human traffic. I so wanted to stop and look in some of the windows – how the Venetians know about dressing a perfectly ordinary frock shop window is alchemy at the very least. The light was fading now and the streets were full of shadows. Eventually we arrived at a quiet square where most of the windows were shuttered except in the far corner where a light shone dimly through the panes and a small wall lantern burned low above the lintel. We could have been in any century here. The eating place was small, with an unremarkable facade saved only from dreariness by the pots of bright red geraniums lined up along its frontage. In the last of the evening sun these had that dusty scent that is entirely southern and to do with heat. From what I could make out of the old lettering across the lintel the place was called Sandolo. Which the Italian told us was the name of a type of boat. This seemed particularly appropriate as, until I'd got a few breadsticks inside me, I felt myself to be a bit boat-like – rocking gently, untethered, anchorless and pleasantly all at sea.

Eleven

Superchery: deceit; cheating.

Reverend John Boag's *Imperial Lexicon*, c.1850

WE ATE FISH. It was a fish restaurant. The owner and his
staff were efficient and cool and the Italian was greeted
without too much effusiveness. Yes – there was a table we
could have, tucked away over in one of the corners. 'In high
season,' he told us as we sat down, 'such a vacancy would
be impossible.'

I made a serious inroad into the breadsticks and felt the
bliss of a little sobering before the first course – *zuppa di
pesce*. I might have had mussels in their shells but I had a
feeling they would shoot all over the place. I wasn't doing
brilliantly with the paper covering on the bread sticks. The
soup arrived and it was delicious even allowing for my
acute hunger. I felt so happy and realised that I had not felt
happy for what seemed like days and days and days . . .
which also made me rather sad. Brando approved and
insisted that we had a very good bottle of wine. The Italian
smiled with his white teeth which seemed to glow in the
dimness and I very nearly asked if I could call him Volpone.
I managed to restrain myself – thank God for the soup and
the breadsticks. He suggested that in the Veneto and for
such a meal, Soave was the best choice. I decided to be
sensible and drink water but the smell of the wine was too
much and I decided not to be so sensible. Why should I? No
one else seemed to be at all restrained. While we waited for

our next course – I had chosen *baccalà mantecato* – the famous and most wonderful creamed salt cod of Venice – Brando prodded our Italian for ideas. No shame, Brando, in pursuit of the cruelties of the world.

The Italian thought there were one or two things he could suggest. For example, 'After dinner I can show you a little-known mouth of truth – I think it is not one often noticed. That is, if you do not mind walking a little way?'

At which a voice, which was, extraordinarily, mine (this was before the *baccalà*), said, 'Oh, can't we take a gondola?' I had always wanted to take a gondola but never actually asked to do it, or done it – so naff – so touristy – so silly – thought radical Robert and I. Now I let out the pink and fluffy in me. Brando stared as if I had suggested hang-gliding over the lagoon. I smiled back at him, shocked and pleased. I might once have concurred in the dismissal of such a showy waste. But now the red rose, 'O Sole Mio', and trailing an elegant finger seemed utterly desirable. I would experience a gondola at last. Brando was still staring. 'Oh, can't we? Please?' Then he blinked his eyes and, of course, said No. The Italian, though much more kindly, said that where we were going it would not be useful to travel by canal. So we didn't. And I felt very disappointed. I looked Brando meaningfully in the eye and said how glad I was that I had spoken the truth about wanting a gondola ride. He offered me more bread. After that I had little to say and just enjoyed the food and the slight fuzziness of the occasion. I felt myself to be a free spirit and ready for anything. Though I wished I had worn slightly more sensible shoes. With the bill paid by Brando – though the Italian attempted to pay – we set off towards the Ghetto near where, apparently, we needed to be.

The night was quite warm but not quite warm enough.

Graciously, the Italian offered to lend me his jacket to drape around my shoulders but Brando just put his arm around me, very firmly, his hot hand warming the top of my arm nicely and the jacket remained safely on the shoulders of its owner. I was rather disappointed. But Brando was, I could tell, irritated that the Italian was so attentive. Usually Brando was oblivious to any small discomfort, mine or anyone else's, and it was amusing to see that, even in the most dyed-in-the-wool gay man, there was still that element of masculine jealousy. I rather liked it. Oddly, I felt very safe with the two of them. And happy. And – in the light of truth and drink – I said so.

'How safe I feel,' I said, 'and happy.'

'Is that unusual?' asked the Italian, all Volpone and teeth again.

I thought about it. 'Well, I haven't felt very safe or been very happy since I started telling the truth. To be truthful.' At which, of course, we all laughed.

'Then why don't you abandon it and be normal again?'

'Because she's a stubborn twit,' said Brando warmly. 'Always was.' He removed his arm as if in punishment.

'No,' I said, 'it's more than that. I've come this far and I can't give up.'

'Can't or won't?' asked the Italian.

'Both. If I can do it, then so can everyone else. Including smiling politicians. Do you know, my daughter refuses to vote? She was able to vote in the last election and just said No. Because she said you couldn't trust any of them. And Johnno did vote, but for the Monster Raving Loony Party. A protest, he said. But it was just lack of belief. Trust.'

'But politics has always been full of treachery,' said the Italian. 'It is about power. Power is the corrupter. When you are powerful truth becomes secondary.'

'You should know –' Brando replaced his hand and squeezed the top of my arm with obvious pleasure at the thought – 'you spawned Machiavelli.'

'Machiavelli,' said the Italian dismissively, 'was a Florentine.'

I laughed and thought, how convenient, to disown a fellow Italian when it suited. He probably applauded the man's political views in the safety of his own apartment.

'And his proposals for government,' said Brando, 'were something like, "When you invade a land and gain territory, be sure to crush the people so they cannot have revenge." Yes? That may have been Florentine once but it's pretty universal now.'

The Italian turned and smiled. 'Or you could say "Stabilise power and then build an enduring infrastructure" – it sounds better like that and it comes to the same. Words can lie so beautifully in matters of politics. Force and Prudence were his watchwords; they sound so good, yes? If he were a Venetian he might have added "and payment".'

Brando puffed an amused smile at the suggestion but seemed to be beyond speech.

'Well,' I said, 'Had he been a Venetian he could also have asked for payment in that peculiarly Venetian way. Like the Merchant of Venice.'

Brando, determined to gather enough breath to do a little pontificating himself, nodded and said, 'Well, we're heading off in the right direction for him.'

'Who?' I asked.

'The Merchant of Venice. Shylock. We're heading for the Jewish Ghetto. My dear girl – why do I employ you?'

'Silly Brando. The Merchant didn't live in the Ghetto. He wasn't a Jew. *That's* why you employ me.'

Brando made a noise of exasperation, as if about to

protest, when the Italian raised his hand most elegantly and said, very delicately, 'It is a mistake very often made, Signor Brando, but the Merchant is actually Antonio. Not Shylock.'

'Shylock is the moneylender,' I said grandly. 'Vital to the economy, yet despised for it. Like now, really. Only it's bankers, not Jews.'

Down went Brando's chest and removing his friendly arm he hurried ahead. 'Well, well,' he said, puffing again. 'Anyway – you did spawn Machiavelli and we've been copying him ever since.'

The Italian laughed. 'You can't expect any politician to speak the truth. Italian, British, Russian, American. Where there's power to be retained there's a problem with truth. It's like tennis,' he said. 'A game won by forcing errors. So politicians have forced lies.'

'Hypocritical humbug,' I said. He laughed. The very white teeth gleamed in the moonlight. They really were remarkable for a man of his age. The darkness gave them a prominence, I suppose. Venetians, very sensibly, do not spend their energy on too much unnecessary exterior lighting. This also preserves the mystery of the place, though at this point I could have done with a bright light or two. It did all seem very dim and deserted.

'Not at all. Would you have had your Mr Churchill announce the date of the invasion plan when asked? Or even acknowledge that there was one? You would have had him shot. Or would you have a politician give the exact details of who and where they are tracking someone suspected of treason most foul? Or even that the nation's finances are sicklier than expected? No – of course not. Forced errors, forced lies. Sometimes they are necessary.'

'And now we've got the credit crunch,' I said, staring up

at the stars. 'Thanks to no one telling us the truth.'

'Hardly,' said Brando. 'When someone earning tuppence gets a mortgage costing tuppence ha'penny, you don't need someone to tell you anything. It's plain as a pikestaff.'

'Says he, who has no mortgage and who has forgotten what it is to struggle.'

'Ah,' said the Venetian, 'the British obsession with property.'

We both ignored this remark as being somewhat fatuous in this most beautifully built-up of places.

'So we blame the bankers? Or people's greed.'

'Bankers,' said Brando firmly. 'Who have nothing to lose. Win, win. And people's desperation. Plain, as I said, as a pikestaff.'

'Plain as a pikestaff. English is so rich in images and metaphor,' said the Italian, smiling away. 'I love to hear it.'

'I unreservedly say we weren't told the truth,' I said, still feeling cross about the gondola. I thought the word 'unreservedly' added a certain gravitas. 'And that is, largely, the problem.'

'There were voices raised. Nobody wanted to hear them.'

'But my dear signora,' breathed the Italian, more fox-like than ever, 'we have always known it. Marx said it years ago, and even wrote it down for us. The absolute truth. That Capitalism holds the seeds of its own destruction, and it is called Greed.'

At which Brando gave another little snort of derision and hurried us along. Over his shoulder he said, 'Somewhat insidious that statement – given that we are in the home of Capitalism and Greed.' And onward we rushed.

There was precious little time to look elegant and at one with La Serenissima but I did notice, which should have been a little warning to my heightened senses, that while

Brando puffed and panted, and I glowed more pinkly than you might call attractive, our Italian was quite in breath. Fit, I remember thinking, he must be fit . . . I stopped to stare up at yet another exquisite facade. In the evening light it seemed tan-coloured, rich and warm, and its Serlian windows, beyond which glinted a gloriously ornate chandelier, were lit from within and glowed invitingly. We all stopped and stared up for a moment.

'So beautiful,' I murmured.

'Very,' said Brando softly.

'Do you know, despite everything we've been looking at, I could forgive this city everything, absolutely everything, because of the beauty it produced.'

The Italian laughed. 'You are becoming a Venetian,' he said. 'Saying one thing, doing another.'

Campari can make you a little belligerent, I find. 'Not at all. I'm simply respecting something beautiful. The sublime.'

'But you know that the something beautiful was built out of exactly what you now feel is so wicked. Banking. Yes? Brought back from the Mongols by Marco Polo, which led to Venice having the first chequebook, the first issues of credit, thereby allowing –' he stood back and gestured grandly with his arms – 'all this. Yes. Here arrived the idea of credit in banking – this city was its very home in the West – and because of that, aspiring Venetians sought to borrow and with what they borrowed to rise, and rise, and build and build, and borrow more and more until –' he clicked both fingers, 'it disappears. In the middle of the fifteenth century – *eccolo* – inflation, failed banks, businesses collapsing, the poor suffering. And did they learn?'

Brando and I waited, both looking a little cross at this invasion of our highly enjoyable sentimentality. Neither of us reacted one way or the other – no nods, no shakes, just silence.

The Italian did not seem to mind at all. 'No. Of course not. This building, any fine building you choose in my most lovely city, shows that they did not. Those beautiful windows you so admire were added on in the sixteenth century – build another floor to impress, more fine acquisitions, more money spent to inflate the image – everything bad forgotten in the call for more credit, more debt, more forgetting that at some time or another it must be repaid. This beauty came out of boom and bust. Yet you admire it. Pikestaff? What do you think of your pikestaff now?'

Brando broke the silence with a little over-careless laughter. 'I think we should move on. But I also think Venice is unique. No one in five hundred years' time will forgive what's happening now because they can gaze in wonder at the bloody Gherkin.'

The Italian looked puzzled. 'Gherkin?'

'A small cucumber, pickled,' I told him, smiling in the same understanding way he had smiled earlier. 'Or a large, phallic modern building in the financial centre of the City of London. It was one of the first high-rise buildings to represent the new millennium's boom times. Bit of an icon, bit of a joke. Shaped like a bullet or a penis.'

'Nothing connected with these troubles can be considered a joke,' he said, suddenly serious. 'And how many new buildings raised to the God Mammon were received with rapture when they were first created? Your Gherkin will probably survive the levity and be as highly praised as a Venetian palace one day. All pains forgotten.'

He was right, wonderfully right – and so clever, so honourable, so far-seeing. Everything was going to be all right one day, and then it wouldn't be, and then it would happen again. And then get better again. Wonderful, wonderful revelation. I wanted to throw my arms around him and kiss him. Either Brando guessed this, or it was coincidence, but he took hold of my arm very firmly and began to march me away. Just as well.

Given that the pavings were bumpy and there were a number of little bridges between our restaurant near the Strada Nuova and the Ghetto, I took off my shoes. There comes a point in a woman's life when the wearing of strappy sandals with heels loses its charm, and I had just found that point. After that, and no longer concentrating on keeping upright, I enjoyed the new terrain. We passed the facades of a remarkable number of large and interesting-looking churches and buildings, less poshed-up than those in the more frequented parts of Venice, and I longed to go into one or two of them. 'You can never underestimate the interesting beauties to be had behind the most crumbling of ecclesiastical exteriors,' I said to no one in particular. Another metaphor, I thought fondly, that the surface belies the reality. Ah well. Onwards we hurried, my feet feeling oddly free on the cold, uneven ground. No gondola rides, no stops in churches, no pauses on little bridges to admire some fine building. What were we doing in Venice if experiencing none of those? What we were doing was going at a lick to find something secret, and I could only hope that would bring frisson enough.

The city has its own special magic in whatever part of it you roam. Now, with so few people around and such low lights coming from the residential buildings we passed, the feeling of being a free spirit transposed itself into feeling like a teenager out on a midnight spree. I had no idea where we were going and was entirely happy to be led. Ah yes, I thought, I always thought of the seventies like this – shoeless, flowers in your hair – how good and innocent it seemed before the darkness to come. And I was also thinking enjoyably about its legacy of Free Love. Free Love and no credit cards in those days, I thought, suddenly sad. Sweetly young and foolish. How much nicer to be that than old and pontificating. I sighed – and I was about to suggest to Brando that we had a little dance, but it was not to be. They were having a conversation.

'It is surely more important for the private citizen to be honest than the politician? On a daily basis it is nice to trust your neighbour. Whereas with politicians it is best to trust none of them. Indeed, if a politician says "I honestly think . . ." you know he does not.'

Brando laughed. 'All right for some and not all right for others?'

The Italian nodded agreement. 'Yes, the weak are usually the ones who lose. In the light of that I have another place to tell you about . . .'

'Oh good,' said Brando. 'Where?'

'But not tonight. One excitement in an evening is quite enough, I think.' And he walked ahead.

I was a little bored now with all this seriousness. 'Piggies,' I said, twirling my shoes and looking downwards, 'I was thinking of piggies.' The Italian looked confused. Brando smirked. 'She means her little toes,' he said condescendingly. We all looked down at my little toes, toes which I dutifully wiggled. 'No I don't,' I said, indignantly. 'I was thinking about George Orwell and *Animal Farm*. Perfect example, those piggies. Some being more equal than others.'

'Erudition as well as beauty,' said the Italian, touching the top of my arm for emphasis. I felt that touch for some time. Brando held his head high and on we went.

Venice by night. The thin alleyways, the far-off sounds, the sudden surprises of window boxes festooned with colour, the yowl of a cat. Without my shoes I had thought I could walk forever. Another Venetian illusion. After a while those rough stones and broken pavings made walking barefoot a chore. Clever this, I thought, as you then need to sit down and very probably have a drink. 'Shall we have another drink?' I asked, seeing a small bar to our left as we walked past a row of small shops. No one paid me the slightest attention. The men were on the scent of one-upmanship. The girl did not count.

Now we had moved into a much darker part of Venice – away from the Strada Nuova and almost at the Ghetto – where the Italian took a sudden turn sharp left down a very narrow alleyway – with a few dim lights at doorways and the usual clutch of inscrutable cats. Of necessity we were walking in single file, this now being the only way possible, and there was a sense of the sinister in the place. My euphoria removed itself and I felt a little less happy and secure. These were the alleyways and not so charming facades where anything could happen and no one would ever know.

'Nearly there,' he said.

'And then we'll have a grappa,' said Brando, who was still a bit puffed. 'And really, Nina, I think you ought to put on your shoes.'

I did as he suggested. Those inscrutable cats tended to be fed very squishy items from very greasy bits of paper. Lovely as the idea of going barefoot in Venice was, practicality was required. But the pavings were even older here, and more uneven. My feet clattered, loud and echoing, and the air was growing chillier. I felt suitably frightened. Where was the Italian taking us? And were we being fools to believe and trust him? Venice has ever been good at dissembling, and Venetians even more so. A cat ran off hissing suddenly and I jumped and gasped. The Italian turned – I couldn't really see his face, save the eyes in shadow and white smiling teeth. 'Ah,' he said, 'you are alarmed. Good. You are safe,' he said reassuringly, 'but that will add to the – nature, er, of the object. We spend too little time nowadays being afraid of things.' He turned away and led us onward.

'I am feeling a bit afraid,' I said, 'To be truthful.'

'In Venice,' he said, and I saw his arm, shadowy, move in a gesture, 'in Venice life has never been very far from the feeling of fear. It is good that the ancient sense of it still lives in us.' I could not be sure if he was being serious or not. I thought probably that he was. But all I seemed to be able to do was giggle nervously – largely at the image we made, ploughing our echoing, single file along this dark and rather putrid place – the fear did not bite very deeply. Just enough.

Then, a window above us opened and a Venetian signora leaned out, calling, 'Caterina, Caterina . . .' I wondered if it were the name for a cat or a daughter or a friend. 'Odd,' whispered the Italian over his shoulder. 'And a little disturbing. The name of the last sad woman known to be – associated, um, with where we are going was Caterina. Yes, very odd.' Then I did feel a deeper chill up my spine. It was the way he hesitated over the word 'associated' – like a wrongdoer choosing his words carefully. It was the first of many little shiverings, not entirely to do with the evening air. Behind me Brando gave another little gasp of amusement. He had obviously given up talking as he could not walk, breathe and talk at the same time. So it felt almost as if I were on my own with this knowing Italian and being led towards who knew what. 'Caterina isn't such an unusual name hereabouts, is it?' I asked. My voice was not exactly firm. In front of me the shoulders shrugged, but their owner was silent for a moment before saying, in a low voice, 'Perhaps.'

I was beginning to feel really spooked when our narrow alleyway finally opened out into a decent little square – very close now to the Ghetto – a square that was one of those rare places up here for being blessed with a couple of trees and a bench. I could see the skyline of the tall, thin houses of the Jews of Venice beyond, and hear the occasional slap of water on bow, so we were close to the water here, too. The state of Venice was cruel in many ways but, as a good merchant society, it needed and therefore tolerated its moneymen and usurers and they had lived here in medieval times in a condition somewhere between protected and persecuted. Capitalism, according to the Bible, was a sin – but not if you had a go-between. Jews, it seemed, had their uses. In much the same way, as objects of barter, had women, I supposed. There was a price for everything then, not so different from now.

Suddenly I thought of Robert somewhere in Florida doing who knew what. In a way that was his payment, the fee for participating in a fully paid-up world. While he bought his ticket to solvency his wife was free to indulge herself in geegaws such as telling the truth . . . And maybe that wasn't all. I took a sideways look at the Venetian and wished I had not, for just at that exact moment he took a sideways look at me. 'We are here,' he said softly, as if he were speaking only to me. I stared straight ahead, bereft now of my Dutch courage.

We sat on the bench. The moon was very bright, the air cool and still, and the night sounds of Venice – the plash of water, the murmur of conversations from open upstairs windows, the occasional sound of a footstep – echoed about us, all comfortingly human. 'It is always a shock to remember that this was the first Jewish ghetto,' I said. 'And in Venice of all places. My, my.' I hadn't meant to sound quite so sarcastic but I wanted to distance myself from that exchange of looks.

The Italian moved – twitched almost – and answered with an oddly stinging tone, 'As you British created the first concentration camps. We all have our dark sides. Even you.'

'Indeed we do,' I said compliantly. 'It wasn't a criticism, it was an observation.'

'Do you have a dark side?' he said, keeping his voice low.

'Oh, we all do,' said Brando cheerfully. 'So what are we here to see? And do you know of a bar nearby?'

The Italian resumed his mild expression and nodded. 'The bar is a good one and just around the far corner. What we have come to see is there, in front of us, beneath that scrolled window. It is a secret letter box.'

'Ah,' I said, with pride, 'it is the secret letter box for denouncing Jewish blasphemy, Brando. We are only a few metres away from the entrance to the Ghetto. I read that one was placed somewhere around here but I didn't think it still existed.'

'It doesn't,' said the Italian. 'And it would not be here in any case – it was further away. That one you speak of was much larger and quite flamboyantly beautiful – the perfection of baroque. The city fathers made the Jews pay for it and the Jews responded by installing the most splendid they could commission – a nice little message of one-upmanship. It was removed by Napoleon. He took it away, he said, in the spirit of beneficence but also to own and admire it. A beneficence that seemed to include wrecking the place. He had certainly read his Machiavelli. But somehow he missed this other one. Very probably the locals covered it up. Who knows how it remained. And it has a special purpose. It is for women. For badly behaved women.'

That made me sit up. I peered at the wall but it was heavily in shadow and I could only just make out a shape. 'What – for women to put notes into or notes about women?'

'Both,' he said. 'To denounce and to declare truth. It was mostly used for people to put notes into *about* women – or those were the notes that counted with the Council of Ten. Come over here and I will show you.'

Some boys cycled past the bench laughing and lurching around, their loudness and their antics breaking the tension of the moment. I stood up.

'Come on then.' I pulled Brando to his feet. He gave a complaining grunt. 'Ah yes, my friend,' he said, half laughing, 'but is it really chilling? And grisly? And deeply unpleasant? I like the ones that have some savage political past, the ones that led the denounced to the garrotte. We've got to get the readers' spines tingling. I want something to make people cower in their bed, goose-bump begetting.'

'Mine already are begotten,' I said.

The Italian said, 'If the women who were denounced were proved to have committed the crime of adultery – which is the only truth this box was devised for, as the Jewish box was devised for denunciations of blasphemy and the drinking of human blood – then it was at the very least the wronged husband's or, in Caterina's case, affianced's right to throw the wicked wife or beloved betrothed into the canal. Usually with stones attached . . .'

'You enjoyed saying that.' I shivered.

'Yes,' he said, and laughed. 'Sensible Englishwomen seldom let their passions rule their heads. Weaker, more passionate southern vessels need the reminder of retribution to keep them in check. I like the thought of making a sensible Englishwoman shiver.'

He knew how to make the words 'sensible' and 'Englishwoman' sound highly pejorative. 'Thank you. Well, I suppose it would concentrate the mind somewhat. You'd have to be mad, or madly in love, to risk it. It gives me the creeps.'

'And makes you shiver?'

'And makes me shiver.'

Brando moved to stand between us. 'The only warming-up you need,' he said, 'is from a glass of grappa. This woman, I can tell you, has never strayed from the path of marital virtue in her whole life.'

'Indeed?' said the Italian, smiling his white smile. Volpone had mutated into Casanova.

'Now,' said Brando, 'come on. Show us and tell us and do your worst.'

The square, like the rest of the places we came through, was only slightly lit and even up close the carved frontage set into the wall was shadowy – but it was, very definitely, a Venetian lion. One of the more curly-haired, less aggressive lions of Venice. 'It looks as if it's kindly and smiling,' I said. And it did. Its mouth being deeply curved and only open a little and hardly anything to be seen of the teeth. I thought it looked positively sweet.

'Yes,' said the Italian. 'Quite as deceptive as the women it worked against.'

He enjoyed saying that, too. I realised, just in time, that I was being played with. Goaded, even. I set my mouth against replying and put out my hand towards the lion.

The Italian grabbed at my wrist. 'Careful,' he said – and seemed to mean it. 'Don't put your hand inside. You might never get it out again. That is the trick of the lion's mouth. Many, many did not. And suffered the consequences.'

I laughed but he didn't.

'Do not mock history,' he said.

I shivered again. 'What happened to them?' I asked, compelled, and yet wishing that I hadn't put the question. Another thought came to mind, which was that I would quite like to go home and have a hot shower and get into my little bed and be that person again, the one who sometimes liked to be in bed by ten with a good book.

Just then the boys came whooping by again, seeming louder and more aggressive, and their ill-lit faces suddenly ugly, like masks of hate, threatening us as they slewed their bicycles around us. Imagination. Venice offers food for it. They were only boys on bicycles after all. A shutter opened and a voice called out something harsh. The boys rode away, laughing, turned the corner and vanished from sight. I reached out and ran my hand over the carved curls and outlines of the head. It was quite small, women's size maybe, and to me still looked most sweet.

'It was the Jews' box for blasphemy that gave them the idea.'

'Them?'

'The state. Of Venice. If you can have one *Bocca del Leone* for a religious transgression, why not for a sexual transgression? By the seventeenth century Venice's licentiousness was well known – something had to be done – and what better way to begin than to make those roving well-bred wives and unvirtuous women come to heel?'

I kept my gaze on the small light above the doorway as he spoke, rather than look him in the eye. I had a strange – if irrational – feeling that he could read my thoughts. And what I was thinking was that it wasn't just the seventeenth-century wives who contemplated leaving the path of marital propriety. When Brando said all that about my never straying from the path of virtue, I felt something of a failure, something of a boring fool. He was right. I never had. Not once. And now I had put my shoes back on and stopped even attempting to be like someone out of *La Dolce Vita*.

'At least they left the likes of me alone,' said Brando, with something between amusement and sourness. 'That's a rare event. Shows they were not all bad. It was usually us deviants as well who captured the imaginations of the hierarchy.' His voice was not entirely flippant. We both turned to look at him. I leaned over and squeezed his hand. Sometimes I forgot the years he had lived through. His nicely Roman broken nose was a result of someone taking a dislike to his holding hands with a lover. Long ago and far away it might have been but I guessed that the memory never quite fades. He once said to me that straight people had no idea how lucky they were to be able to do the normal things in life, like link arms with their husbands/wives/lovers without someone, somewhere, spitting on them.

'No, dear Brando,' I said. 'Just for tonight we shall concentrate on the iniquities of women.'

'The box for secrets was not only, as I said, for denouncing women. It was also for women to tell truths about themselves. To perhaps request mercy, or release from a vile marriage or some unwonted contract of betrothal. And occasionally these secret requests were taken note of and fulfilled. But not always.'

'Why doesn't that surprise me? Keep the women on their

toes. One day it's OK to be naughty, the next it's off with her head.'

'Let's hear the story,' said Brando, and tapped my arm warningly.

The Italian laughed. 'Certainly. It is what we are here for. So then, Caterina, daughter of a humble gondolier, certainly not of high-born stock, which is unusual, in 1622 was seventeen – and beautiful. She was said to be more beautiful than the Doge Priuli's mistress, which did not please either the mistress or the Doge. Caterina was seen – I would guess not without some bribery – by Francisco da Lometti as he passed by her father's house. The da Lomettis were one of the wealthiest families at the time and he was their eldest son. Most eligible. She came, he saw, she conquered. The state of Venice was furious. Certainly the mothers were. The daughter of a gondolier? It could not be. And soon after the betrothal the letters of denunciation began. Accusations that Caterina was still having an affair with her erstwhile lover, a young metalworker. That she was an insatiable whore – the Venetians liked the mythology of the insatiable whore – what men would not? That she entrapped Francisco only for his money and was making a fool of him all over the place. It is quite true that he was older and not handsome and that she – being young and beautiful – very probably had many admirers around her after her betrothal, it was the courtly way, but apart from these letters and the testimonial from one tortured youth – the metalworker's brother – nothing points to her being anything but proper in her behaviour.

He paused. I felt tears welling up. Beauty was never easy on the owner.

'Go on,' I said. 'What happened? Was she saved? Did she become a nun?'

126

'Well, the deed was done – the spirit of Othello was invoked – and Francisco da Lometti was brought to the *Bocca del Leone* by members of the Venetian oligarchy – no doubt encouraged by their wives – and so was Caterina. She was asked to place her hand in the lion's mouth and swear that she had done nothing wrong. The story goes that if someone tells an untruth while their hand is in the mouth one of several things will happen: it will be bitten off, or it will be hurt in some way, or it will become caught there with its owner trapped by the lie. Or – unlikely – the hand can slide out again quite unharmed. So then Caterina cannot escape this test. In she puts her dainty little hand, and swears her sexual fidelity to green-eyed Francisco – and immediately she screams in pain. Everyone jumps back – except our poor lady who is trapped, held there. They pull her; still she remains trapped. She weeps, she swoons, she swears, all to no avail – they will have their justice. Or Francisco will. Her hand is greased with pig fat until, eventually, the poor little damaged hand is released. And then she is marched to her death. Not drowning with stones, either. Not for a Venetian aristocrat's affianced. No, something altogether more picturesque. Strangulation. A favourite way to dispatch the grander sinners of Venice. Francisco got a dispensation from the courts and watched her die. There is a painting of the event by Scagolino buried somewhere in the stores of the Accademia.'

Both Brando and I moved closer to each other – nearer the dim pool of yellow light from above the doorway. 'By garrotte?' whispered Brando. 'Not with the hands?'

The Italian nodded. 'Too cruel,' he said, with feeling. 'Cruel times,' he added. 'In the days before the new Doge Priuli arrived, just to give a flavour and to set the scene, scaffolds appeared each morning with bodies hanging by one leg. No one was told why. No edicts appeared, no proclamations. Just the bodies. And soon enough they stopped appearing, again without word. It was the Venetian way of reminding its people that life could be shortened for no good reason. That the state did not have to explain its executions and that its executions could be as cruel as they chose. Caterina would know that message as everyone else did.

'Poor little Caterina,' I said, and I tucked my arm into Brando's. He, rallying, gave it an excited squeeze and said, 'Good stuff. We must get a reproduction of the painting. Thank you for a marvellous story.' He slapped the Italian on the back. 'My skilful assistant here will work it up nicely. And now – a grappa for us all.'

I wiped my eyes, not that either of them had noticed, and asked, 'Do you think they really believed it or do you think it was just expediency?'

Brando rolled his eyes, as if to say, who cares after all these years . . .

But I really wanted to know. 'They didn't like Caterina's humble origins – and expediency is another word for lying, isn't it? What Voltaire meant by things being for the best in the best of all possible worlds?' I looked up at the Italian. 'Or Machiavelli?'

'Didn't anyone defend her?' asked Brando.

'Who can defend one human being against the might of the state? And only a woman.' The Italian smiled with unconvincing apology. 'Maybe money changed hands. Something helped it, for the state of Venice was not always dishonest even to save its own face. In the very next year they publicly pardoned the Doge Foscarini. He had been set up in a political lie and executed for treason. They very publically pardoned him and very publically announced that they had made a terrible mistake – they had been hoodwinked by treachery.'

'But he was already dead.'

'They could have kept silent. But no – they declared his innocence to the world. And their culpability. This was honourable, I think.'

'But he was dead.'

'Indeed, Signora Nina. But nevertheless – they confessed. They dug him up and buried him with full honours. And it was your ambassador to the Venetian court – your Henry Wootton – who wrote at the time that it would have been much better for the state if the Venetians had kept the truth to themselves. An *English* politician. Not a *Venetian* politician.'

I stared at the lion which continued to smile its sweet smile. 'A few years ago a highly respected English politician opined, when some wrongly accused Irish terrorists were released from prison, that it was better that the truth should not be made public rather than the judicial system be seen as flawed. And that was only thirty or so years ago. The more you look at the world the more you see lies.'

'Well, well,' said Brando quickly, 'the Doge was exonerated, Caterina was topped in a most gruesome way, and now for a grappa.'

'Caterina's story, of course, is the story of very many such incidents through the years. That little opening will have accounted for many lives . . .'

The Italian leaned back against the wall and crossed his arms as if waiting for our comments. The boys cycled back, whipping past us, whooping and hollering, staring over their shoulders before they turned the corner again, leaving behind them a deafening silence as only the sudden loss of noise in a deserted place at night can do. Another pair of shutters slammed ill-temperedly. And Brando yawned. But I – I suddenly felt a touch of real fear in that dark silence, real fear balanced by the daredevil edge that the tail end of too many Camparis can bring – and it seemed to me that the only way to overcome the shivers – and the power of the thing – was to put my hand into the wall and break the myth. After all, I was no Caterina, he was neither Volpone nor Casanova and this was the twenty-first century.

I stepped forward, released my arm from Brando's, and pushed my hand towards the gap. Both men moved quickly to stop me with gratifyingly worried looks – and I laughed at them. Here I was in Venice at this hour of the night with a tantalising stranger. All that talk about infidelity was exciting. Prove it, I thought, prove it. I wanted to show that Italian something of my dangerous side. I might be an identifiable Englishwoman Abroad sitting alone in the piazza, but he had laughed, oh delicately enough, but I'd show him. Oh yes I would. I was as capable of being as daring as any woman, and it was not fear that made me resist him, it was my wish. Why, my hand would slide in and slide out without so much as a scratch. Thus spake Campari. So I laughed at them both and pushed my hand further towards the gap that lay between those harmless-looking jaws. I ran my fingers around its lips.

Somewhere in the dark close by, two of those ubiquitous night-time Venetian cats decided to have a loud spitting and howling spat – right behind the doorway – so close that it seemed to echo out of the lion. I jumped, stumbled – and my hand was suddenly in there – right up to its wrist – without my consciously trying. Both men leapt forward, but it was too late – and as my hand went down into the depths behind what would, normally, be Leo's little uvula, something grabbed at my hand and held it fast, squeezing until I cried with pain. At which point – cats still yowling – I fainted clean away.

Twelve

Pelch: faint; indisposed; exhausted.

John Brockett's *Glossary of North Country Words*, 1825

IT WAS JUST more comfortable to keep my eyes closed and stay in the dark space chosen for me. I knew that all around me were forces who would have me leave it but I would not, I would not. I also knew very well that I was dreaming and in a completely different place from the kindly dark one. I told myself very sternly to wake up, that I was not in my bed in London, or at La Calcina, that my mother, my daughter, my husband, my best friend and the couple at the doctor's and the person in the shape of a nun with the car, were not all grouped around my bed with grievance and disapproval etched into their watchful faces. I was ten years old again and had committed a silly misdemeanour that meant I needed a good telling off. Which I was about to get once I opened my eyes. So I lay there quite resigned and waited for someone to start.

Robert, dear Robert, stepped forward first. He did not, I was surprised to see, look very suntanned considering he had just flown in from Florida. But he looked as young as he had when we first met. Perhaps that was what a holiday away from me did for him? I did not like this dream. He gripped the edge of the bed rail, looked down pityingly, shook his head and opened his mouth to speak. Instead, out came a loud and quite unacceptable gout of laughter,

132

followed by another. I was being ridiculed. I was bloody well being torn a strip off for trying to do something decent in this world. I struggled to sit up and pull his ears – an odd aspect of violence hitherto untried – but then he moved away. Clever. He knew he had gone too far. Like the Cheshire cat he seemed, with all the others, to begin to fade away. Cats, I thought, hmmm, what was it about cats? And were they all going to step forward and laugh at me for upsetting them? If only I could move I would run. And then another laugh broke up the thought, I lost the thread, tried to regain it, couldn't, felt very cross – and slowly, slowly, I felt myself being forced to wake up. One more laugh and my eyes were open into slits, with a light shining into them that really was offensive. 'Turn it off,' I said. 'Or I'm not coming.'

A hand moved under my head. 'Come on,' said Brando's voice, strangely tender. 'Wakey-wakey.'

My eyes closed. I was quite comfortable and the laughter, which I now knew to be Brando's, was galling. 'Why are you laughing at me?' I asked. The hand moved in a comforting gesture. 'Not at you. Not even with you. I was just thinking that those boys deserved a damn good fright themselves. They certainly gave you one.'

'Boys? What are you talking about?'

'The boys on bikes.'

I was very irritated by now. Everything was nice and foggy and Brando was making it all clear away, which I didn't want. But eventually I opened my eyes wide.

I was in the square. Lying down on the bench. The light in my eyes was the moon which shone very brightly, straight ahead in the dark blue sky. There was a pain in my hand. Somewhere around the marriage finger. Strange. I moved my eyes. There was Brando, looking down a bit like a moon himself and smiling at me. I was stretched out and he sat sideways next to me with his hand beneath my head. I seemed to be wearing a shroud which was a very jolly thought. This, on closer inspection, was Brando's ochre jacket. God, I thought, I must be dying.

'The Italian's gone to get you a drink of water. Personally I'd have thought grappa was a safer bet but we can get that later. Feeling better?'

'No,' I said, for shame and humiliation suddenly arrived, 'I feel like a prat.'

For once Brando was kind. 'Not at all,' he said. 'Those boys grabbed your hand inside the opening and you fainted. I should think your heart must be in excellent shape. If you didn't die from it then, you probably never will. Whereas I and my Italian friend were very much in danger of shuffling off the mortal. Fortunately you didn't hit your head as you went down because he grabbed you and saved you. All very romantic, it was, swooning and then being carried by a gallant Italian to a Venetian resting place. It looked exactly like something out of a Victorian melodrama.'

'How did the boys . . . ?'

'It's the wall behind the box. They've reopened the hole. That, apparently, in years gone by was how they made the mouth work – if they wanted it to work. It had been bricked up but the boys opened it again. Maybe it's where they keep their pornography, away from the searching eyes of their Italian mama. It was all quite funny really – you being so bold and then that happening – we both –'

'You both laughed. Yes, I heard you. Thanks.'

I sat up. The boys were peering round the far corner of the square and immediately vanished when they saw me looking at them. 'Little bastards,' I said. 'They should be locked up.'

'Hardly,' said Brando, the voice of reason. 'They were only playing around. They weren't to know you would pass out with fear. Boys will be boys,' said Brando, rather too happily.

Of course he was right. It was the sort of trick you'd read about in a William Brown book and chuckle over. But I had been so scared. If adrenalin is said to be good for the system I was, as Brando said, due to live for a very long time. I relaxed my head back into his hand, still feeling swimmy. 'And if they come anywhere near me they'll find out that girls will be girls, too,' I muttered.

I raised my throbbing hand. My wedding ring was badly mangled – it was Robert's grandmother's ring originally and was already thin when we were given it – and the finger was red and swollen. I rubbed it. Somehow it seemed as if I had been given a lesson in something, only I didn't know what. I certainly didn't feel brave and daredevil any more. And I blushed to remember what I had been thinking when those little demons struck. 'Oh dear,' I said feebly and out loud. I suddenly felt exhausted with it all. Brando misunderstood and said, 'Yes, sorry about that. We had to extricate your hand once the boys ran off. You were away to the woods and I pulled it a bit hard. The gap isn't that big, and according to our Italian friend, part of the devilment of the box was that you could slide your hand in quite easily, but because of the way the knuckles are set, it's much harder to get it out again. Hence the myth of the captive hand of deceit, I guess, even without them hiding on the other side. But you're all in one piece – and so is the ring.'

He looked at me quite hard when he said this last so I sat up a little more and looked about me. Running footsteps clattered through the square and out of a little side turning came the Italian. He held a bottle of San Pellegrino and what looked like a coffee cup, over which he held the palm of his hand.

'Ah,' he said when he arrived at the bench, 'you are back with us. Good.' And he held out the bottle of water, unscrewing the cap with a slight fizz as he did so, and manoeuvring himself nearer to me than Brando. 'How are you feeling?'

'Like a fool,' I said, taking the bottle. 'A very big fool. And one with a bruised ego as well as bruised knuckles.' He took my hand with his free one and ran the ball of his thumb very lightly over the grazing. It felt a little too pleasant, too familiar, but I let him.

'Not at all, not at all,' he said, 'It was very frightening to have those boys hold you like that – I, too, would have fainted, I am sure.'

Well, it was nice of him to say so but I didn't feel like smiling very much. After all, it was his silly storytelling that made me so nervous in the first place. First law of recovery – find someone else to blame. I handed him the bottle and sat up a little straighter. 'What's in the cup?'

'Grappa,' he said.

Brando said, 'Ah good,' and reached for it, but the Italian moved his hand away and offered it to me. Since it was somewhere between him and too much of the red stuff as to what had caused me most pain, I declined. I sat up completely and handed the jacket back to its owner. Brando took both cup and garment, drained the first and stood up to put the other back on. The Italian renegotiated my hand and took it in his own. He studied the swollen finger and touched the wedding ring in its newly mauled shape. I withdrew my hand quickly.

'I am sorry you were hurt,' he said. 'But I know someone

136

who can make the ring look like new again. If that is what you want?'

Without looking away from the finger, I said, 'No – I'll keep it as a reminder.'

'Of what?' he asked.

'Of what can happen to an Englishwoman in Venice when she gets her knickers in a twist.'

The Italian looked puzzled.

'A metaphorical term,' I said. 'For getting a bee in my bonnet. Being carried away for a moment . . .' He looked even more puzzled. 'I thought you loved the richness of English?' I wasn't being very nice but I didn't feel very nice. 'Or you could say what can happen to an Englishwoman when she gets on her high horse . . .'

I smiled, showing all my teeth. So did he. 'Bees,' he said. 'Knickers. Horses. I think you are delirious.' At which we both smiled, understanding each other completely. The moment had passed. I felt him ease his grip on my hand. Brando muttered something further about the eternal treasure chest of the English language, and handed the cup back to the Italian who slipped it into his pocket. Then, still smiling with those white, white teeth, he also stood up, leaned down with his arm crooked, and indicated for me to take it. I saw that the top of his hair was thinning and that he had more jowls than I had noticed before in the piazza. Good. The days of Free Love and bare feet floated out of my mind and I was left only with even more of a feeling of foolishness. Had I really contemplated . . .? Did I really . . .? I looked at him. He wasn't even, really, attractive. Well, not as attractive as Robert. Robert. Why wasn't he here with me? And then – in the city of water – I began to cry. Great big tears and shaking shoulders and quite unable to stop. Reaction, I suppose. Both men were instantly thrown into confusion – and between being patted and squeezed and cajoled and having the bloody jacket thrown back around my shoulders and patted some more, it felt like taking part in flyweight boxing.

'I think I'd just like to get back to the hotel, if that's all right,' I said, the tears refusing to stop. Brando produced a huge pink handkerchief, so big that it made me feel little and Alice-like and even more vulnerable – and the tears increased. Both men had a wild look about them now, especially as one or two windows were opening discreetly and Venetian eyes were sizing up the situation.

'The hotel? Certainly,' said the Italian briskly.

'Are you sure you wouldn't like a grappa first?' said Brando wistfully.

'Certain,' I said. 'Just the hotel and my bed.'

'Of course,' said Brando with relief. Glad to be shot of me. And off with me they marched. Behind us the boys made their tribal noises of joy at their victory and cycled around the square – the cats joined in, while the sound of the windows and shutters opening and occupants shouting and then the banging of them closing again and being bolted against the night were the only sounds to rise above my sobs.

The concierge looked at me in dismay and the Italian explained to her that there had been an accident to my hand. She immediately suggested a doctor, to which I shook my head. She then offered to get some warm water and a sponge but I was past accepting kindnesses. I just wanted the fussing to stop and to be left alone. To anyone who has ever contemplated stepping off the straight and narrow of their marriage and having a fling, let this be a warning. All I wanted, all the way back to La Calcina, was my husband's arm around me, not Brando's, and my hand in his, and not loosely held by a stranger. I wanted the comfort of Robert's familiarity as I made my way up the stairs and opened my door, and I vowed that if I had to tell lies in future in order to have those twin connections, then lie I would. A bedroom had never felt lonelier to me, a bed more empty, a city less of a place I wanted to be. But adrenalin from fear, and its aftermath, will always produce sleep – we are but animals after all – and I did fall asleep as soon as my head touched the pillow. The last thought I had was of how much pain and upset I had caused everyone and I wondered if it had really and truly been worth it. I decided that it had not. Machiavelli was probably right. The last image I saw before sleep descended was of Winston Churchill in a tank. And fortunately I was well away in the land of nod before I had to think about it any further. One thing was absolutely certain: truth was dangerous.

Thirteen

Forswart: exhausted by heat.

Reverend John Boag's *Imperial Lexicon*, *c.*1850

I WAS WOKEN the next morning by the ringing of my mobile phone. I'd been drifting in and out of sleep as you sometimes do with a bit of a hangover and after a shock. The room was filled with sunshine and for a moment I thought I was still dreaming, but no – it was probably Brando with orders for the passing of my time usefully. I welcomed the idea. Anything to get through this day and then I would be setting off for home.

I grabbed the phone, threw open the doors of the small balcony and leaned out over the Zattere as I answered. But it was not Brando – it was Tassie.

'Mum? I'm going to book my flight home,' she said. 'I'll confirm it with you but I'll probably be coming into City airport via Schiphol on Sunday at about six in the morning. It's the cheapest flight I can get.'

'Well, that's great, Tass,' I said, not thinking it through.

She sounded stony. 'No it isn't,' she said. 'I'm coming back to save your marriage.'

All my resolution of the night before melted away in the morning mist. Had I meant my undertaking to re-embrace equivocation and untruth in the cause of human harmony, this was the moment. I would have said that I was sorry I'd been such a twerp and that it was all going to be fine, now. But there was just something in the way Tassie said 'Save Your Marriage' that made me *furious*.

Youth has a way, wonderful really, of persuading itself that Age is mentally retarded. The perceived role of one's children in the great rolling world of books and film and television and stage is to be wise where we are foolish, sage where we are ignorant, benign where we are full of evil intent. Children, even very young ones, are no longer seen as cute and whimsical – or naughty and worse – they now represent fresh pages on which to write experience – they are now the gods of enlightenment. Where once, in *To Kill a Mockingbird*, Atticus Finch was the moral hero and the daughter, Scout, learned truth through observing him and others, now it would be Scout who would give Atticus the big truth. And where once Young Raleigh would have sat at the knee of a knowing sailor to learn his experienced ways, now the knowing sailor would find wisdom issuing from the Young Raleigh's mouth. It is called middle-class fear of one's children. And unfortunately, Tassie – and very probably Johnno (though it was extremely hard to gauge from his grunts what our son thought) – was of this frame of mind. Tassie alone, it seemed, knew the secrets of the world and how to behave as an adult – and – yes – we had indulged her in her conviction. Middle-class parents are indisputably afraid of their children. Johnno? Well, Johnno was a boy-bloke. He simply had contempt for everyone he considered old unless they drove a very new, very fast, very big BMW. While at the same time wearing a T-shirt saying 'Save the Planet'.

'Don't be silly,' I said in a new and excitingly firm voice. 'There's nothing wrong with our marriage. Stay where you are. Please.'

'Why – don't you want to see me?'

Youth also has a way of making you feel a shit whichever way you deal with things. I couldn't lie. I'd come this far. 'Of course I want to see you. But you don't need to come back early for our sake. We'll be fine. Really.' At that moment I made up my mind that no matter what, we would be fine.

And then one of the gondoliers called out in unmistakable dialect: 'Gondola, gondola!' And Tassie said suspiciously, 'Who was that? Where are you?'

Quick thinking amazed me given that I felt rather unwell and I said truthfully, 'Just doing a bit of research for Brando.'

'But it's eight o'clock in the morning.'

I stepped back into the room and closed the long windows. 'I know,' I said happily, for this was truth. 'He's a real slave-driver.' She did not ask where I was. I didn't give her a chance. At this point she would probably regard a trip to Venice as mother enjoying herself while father languished in solo Floridan misery. 'Now look, Tassie,' I said, in a tone of voice I had never used with her and which had the effect of shutting her up. 'Now just look here . . .'

After some persuading, our disapproving daughter agreed not to book the flight until she had heard from both of us once Robert was home. And after I pressed the phone's off button I felt deeply ashamed. How could being truthful hurt so much? And why, fool, did I ever think it was going to be easy. I then tried Robert's phone. Zilch. It was 2 a.m. in Florida. Where was he? Usually when he was away from home he kept his mobile on all the time. Well, at least he would know I had tried, again. A bubble of resentment rose above the longing and remained long enough to register. Then it was gone. I couldn't think of a message that didn't sound either pathetic or reproachful so I didn't leave one. It would be all right, surely, once he was back. It would have to be. Together, I thought as I studied my unattractive tongue in the mirror, together we go forth into the light. I remembered my mother, too. How was I going to face her ever again? I would change my flight and go home today. This city of deceits was too disturbing for an already disturbed mind. Much better to surround myself with the ordinariness of home. I rang the airline. Once the flight was settled I felt much better. Certain that this was the right way. I rang Brando and left a message about the change of plan. Then I had the swiftest shower possible, washed away both the real and the metaphorical dirt, donned cool clothing and a large hat, kissed my poor bruised finger, and went out, blinking in the sharp morning light, before I could think about the decision any further.

On the vaporetto the phone rang. I hoped it was Robert but it was Brando saying that if I hadn't changed my flight he was going to suggest that I did. 'You are all over the place, Nina,' he said. 'Your mind is elsewhere. Best you go home and get things sorted out.' This was marvellously understanding of him.

'Thanks,' I said.

'Don't mention it. Oh – and our Italian friend has just rung – unearthly hour – to ask how you are. How are you?'

'Extremely well,' I said, for I suddenly felt it. 'Do you want to meet? I'm on the vaporetto going towards San Marco.'

'Well, meet me at the stop for the Giardini as soon as you can. There's a house of ill repute there with lewd carvings on the loggia – they apparently denote the worst kind of excess. Our Italian friend told me about it as penance for causing you so much pain. I said it was nothing at all. Was I wrong?'

'No,' I said, clear as a bell. How beautiful the world looked.

'Good, because I told him you were flying home early this afternoon.'

'My flight's this evening.'

'Your point?'

'I'll wait at the stop.'

Oh Venice, I thought as we chugged along, with your blue sky and your sun on the water, how could you be so bad?

Sant'Elena looked beautifully cool and empty of people though the day promised to be another hot one. The vaporetto was crowded and I kept seeing, perhaps like a guilty chimera, the Italian's smiling face. I was relieved to get off the boat and wait for Brando who was unusually prompt. Human vileness seemed to stir his stumps like nothing else. We walked from the vaporetto stop in silence, Brando following his map and humming the tune from the night before, 'Eleanor Rigby'. Very irritating. But it was best to keep the day harmonious after what we'd both been through. There was no knowing what Brando would come out with if I spoke too sharply. So I smiled at the day around me and steeled myself for whatever it was we were about to discover. What was it about sex, religion and money that created such unpleasant reactions in all societies? I have no answer, but so they do, all over the world. And what is our fascination with them? There but for fortune . . .? Witness poor Caterina's story, our own dear burned bishops, the tortured concubines of Peking, the suttee of Calcutta and the cheering, blood-soaked crowds of eighteenth-century Paris. Venice, like her sister cities, was no slouch in matters of pleasure, pain and cruelty. Yet we love her. *Nota bene*: being nice doesn't necessarily get you admired.

As we walked I asked why a house of ill repute should be interesting enough for Brando's book. Surely there were hundreds of the places here, there and everywhere – oldest profession, that sort of thing. He was wearing a very large hat himself, straw, broad-brimmed, with a pink-and-green bandeau. Beneath it his eyes gleamed and his face was all smiles. 'We have to include one in each city, I think. And this one is little known and will – so I'm told – provide some interesting pictures.' He tapped his camera and looked pleased. I cheered up. Home tonight.

The building was tucked away to the north of the city in an area without canals and mostly residential. An unremarkable place. I suppose that makes good sense, to put a remarkable house of ill repute in an unremarkable place. And perhaps when it was founded the whole area had been very different.

'That looks like it. Sticks out like a sore –'

'Brando,' I warned.

'– thumb,' he said, innocently.

From a distance the whole building seemed uninhabited and, like much of early Venice, elegantly decayed. The house attached to the loggia was long and low, only two storeys, with an ornate pediment and crumbling, pale plasterwork. Whatever grandeur it had once offered was no more – any architectural hubris had died in the decrepit facade years ago. Parts of it were shored up with timber buttresses and all around it were fences and notices of trespass and wire. If you blew too hard, it seemed, it might fall down. 'Palladian revival, the newer bit,' I said. 'But the loggia's much earlier.' I thought it was beautiful. Brando pulled a face.

'Always looking to the past, the later Venetians,' he said. 'The city was dying on its feet by the time this part was built. The loggia is charming – and that is where, so I am told, we will find the reliefs. But there was supposed to be someone here . . .'

As we came nearer we could see that, although it was decayed, it was not uninhabited. A face appeared for a moment at the corner of a glassless window – and then vanished. We stepped around a hole in the panelling of a wooden fence to where a flimsy and very half-hearted wire fence sagged at the front. If it was put up as a final barrier, it wasn't. Lying on its side was a tattered, tipsy-looking poster with the outline of a guard dog. I called out asking if there was anyone at home as we pulled back a corner of the wire and walked over uneven pitted tiles to the loggia's front. A cracked voice called back, not very nicely – '*Ola! Ola!*' I thought it was the voice of an old man, but when the owner emerged from behind a rotten wooden door that probably saw light before the sumptuary laws, it was an old woman. And, like any Venetian, though she might be old, stooped, poor and possibly dispossessed, she still had style. Long hair, inadequately hennaed, untidily pinned and falling in thin, greasy curls with crazy woman big hooped earrings dangling were entirely incongruous above the plain black of her dusty dress.

'What you might call a magnificent ruin,' said Brando out of the side of his mouth, as he held his hat and bowed wonderfully obsequiously. Diplomacy rather than deceit saved me from saying 'Just like you'. But there was something grand about her and I had to stop myself from curtsying. Instead I held out my hand and advanced.

Brando was quicker. He held out his hand all right but it was holding a fifty-euro note. '*Biglietto*,' he said. Clearly the Italian had given him detailed instructions. The old woman smiled more civilly but her eyes were watchful. 'We wondered,' he said, as he moved nearer like a man stalking a dangerous dog, 'if we could see over the place –' he gestured – 'and ask you some questions? For a book I am writing. In English. I am told you have been here for many years as its custodian?'

La Vecchia obviously understood not one word but she did understand the money and took it immediately, putting it somewhere very safe within the folds of her dusty black skirts. Then she backed away towards the old door. Brando looked at me. I translated what he had just said, more or less, moving forward all the while. Suddenly the old woman held up her not entirely clean hand, palm outwards, and called, '*Fermo!*' And stop we did. All three of us frozen like a tableau of refusal. Now what?

But Brando was perfectly calm. He gestured at the building again and said, over and over as if soothing a child, '*Bella, bella – bella casa*,' and he smiled and smiled at the old woman until she could do nothing but agree that it was, indeed, *bella* and that she was gratified. Her smile was, for all its wrinkles and discoloured teeth, charming and it was easy to imagine that she might once have been *bella, bella* herself. Brando gestured to the low wall that ran along the front of the loggia, suggesting that we might sit in its shade – the heat was becoming fierce now – and the old woman nodded – still smiling.

We sat. I looked up at the carvings – they were old, some had been vandalised, some just worn away, but if you looked really hard it was plain to see what they were all about; copied, maybe, from old Roman tablets and plaques seen in the ruins of ancient towns dotted around the Italian countryside. The medieval mason knew exactly what was required. They were like some of the more hidden artefacts in Pompeii and Herculaneum, though those were finer wrought and better preserved. Titillation and promise of the pleasures within. A tradition as old as time and perfectly fitting for the oldest profession. I've always thought that Roman pornography was easy to look at because the women and the men are treated as equals. Participation is obvious on both sides. The Romans might treat their women as lower orders in society, but it seemed as if they were equals in the bedroom. I wonder what changed it? Constantine taking on Christianity, perhaps. I could see Brando eyeing the reliefs but he was much more concerned with ingratiating himself with La Vecchia. She reminded me of the Giorgione portrait of the old woman who says, 'One day you, too, will look like this.' I thought of my mother and the very idea of her using henna and wearing golden hoop earrings was so funny that I couldn't stop a little trill of laughter. The old woman gave a little laugh in response – woman to woman – and the atmosphere became instantly more relaxed.

Now our hostess nodded to us again, but a little more benignly, and then went back through the old door returning a moment or two later with a very ancient kitchen chair – Brando immediately leapt to his feet and settled the chair for her and bowed that she should sit. He was – is – the most elegant of men despite his girth – when he wants to be – when he wants something – and I was reminded why it was that he had such success in his romantic pursuits. He was like a caring and considerate ballet dancer as he moved about her. Then, when we three were settled, I began to ask the old lady some questions. First I told her, as Brando instructed me, that there would be more money at the end of the interview. And said that we had been sent here by the Italian, something that she seemed to know already. Without any apparent hesitation the old lady began. I wondered to how many she had told the tale. Or maybe it is just the Italian way. *The Decameron* tales of life, death, love and survival were all in the story she told.

Her mother had brought her here in the last years of the war. They came from the mountains and were driven out by hunger and homelessness. Her father had been killed fighting in the Liberation Army at Monte Cassino and her mother was in despair. She was quick to say that mountain people had an understanding of survival no matter what was required of them. Her eyes were very sharp as they looked into mine, as if she dared me to defy what she was saying. I nodded. Well – there was her mother widowed and alone with her only surviving child – Claudia – the old woman who was then just seventeen. Her father was dead, her brother, a Fascist, had been killed by partisans – and it was safer to come down to Venice. The families of Fascists expected to see a bad time of it when the Allies arrived, even if they had changed sides. An acquaintance told her mother of this place. There was no other option except death. And the house was always looking for women. So they arrived.

At this point I asked her to stop for a moment while I told Brando what had been said so far. He nodded and pursed his lips and clucked sympathetically and then gestured that she should continue. There was not a lot more to say. Her mother offered herself and they laughed. Here the old woman shrugged and pursed her lips in that universal gesture of *so what* – she was intelligent, she said, and could put two and two together perfectly well. In the end she persuaded her mother that it was for the best. At least they would live. The house was well used by Germans at the time and they were decent enough with a certain discipline about them, a code. But as the British forces broke through in Salerno and moved on up towards the north, the Germans moved away and times became more difficult. They waited for the Americans and the British to arrive, expecting life to continue in much the same way if they kept her brother's politics out of it and spoke only of her father's honour. The old woman smiled and rubbed her hands. 'A house like ours was always required. We were not likely to perish.' No one, it seemed, expected life to change at all for the women of the house.

Her mother took her solace where she could (here the old woman shrugged and made a gesture of drinking) and became the self-elected manager of the place. I wanted to ask her if she could remember how she felt about her mother giving her up in this way, how she felt about the experience of it all – what had it been like to become what she became. But of course I could not. And Brando was not interested in the sorrows of the situation. Nor, it seemed, was she. Whatever her experience she had dealt with it. I could hear Tassie saying to me or her mates or Johnno, 'It's happened. Get over it. Move on.' I guessed that this old woman had done just that and I wondered – briefly – how Tassie would have coped – never mind how I would have done. A few banks going to the wall and a bunch of politicians telling lies began to lose its importance against this real truth. As for me – what was trying to tell the truth for only seven days compared to all this? Should the mother have owned up to her Fascist connections and been shot just so she could put her hand on her heart and say that she had never told a lie? Or died rather than trade her daughter? One thing was certain, I'd never end up sitting on a chair with anything approaching these realities.

'What kind of services did they offer?' said Brando, looking up at the wall plaques. Depicted were positions I couldn't imagine even a limbo dancer achieving, men in states of ecstasy with their heads thrown back and their legs agape – and animals. 'Animals?' said Brando wonderingly. '*Animals?*' 'I wouldn't take those too literally,' I said. 'They are based on Roman ideas.' I looked at the signora who looked straight back at me. 'You'll just have to guess. I'm not going to ask her for details. I wouldn't know where to look, and anyway, my Italian isn't that good. Or bad. Those images are less true representations than hooks to draw you in.' I peered. 'I very much doubt if they were really able to enjoy the intimate companionship of ducks. Even such large ones.'

He smiled and said, '*L'anatra grande*. It has a certain ring about it . . . I wonder.' The old woman laughed and shook her head. '*Anatra? Anatra?*' She made an eating movement with her hands. I signalled with my hands that the ducks were, indeed, very big. 'No, no,' she said, her Italian amused and emphatic. 'We only ate the ducks. And in truth they were exaggerated in the pictures. Really they were very, very small.' I did not need to translate this for him. She obviously found Brando's disappointment delightful.

Venice, she told us, was not a bad place to be, if you were going to be somewhere like this, for the city had no scruples and was used to the ways of such a house. There was a decency about it and the Venetians saw it as just another aspect of trade. The services were not cheap.

'Services?' said Brando, understanding the word. '*Servizio?*'

'Casanova.' She laughed coarsely and made the gesture of opening and reading a book.

'She says you can read Casanova on the subject. And I've got Pallavicino's history of a *puttana* for you. And our home-grown Mary Wilson's *Voluptuarian Cabinet* – you'll have all those to look at. And if that doesn't inspire you – well.'

Brando looked satisfied and for some reason those sad lines of Oscar Wilde's came into my mind, images from the harlot's house.

> Sometimes a clockwork puppet pressed
> A phantom lover to her breast . . .
> . . . Then, turning to my love, I said,
> 'The dead are dancing with the dead . . .'

The signora continued. The northern Italians, she insisted, had class, had culture. It was the little dark men in the south of Italy, *il contadini,* who were bandits and vagabonds. But this house had always maintained a certain quality of customer. Over the years officers and the better class of men came here – first the Germans, then, eventually, the British and Americans who were mostly generous and good, and then the Italians – of a certain class – and finally the Venetians themselves as they picked up their old prosperous ways. Her mother had looked after the house and became quite wealthy, dying at a good age despite the grappa. After which Claudia took on her role and cared for the place, keeping it fit for the more refined gentlemen of Venice. The Germans came again of course, only this time they were not soldiers but travellers, with money in their pockets and fat bellies, very fat bellies – sometimes, said the old woman, their bellies were so fat it was hard to find the *cazzo* – at which she laughed and slapped her knee and held up her hand to indicate something very small. Then, with the good Germans, came Swedes off the cruise ships and tours and the money was good. The house and Claudia prospered anew. The city of Venice, though modern and part of Europe now, still understood such trade and did nothing to stop it. Indeed, in partnership with the man who now owned the place, the city fathers put up funds to restore the building. There were few original early Renaissance buildings left – Palladio and the baroque saw to that – and this loggia was very fine and worthy of repair. A new mason was employed to start returning the old decorations to their original designs and the rooms were to be refurbished. There was even a plan, nothing to do with the city fathers, of course, to increase the girls from six to nine with a new annexe. Good times, the old lady said, good times were coming again. But –

But before all the splendid plans could begin, the world turned upside down. She shrugged, raised her hands, as if it was the most foolish thing in the world. Money that was forthcoming, in a devious but nevertheless committed way, from the city was withdrawn. Until now everything had cheerfully been done on the nod and wink – but with the European Union becoming stronger – here she spat – things changed. Even in Venezia! She spat again. Without their interference, she assured me, the money would have been found somehow. No questions asked. But the owner could no longer raise the funds to restore the place, the city said it could not find the money and would not if it continued in its capacity as a bordello. 'What do you expect from a place like Belgium?' she said, with contempt. 'All they do for pleasure is eat chocolate.'

I translated this for Brando who thought it was wonderful and laughed and laughed. The old woman laughed too, before declaring that she had – even so – refused to give up and lived on here. The man who owned the building paid her a small stipend but he could do nothing. Trade was banned, the rooms closed, the girls dispersed. The house began to fall apart. A municipal bigwig came to persuade her to let the city take on the building and make it beautiful again and she could move to a nice little apartment nearby and end her days with the comfort of modern amenities. Here the woman laughed again and mirthlessly. 'The man, a city grandee, they sent to persuade me,' she said, 'was one of our best clients until all this happened. I would like to tell someone about that.'

'In a *Bocca del Leone*?' I said.

Her old eyes widened. Then she nodded. 'Venice has always been good at such secret places,' she said.

Brando was not, of course, interested in the decline of the place, he wanted to know what made a successful bawdy house – why, for instance, her business was so long-standing and so classy. What was it they offered that made them exceptional? The old woman smiled at him and asked why it would interest one such as *him*. So I explained all over again that it was for a book of shocking facts and stories about Venice. The old woman said that it would need to be a very big book. Then we all laughed. But she would not tell her secrets. There was no brutishness, she said. There was no damage done. It was all within reason, which is why the girls stayed. And it was, in the end, up to them how far they chose to perform. Some – she inclined her head – some were more adventurous than others. That is all. Brando leaned forward questioningly. The old woman smiled at him a little severely. 'Yes,' she said, 'very, very adventurous. Some of them.' She turned briefly and nodded at the wall with its carvings. The house itself, she suggested, is the secret and you must use your imagination – just as those who paid to come here used theirs. 'My profession,' she said, 'is an honest one. We offer a service and we fulfil it. You bring the fantasy and we fulfil it. How many other professions can say so?'

'*Banchiere? Politico?*' I said.

She nodded her head emphatically. '*Si, si, si.*'

I translated for Brando who only said, 'Enough of the Holy Fool, what made it work?'

'Two-way contract,' I said.

'I don't want the philosophy,' he said, like a grumbling child, 'I want examples.'

I translated this for the old lady who looked at him and said, via me, 'Use your imagination.' She raised her hands once more at the wall in a gesture of explanation. 'That is what we did, after all.'

Brando stared at the wall reliefs as if willing them to come alive. And then he indicated his camera. The old woman nodded and he got up and began to prowl around. We both watched him for a while and then I asked. 'You have children?'

She shook her head. It was, she said, denied her by very reason of this life, this house. What she had wanted was a husband and children. That, she said, looking at me with the first hint of sadness in her eyes, regret in her voice, was all she had ever wanted. We were both in deep shade now. Beyond the loggia the sun beat down on the scrubby bit of land that had once been a garden of sorts – the lilies were in bud beneath a weight of vine and creeper and there were the trumpet heads of pink and orange poking their tired shapes among the weeds. It looked forlorn, in keeping, I thought, with an old *meretrice* past her best, with her head lost in memories of when she was young and desirable. The wire netting winked in the brightness looking hot and forbidding and a brave rat or two ran across the opening, wanting shade or dampness, or who knows what. The rats of Venice outnumber the inhabitants, it is reckoned, by twenty to one. And they are big. Much to feed on, presumably. No wonder Venice loves its cats.

After a little wait – a little creaking around in her chair from the woman – and a little more polite conversation about the state of the world in general and Venice in particular – Brando returned from his tour. When he was seated again she raised a bony finger, looking even more like the Giorgione portrait, and said firmly that she could tell us one thing, one certain thing, about success. I translated for Brando and he leaned forward to listen. She said that age had nothing to do with it, nothing at all – because it was all in the head. *In testa*. She tapped hers to make sure we understood. Yes, she said, even truth is in the head. And we only hear the truth we want to hear. Then she sat back and smiled almost saucily. While he has been with you, you have made a man feel that he is big as a satyr with a wine cup balanced on his prick – she laughed – now that is imagination, you see. But when you return him to the real world it is back to reality. He must, after all, go about his business comfortable in his own trousers. She laughed really heartily at this. Brando blinked. So did I.

Once you start thinking about honesty in life, everything seems to connect and everything that connects seems to undo your presumptions. Maybe the oldest profession was the most honest? Claudia had used the words *onesto, integro, probo* many times in the course of the interview and they had never seemed artificial. Truly, truly the world had turned upside down.

'Quite right,' she said. Then she looked at my hand, at my wedding ring, and smiled – not entirely sweetly. 'You are married?'

I nodded.

'Happily married?'

I nodded again.

She clapped her wizened mouth shut with a snap, puckering her chin, and looked at me sourly, and then Brando, and then back to me again. 'How long?'

I told her.

'Marriage,' she said vehemently, 'is the least truthful state of all.'

'What does she say?' asked Brando, responding to the emphasis.

I told him, still thinking about it myself.

'Do you want me to explain?' she asked.

I said I thought I understood.

Brando gave a chuckle of sardonic pleasure. She turned to him and said firmly that she expected there had been many a young man who had not, quite, told him the truth of his actions. And had he, Brando, really taken pleasure on every occasion he had found himself in bed with a lover? His *cazzo*? Had it always performed properly? Did he think the colour pink was suitable on him, a man with such florid cheeks? Brando understood about a quarter of it all. I made sure, by translating for him very carefully, that he understood the rest. It shut him up nicely.

Now we both sat there in that hot, dry and shadowy loggia trying to put a good face on it. But she was saying no more. She stood up, either the chair or her joints creaking, and walked along the deeply shadowed walls of the building – indicating each carved panel. 'It is all here,' she said. 'You do not need me to describe our skills. There are and always have been only seven orifices. They are all there in their various ways. I hope your photography is a success.' And with that she returned to her chair, closed her eyes, nodded and said no more. Brando placed another note into the woman's hand which, like its sister, with remarkable deftness, was hidden within those black folds immediately.

The heat was intense now, well past midday, and even though it was April there was nothing cool on the slight breeze. She sat, eyes still closed, and flicked her hand at us dismissively.

We thanked her, to which she nodded again but did not open her eyes, so we wished her good luck, and left.

'I need a stiff drink,' said Brando.

'I wondered what you were going to say.'

'Don't be so vulgar,' he said.

And then, as we walked back towards the Schiavoni in the chequered heat, he kept repeating with admiring wonder in his voice, 'A satyr – with a *wine cup*?'

'Trust you to remember that. You should be so lucky.'

'So should you. And your new Italian friend? I wonder – how is his *cazzo*?'

'I wouldn't know. Nor do I intend to find out.'

'That's not the way it looked last night.'

'That was just the Campari.'

'He was attractive – in a straight up-and-down way. And highly respectable – a director of that most prestigious museum – and anyway, he thinks you've flown already. You are safe from temptation. If that's what you want?'

'Stop stirring, Brando. It was merely the Campari and I'm back to being a respectable married woman today. And a truthful one.'

To which he, much amused, said that I'd have made a

very poor whore if all I could do was tell the truth to the hopefuls who had the misfortune to come to me for a bit of fun. And that anyway, I seemed to have lost my capacity for fun, or what capacity I once had. In fact, Brando said, I was dull and respectable nowadays. Just as well that I was going home. He was better enjoying the city without miserable me. The old woman's words had obviously stung him. That, and fear of age perhaps. And, despite my telling myself that he therefore wanted to sting me, his words went in. Very definitely went in. Indeed, truth hurt. I was dull. I had no spirit of adventure. I should have gone to Florida, it was the kind of safe place suited to a dullard like me.

'I wonder who the owner of the building is,' I said.

Brando looked at me in a kind of baffled wonderment. 'Well, your Italian of course.'

We walked until we found a little bar in a nice shady square. I had gin and tonic. Campari was not, yet, to be tolerated. I felt absolutely wiped out, though whether it was from the heat of the sun, or whether it was from the heat of the experience, I couldn't say. Suddenly, as I looked about me at the beautiful old facades of this little square with its ochre and terracotta walls, its elevated windows and the rush of the crowds passing through, and across at the light playing on the buildings and the glistening of Salute's golden dome in the distance – it all looked so picturesque and delightful. Telling small lies was hardly significant when there was so much else going on that was cruel or unjust or misery-making. Venice knew very well that when banks fail, the city fails. When cities fail, the world begins to crumble. She had suffered a slump all those hundreds of years ago, and now look at her – a shell of her former glory but functioning, certainly functioning. So he was the owner, that wily old Italian Casanova, that foxy Volpone. It made me feel strange all over. I didn't like it. Suddenly I really wanted to be home so badly it felt like a pain. Safe, I wanted to be safe. Dullard, dullard, dullard. But in the secret places of my thoughts . . .? Perhaps not. Perhaps we all have a fantasy about what we could be like – and it's best kept that way, just a fantasy. It is certainly not a truth that has to be told. How right the old woman was about *that*.

The heat was enervating, the place was enervating, sucking the common sense out of anyone who dared to dally. I just wanted to be back where I felt secure and unchallenged by old crones with too much wisdom and too much experience and too little ordinary happiness to assault the senses. And my hand, particularly my wedding finger, throbbed. And I was getting superstitious – which was reason enough to embark for home and quickly. Nothing like the carefully tidy front gardens and little brick paths of a London suburb to make you rational again.

'I think my life is too easy,' I said out loud. 'Even all this financial stuff isn't going to affect me very much. I am immune to difficulty. And I shouldn't be.'

'You have said some stupid things in your life, Nina,' said Brando, 'but that takes the biscuit. The whole point about life is to make it as easy as possible, for you and – without putting yourself out too much – for everyone else.' He paused, and looked up at the pure blue sky. 'I wonder why we say "takes the biscuit"?'

'Almost certainly nautical,' I said. 'We're an island race. The sea is in our blood's vocabulary. Nautical. It'll be nautical.'

'Ah,' he said, '*that* is why I employ you.'

Brando bought himself another grappa and a *Times* and settled down to read. I settled down to think. And when

Brando's phone beeped and he answered, he gave me a look as if to ask if I was here or not – at which I emphatically shook my head. I guessed it was our Italian friend. But I had much to think about, much, and I didn't want any further craziness entering what was already a state of confusion. Brando walked off chatting to him for a while. I heard him thank the man for the interesting excursion – and suggest they meet for an after-dinner drink. 'No, no, she was absolutely fine. Yes. She's flying out about –' He looked at me. I flapped my arms. 'About now, I think. But I'd love to meet for that drink later. And talk a bit more about –'

Good. He could go on his own. While I flew home to my beloved suburbia. As I watched the people of Venice come and go and thought about infidelity and *onesta,* etc., in all its many guises, I remembered those salient lines from Dorothy Parker –

> Helen of Troy had a wandering glance;
> Sappho's restriction was only the sky;
> Ninon was ever the chatter of France;
> But oh, what a good girl am I!

How well our old woman knew the fires of desire and suggestion. I had a sudden, unpleasant image of Robert visiting a house of ill repute in Florida (Did they have such things? Of course they did), which left me wondering – how idle is the idle brain – if that wouldn't be preferable to his meeting someone in a bar and actually *liking* them. At least if he had to cough up some dosh he might feel less inclined to fall in love. I heard Brando say, 'Yes – pity she had to go – her husband . . . all a bit difficult at the moment for them. But I shall see you later and look forward to it. Goodbye.'

He put the phone on the table and picked up *The Times* again.

'Brando,' I said suddenly, 'have you ever paid for sex?'

'Every day of my life, sweetheart,' he said cheerfully, and went back to reading the paper.

Fourteen

Ambiloquy: the use of indeterminate expressions;
discourse of doubtful meaning.

Samuel Johnson's *Dictionary*, 1755

IT WAS THE middle of the afternoon and I was packing slowly, longing to be gone. As I folded and smoothed I thought about truth generally. It was a such a hydra, it really was. And not one I could imagine taming – for long. And at least I had tried, and would go on trying. Only another few days to go. But maybe just for this one week I could square up to some of the great names? After all, George Washington might be known for his truthfulness but, frankly, the cherry tree was – or rather was not – there – the axe was in his hand – what else could he do but own up? He couldn't very well say the tree fell over and the fairies took it away. Well, possibly he could if he were my son – in fact it's a racing certainty he could if he were Johnno. But George? He had to own up. There was the felled tree. So he's scarcely a decent example of taking the hard road to honesty. Literature does better than fact in the matter of truth's dark side. Fiction may be one big lie but Hardy's Tess is much more of a warning because she finds out that truth-telling comes with its scourges. Poor, poor Tess. She tells the truth to that moralising, dewy-eyed fool Angel and eventually hangs for it . . . Hardy's message? Keep shtum.

Even in the greatest of all literature – the Sophoclean

163

model whence all drama derives – there is no advertisement for the better side of veracity – none at all. Oedipus is certainly no incentive for the digging out of truth. Or the joys of having your own, tame Oracle. Oedipus. Polluted outcast. Destroyed with the guilt that the truth provided. Poor old swollen foot. A man beset by the gods, advocator of truth and finally blinded by it. *It's not my fault* cuts no ice with truth. I should remember that, I thought, rather than parading all my new-found transparency. Personally I have always thought that the great flaw in this Grecian tale is that Oedipus, having solved the riddle of the Sphinx for Thebes, then gets married. If he knows he's destined to marry his mother you'd have thought he'd steer clear of that union altogether, just in case. I know I would. But that's those boys for you, they just won't be told. Lust, I suppose, lust and the desire for power. Marry Jocasta and you will be King. So maybe he deserved his exile. Any right-minded person would have steered clear of tying the marital knot on the grounds that you can't be too careful. But not in old Greece. Marriage, I thought, looking down at my poor bruised finger all puffed up around my wedding ring, it always seems to come back to that. And the room was getting hotter despite the open windows.

Robert and I liked Jack Nicholson. Robert, I imagine, liked him because he could fantasise that – had things been a little different – his life could have been just like that. Women dropping at his feet, wonderful set of teeth and happy hedonism. Whereas I just drooled, mostly, and if pushed might manage to say that I also thought him a fine actor in fine films but, really, this was, largely *untruthful*. About as *onesta* as I imagine it is to look at Marilyn Monroe on the screen if you are of a male heterosexual persuasion and to declare that you only think of her in the same light as Sybil Thorndike. Anyway, there I was in a heap on the bed, thinking about a Jack Nicholson film, *A Few Good Men*, and remembering his lines and the way he delivers them and thinking that they sum up the dichotomy perfectly. 'You can't handle the truth,' he says to his interlocutor, who happens to be Tom Cruise, but never mind, 'because you sleep under that blanket of protection which I provide and you'd rather not know how I provide it . . .' He pauses. Tom Cruise tries his little best to act a response and fails but Jack is acting for both of them here. '. . . You can't handle the truth: because somewhere, deep down inside yourself, in that place you don't talk about at parties, you know you need the bad stuff to protect the good stuff.' Tom Cruise grips his little fists, clenches his tiny jaw and turns on his little high-stacked bootees. Jack wins.

It was while I was dwelling on the additional struggle of truth with honour, and how badly I had misjudged the Italian in thinking he had any honour to him at all, that my stomach gave me a little tickle. Most improper of it. It happened again when I could not stop thinking that, compared to Jack Nicholson, physically the Italian was chocolate chip. How strange, when there were older men who looked like the Italian, that so many perfectly wise and excellent women found a balding Lothario with little piggy eyes and absolutely no regard for delicacy where the pursuit of sex was concerned entirely seductive, to wit one Mr Nicholson. I had no doubt that the Italian would have more finesse. Much more finesse. It was around that point that my stomach suffered the tickle and the telephone in my room rang. It was the concierge. I had a visitor. It would be Brando, I thought, and I said she should send him up. A little while later there was a knock on the door. It was not

165

Brando. It was the Italian. With a small posy of lilies of the valley and an expression of tender concern.

At the sight of him and the realisation that a) it wasn't Brando and b) I was supposed to be on a plane and c) I wasn't wearing very much – quite a small T-shirt over unpretentious knickers – I did the only thing possible under the circumstances and squeaked. The Italian put up his free hand, palm outwards, as if to say that I should not be anxious. And then gave me the quickest and undoubtedly most calculated look of approval – true or not – before turning away. Irritatingly, I was pleased. I wanted to ask him to wait downstairs but not much came out except another squeak or two which may or may not have been the question 'What on earth are you doing here?' as I scrabbled in my half-filled case for a skirt. He might have had the decency to turn away, but not, I noticed as I did up the zip, to offer to leave the room. 'You may turn round,' I said, with as much dignity as possible. He did so. He was smiling. I couldn't help admiring his teeth all over again, all the better to eat you with, my dear . . . Or rather, at first he smiled and then he shrugged with that look of the little boy who has done something wrong and then he moved towards me with the flowers held out. They smelled exquisite. He said, 'I am here to say that I am sorry. And I was told it was all right to come up . . .?' I tried to look casual and at ease. 'Oh yes,' I said. 'But I thought you were Brando.'

I took the flowers. Their scent was sweet and fresh in that hot little room. By then, and despite the open window, the air had grown even heavier – and I pointed to the chair set against the far wall. 'Would you like to sit down?' How formal. The whole thing was quite mad. And what was he doing here? He removed the papers and books from the seat, took off his jacket – which he hung over the back of the chair – and sat down. His shirt was open at the neck. He crossed his legs, folded his arms and looked convincingly relaxed.

'I am so sorry for what happened last night,' he said. 'I feel it was my fault. And it spoiled our – our new acquaintance, which is a great pity. I wanted to take you for lunch today but your friend said you had flown home.' He gave me a candid look. 'I knew that not to be true since there are no flights in the early afternoon and I knew you were at Casa Giovanni in the morning. So I came to apologise after all.' He did not look particularly contrite, I thought. He raised an eyebrow. 'I also knew that you must be very angry, or very upset, to have told me such a lie.' I flushed, or blushed, and I could not be sure if he was teasing me or not. I decided to ignore the remark. I also decided not to look at him.

'Oh well,' I said, staring at the wall above his head, 'I expect Brando got muddled.' And then I thought about truth. 'No. I expect he thought he was protecting me.' The Italian nodded. He did not seem surprised at the notion that he was someone from whom I needed protecting; indeed, he seemed to think it was a perfectly fair comment. I felt a small and pleasing flutter in my stomach.

I tried to do the reverse of good therapy and think up an anti-gratitude list – he has thinning hair, he has definite jowls, he is nearer sixty than fifty and he is a playboy, without the boy bit. A playgrandpa then. But none of it helped. He was wearing all the right clothes again – the Italian linen, pale biscuit-coloured suit, impeccably sky-blue shirt, soft pale leather loafers. You just knew he could quote from Dante if asked. It was hell. And then he smiled and with his head on one side, asked, 'And how did you enjoy meeting with Mama Giovanni?'

'She's your *mother*?' More squeaks.

He laughed. 'No, no – it is merely a convenient, a courtesy, title. Honorary. My own mother would be very upset. She would, as you might say, turn in her grave.' He looked, waited, and when I said nothing and fiddled with water, glass and flowers, he asked again. 'Was it helpful?'

'It was,' I said.

'Good.'

'It showed that the underbelly of this beautiful place is as corrupt as it ever was.'

'And the pictures on the walls – fantasies, deceptions, enticements?'

'No,' I had to concede. 'Not deceptions. Fantasies, enticements perhaps.' The words he was using were not helping the heat in the room.

'Mama Giovanni is worth meeting and remarkable in any sense. I always think she would have made a fine Mother Superior.' And of course it was my turn to laugh because he was right.

'I'm glad it amuses you. I wanted to give you something special for your book. As far as I know the house has never been mentioned in – well – acceptable guidebooks. Smollett did not even visit Venice, and although Goethe came here he says nothing of such places. He probably visited one or two along the way – he, too, came on his Italian journey when he was having a life crisis . . .' He paused. We looked at each other. Pointless in denying it. 'And I hoped that it would be a useful visit – and a kinder memory than the unfortunate experience with the lion's mouth . . .' He looked at my hand and made a little moue of sympathy.

'But you own the place,' I said, accusingly. 'You live off immoral earnings. Or you did.'

'I lease it to the old one,' he said. And then he smiled.

'Morality? You pursue truth and now you pursue morality. You *are* high-minded.' And he looked irritatingly amused again. 'But no – my *father* lived off immoral earnings, if that is what you want to call them. I have never owned it as a working business. Only as a property. I had thought it would become a wonderful home, a glorious home in fact.' He laughed and looked at me in a bold way that was very disturbing. 'Somewhere that would be quite as impressive as the building you so admired on our walk last night. And now I shall pay the price for that. It will take a great deal of money to restore and all of it will be from my personal purse, which I have not got. So it will languish. No more credit.'

'So you are just the same as . . .' He moved a little nearer and my voice trailed off.

'Did I ever suggest I was anything else? But at least you have the story of it, the existence of it, for your book. And in the meantime I can look at it and dream. You have it for your book as – what is the word? – as a scoop, with my compliments.' He bowed. I was not altogether convinced that his graciousness was without irony. However, I decided to be equally gracious. 'That was nice of you,' I said. 'But Brando is something of a dilettante. I'm not sure when the book will be finished, if ever. It's likely to be an unfinished business with him, scoop or no scoop.'

'Ah,' he said. And then waited.

I went on folding things and self-consciously rattling on, speeding up. 'Yes, he's too rich, that's the problem, and too interested in the pleasures of research without the pain of actually writing any of it up. It can be very frustrating at times – I like to get on with things, I'm not a good one for unfinished business, not at all, I like to get going and finish the –' Then he stood up. And I stopped talking. And packing. He walked over to me and put his crooked finger under my chin and stared right into my eyes and said, 'We have some unfinished business, do we?'

How long can a moment be? A picosecond? An eternity? Both. Enough time, certainly, for me to think that this was probably, marriage or no marriage, the most perfectly romantic moment in my life – a sweetly hot bedroom, scented by lilies of the valley, in Venice, overlooking the canal, about to be made love to by a tall, dark attractive near-stranger. The *sine qua non* of seduction, I discovered, is that it is most seductive when enacted by one who is experienced in the art of it, and when the one being seduced is aware – exactly – of the possibilities of the situation while being in a safe pair of hands. One of us needed to have a safe pair of hands and mine were all over the place or, rather, coyly and chastely still. The Italian was serious in his pursuit, as I had no doubt he was in all his pursuits, of which there would have been many. And what, exactly, was wrong with that? What is it about the value of chance in love and sex rather than planning, I thought (feeling it was all unreal anyway, some sort of a dream maybe) that overrides something planned as a better way to success? There was no tiptoeing around this eternal picosecond and I did not move away. I did not want to move away. The flowers, the scent of him – not – thank the stars – aftershave but a faint smell of heat and skin. Robert wasn't here and he wasn't even on the end of a telephone. I'd been abandoned by him. Forlorn. Here was someone who – well – here was someone. That was it and that was everything. No aftershave, I thought, how clever, as we both seated ourselves, very slowly, on the end of the bed and faced each other.

'It is warm. For April.' He undid another button of his

shirt. He moved closer. I agreed it was warm. Our thighs were now touching. They were also warm. I looked across at the open window and the sky beyond. Blue, clear, with the waters of the Giudecca rippling and twinkling below. He kissed my neck. The blue sky was oddly full of stars or little explosions and I thought I might hiccough. Certainly I felt dizzy for a moment and I recognised the sensation of thrill. Of non-married thrill. It's so nice, I thought dreamily, it's nice. Then the fingers of my hand seemed to be attached to his shirt and undoing yet another button, almost of its own volition, and one of us made a little noise. Me probably. He was far too assured to make indelicate noises, whereas everything inside my body seemed to be moving around and demanding attention, none of which it was getting and all of which it anticipated with rare eagerness.

His fingers were now stroking the top of my arm under the T-shirt sleeve. My bones were no longer rigid matter but made of water and, almost idly, I wondered if I'd ever asked Robert to do the same, stroke me like this, and then with a sharp little pinch of my heart I dismissed him and instead I smiled up at this stranger. Seduction is also about surprise. Oh dear, I thought, smiling and smiling still, I had – even more surprises – undone all the stranger's shirt buttons now and for the first time since my marriage I ran my fingertips over another man's naked skin with sex in mind. It felt different, new and responsive – just as my skin was responding to his touch. Someone else's skin, masculine, I thought, has a deeply seductive feel to it.

It was all taking place like some perfect motion – but I wondered what would happen when this stopped, as it must, and all the other stuff started – the practical stuff – the socks, the shoes on him, the skirt, the bra, the T-shirt on me

– how to keep this beautiful rhythm and get undressed. I moved away wanting to begin. He was smiling, eyes very close to mine, lips near – my lips near to his, also smiling. He lifted my hand to his mouth, kissed the knuckles, stroked the bruised part with his thumb. I was most wonderfully compliant – quite resigned to the whole thing – lost in it all. 'You are quite sure?' he said quietly. 'Oh yes,' I said, 'quite, quite sure.' Those bits of me that should have behaved with the propriety of a married woman, did quite the opposite. Those bits of me that should have remained chaste and thrown him out for his perfidy, did not. 'Quite, quite sure was the absolute truth.' With what I was thinking, I belonged in his whorehouse, a thought that made me all the more aroused. How could it not in this lily-scented, heat-ridden paradise of romantic sensuality? All considerations had gone. This was living in the moment. This was what happened when your husband let you down. Funny how – even at the point of no return – you make a justification for what you are about to do.

I lay back on the bed, quite, quite sure. And he lay beside me, turned towards me, and put his hand to my face. I touched his hand with mine. I could no longer convince myself of his jowls or anything else undesirable. Right then he was entirely and supremely It. 'Your poor bruised finger,' he said. I felt utterly sorry for myself and for my poor little bruised finger. Robert was a brute, Robert had not understood anything – why, even now Robert was probably in a high-class Florida brothel without thinking about me at all, or at a bar somewhere with his hand on a plastic blonde's . . . I looked down at the other hand belonging to this stranger, which was stroking just above my knee. Yes, I thought, that's probably what Robert is doing, too. Oh, to have left me alone, to have left me alone.

And here was someone who really wanted to be with me. And really, really wanted me. 'I feel very cherished,' I said.

'Good.' He smiled. 'Very good.'

It was as if I were a child again and being praised for doing something right. I felt even more cared for, even more vulnerable, even more trusting. She who normally cares for others is being cared for herself. Very seductive. Sex is whatever we want it to be and I wanted it to be a yielding thing, without any responsibility on my part. Probably because that way it wasn't my fault, any of it. I was the passive receiver and therefore I was not answerable. He took my hand and began to kiss the fingers one by one: poor me, poor me. I opened my eyes and looked into his which were beguiling, intent, and so I smiled a reply. A smile of invitation, a smile of aquiescence, impatience even. I had no conscience, only pity for myself. He released my hand and I moved a little closer to him. The heat of the room made our bodies slither as they touched. Casanova, Volpone, who cared? It was perfect for Italy, perfect for Venice on this most perfect of afternoons. Who made *Love in the Afternoon*? I wondered idly. Eric Rohmer. Why shouldn't I have this beautiful time, this siesta heat? Ovid praised those afternoons when Corinna came creeping into his bed in the shaded sultriness – May my siestas often turn out that way, he says. I looked up, thinking, And mine.

I touched his bare chest with the palm of my hand, feeling quite bold. He closed his eyes and ran his fingers over my neck and shoulder. So far, I thought, he's not at all bad for his age; in fact, he was quite good for it – slightly tanned, slightly hairy, very different. I wondered what he would think of me. Was I good for my age, too? Did it matter? And then, as I watched my hand moving so easily across his body, the sun glinted on the dented gold of my wedding ring like a little shaft of fire and I thought, Ovid would have removed it before we began. Ovid always took the right steps to ensure satisfaction . . . Ovid, at least in his poetry, judged seduction and the preambles to lovemaking perfectly. There would be no wedding ring as reminder if Ovid were here to seduce me.

I tried to keep them closed but my eyes snapped open. There was the old gold ring again, dented, accusing. I felt cheated but all I could do was sit bolt upright and say, 'I can't do this.' He opened his eyes wide, looked at me startled, said, 'Of course you can, *cara*, of course you can – it hurts no one.' But when he took my hand and tried to kiss it again, I did the only thing a woman can do under those circumstances – I began to cry. Poor me, indeed. He made all the right noises, made all the right moves, and I should have succumbed. I wanted to succumb, very much. But at the point of being touched again, with that little old ring glinting, I did the only other thing a woman can do under those circumstances – I apologised and moved away. A good seducer knows when it is final. I was still weeping and apologising as he dressed and left. He assured me that I must not be upset, mopped my eyes with a pure white handkerchief, and departed – I suspect in some relief. When the door closed I positively howled. The child had lost its toy.

Out onto the balcony I tottered and watched him walk away, striding away really, along the Zattere, and I cried all the more. Then my phone rang and for the first time ever I thought, Please don't let it be Robert. It wasn't. It was Brando. Who thought he might accompany me to the airport as he would enjoy the journey back and forth across the lagoon. He was bored, clearly. 'You sound – odd?' he said.

I looked at the now diminutive figure with its jacket slung over its shoulder, the blue shirt bright in the afternoon sun, a hand casually in its pocket, going away, far away, and the tears continued. 'Just got something in my eye,' I said. Which was more or less true.

So. *Truth? What is truth? said Jesting Pilate. And would not stay for an answer* . . . In the end you must face the mirror. That was it, and that was all. I snapped the suitcase shut. That's how it is. Do your best, I thought, as I set off down the stairs. Do your best as I waited at the vaporetto stop. I arrived at the other side and walked to where the water taxis waited. Brando was there, looking extraordinary in a pink-candy-striped jacket and sky-blue trousers and the sight of him cheered me up. Dear, familiar Brando. I was comforted. Do your best, I thought, as I watched Brando handle my case onto the deck. Mother's favourite maxim. Just do your best. And even as I stepped onto the boat, I momentarily froze. But Brando and the conductor hauled me aboard. Mother, I had suddenly thought. Oh God. Home to London and *Mother*.

Mother – Tassie – Johnno – Robert's slumped shoulders at the airport – even those innocent and ordinary and thoroughly nice people at the doctor's surgery. Oh God, oh God . . . And the *nun*. And then there was Toni – how could I ever face Toni again? But that was what I had to do now. Face it. All of it. With the sword of truth, too, to quote a well-known politician and liar, reformed. So I settled my face towards the open lagoon. And towards the hell that would certainly be arriving home.

Fifteen

Steehopping: usually applied to women, but not always; not used in any other sense. 'Her is always steehopping about. Better fit her would abide at home and mind her own house . . .'

Frederick Ellworthy's *The West Country Book*, 1888

ANY FORM OF travelling alone provides a golden opportunity for thinking. Which may be why so many passengers like to get drunk. Thinking, especially over a long and enforced period of idleness, can be extremely depressing, especially when you are thinking about what a fool you are, and what a fool you will continue to be because you can't change it. I wondered how I felt about the Italian. Did I mind that I had thrown in the towel, or was I pleased? Telling the truth to others can be hard enough, telling it to yourself takes immense courage. I had two gin and tonics in the short time it took to fly home. The pursuit of truth had certainly rekindled my propensity for alcohol. I'd consumed more in these last two days than I had in a month. I winced at where the Campari had nearly taken me. Even so, a little bug whispered in my ear that – well – where it had nearly taken me was an achievement of sorts – for an Englishwoman of certain years. I lingered over the thought for a moment, and then put it away from me. Two gin and tonics may blunt one's intellect, but it does not cure it. I set foot back on English soil feeling like shooting myself. And I still didn't know if I regretted not turning into Corinna.

176

I could do very little immediately about my husband who would not be home for another three days, nor my daughter whom I hoped would not be home for some time, indeed, not come home until her allotted time. (I could imagine in the years to come when she, cradling my first grandchild to her breast, would weep to remember how I had forced her to return from her longed-for travels with my selfishness. Better by far she never had such an opportunity.) My best friend I could do nothing about, because Toni was currently in Edinburgh and would not be home for another forty-eight hours. I'd rung Arturo, dear unsuspecting Arturo, and asked. My truthful and unkind treatment of society at large, which focused on those poor souls at the doctor's surgery, could not be rectified either, well, not straight away. And in any case, they were racists, even if they didn't know it. If ignorance is no excuse in matters of breaking the laws of the state, neither was it an excuse in matters of breaking the laws of Nina. Yes, racists were fine to be left. In fact, it would only open old wounds to try to do anything about them.

But there was one offended person I could do something about immediately, one offended person who was no doubt, at this very moment, as I stepped off the plane, sitting grimly on her unremarkable settee thinking dark thoughts about her only daughter and her daughter's lapse into perverse and wanton lunacy. Hence the continuing feeling that it might be beneficial to shoot myself. Though I did think that of all the various confrontations that lay ahead, the one with my mother might be the easiest to deal with. If I hadn't thought that way I would never have found the courage. Better get it over with tonight.

Delaying tactics are extraordinary. Subconscious delaying tactics are not only extraordinary, they are believable. I got off the bus at the airport car park at what I thought was the right stop for my row and number – C 47/48 – but it was not. I had already made up my mind that once the suitcase was stowed and I was sitting inside the car, I would take out my mobile – yes, yes I would – and I would phone my mother. I would drive straight over to see her. That was the plan. I discounted the gin and tonics. By the time we had circled, landed, waited for baggage and come through customs, it was a long time ago and much water had been consumed in the meantime. So – having made this monumental decision to go straight to my mother's house it was hardly surprising, really, that I lost the car completely. Up and down the rows I trundled, pulling the suitcase behind me in the eerie half-light, rather enjoying the justifiable delaying tactic and not minding at all when I got very strange looks from people whom I passed several times. One cheery man called out that he'd been there and got the T-shirt and that the thing to do was to keep pressing the zapper. Eventually I'd be near the car and hear it cough its locks open. Damn him. I did what he said and – all too soon – I was back in the car and back in the land of reality. With no gun handy, I made that call.

My mother was frosty – unsurprisingly – and muttered something about watching *Springwatch*. I said it would be over by the time I got there. At least she would be in a good mood after all that carnal activity with birds and rutting deer and whatnot. She was not in a good one currently. 'So, dear – Venice and that homosexual was *much* better than Florida and Robert? Well, of course it was . . .'

Like a depressed knight I cut my way through the thorns, told her I was on my way, and drove towards the house I grew up in. Though I was sure my mother would question whether I had actually grown up at all.

The gate squeaked as it always did to tell my mother that

I had arrived. Usually she opened the door in a kind of triumph before I'd had time to ring the bell – but not this time. I pressed the little white button and the familiar chimes rang out. Deep breath. Door opened. Mother stood there straight-backed in a dark green twinset, reading glasses in her hand, floral apron around her still slender waist, the very picture of domesticated grandmother at ease. She did not smile. I, on the other hand, was grinning like a hopeful in a beauty contest, and couldn't stop. She indicated that I should go past her into the hallway. Which is what I did. And we then went, oh mercy, into the *front room*.

'*Springwatch* over then?'

'Only just.'

'Was it good? Nesting boxes and blue tits and things? Deer? Rabbits?'

'Did you bring the *mostarda*?'

Fuck.

'No.' And, of course, I was about to say that it had been confiscated at the airport when I remembered rotten old truth. 'I forgot. I'm so sorry.'

Advantage, Mother.

'I'll get the coffee,' she said. 'It's just made.'

While she was out of the room I looked at all the familiarities. Damask curtains in a non-colour, the cherry-wood china cabinet whose contents I had so longed to play with as a little girl – the key was in it now, though in the days of childhood it had been well hidden. A livid, patterned rug on the floor in front of the fireplace with its non-existent open fire. She now had a strange brass-framed panel that had a series of white flickering flames that gave out no heat whatsoever. Much cleaner, apparently. I did not, when I first saw it, say that it was also much colder.

What else? Well, there was what my mother called a serviceable suite – beige dralon, lumpish and comfortable and too large for the room. Perfectly pristine, everything. And colourless. It was no wonder our house was painted in all kinds of colours, even the wooden furniture. After living in this non-provocative Narnia, colour was all. How reactionary we children always are. How we think when we do things like paint two walls Bloomsbury Green that we are breaking new ground – when in fact we are just throwing our familial-psychological stuff away. And Robert, I thought, suddenly feeling a bit teary, Robert had never once objected in all these years to bright walls, painted floors, singing graphics and rainbow blinds. Tassie had, of course. She would go the other way. I looked around. One day, I thought, when she has a home of her own, it will look more or less like this. Oh, more modern, but cool, definitely cool. Even there, with the decor, I'd thought I was being true to myself and you know what? I was being anti-parent really. Johnno didn't seem to notice, fortunately. He just never pulled his curtains and painted two of his walls black. Any floor covering had long since been hidden under a mound of unmentionable matter. He would have painted the whole room black but the paint ran out. Strange how it never occurred to him to go and buy another tin.

The photographs in this nerveless room were poignant, too. All lined up on the top of the oak sideboard. All perfectly symmetrical and dusted. Laurence and me on the swing in the garden, Dad behind, both of us children looking out with ten- and twelve-year-old eyes eager for the world; my mother holding Tassie in her arms after the christening (a small rise of irritation here; I had wanted to wait until Tassie could make up her own mind but my mother wouldn't hear of it and so we conformed – Robert the (atheistic) peacemaker); and then that picture of Robert and me on our wedding day looking so happy and young and as touching in its way as the picture of Laurence and me on the swing. Photographs often lie, of course – you could go through Henry VIII's photo albums, no doubt, and see nothing but happy family snaps – but this picture of the two of us did not lie. We were happy that day, and – despite the usual ups and downs and occasional marching out of the house by either party – we had continued to be so. As marriages go it was a good one. Probably I was helped to see this by having a best friend who was having an affair. It concentrated the mind. Robert would do, Robert would do very nicely, and I believed he felt much the same about me. Oh, we had our fiery moments and we had our cooler times – but we smouldered along together and occasionally burst into flame and that was just fine. This latest bit of behaviour, though, for some reason, had gone deeper than anything before. I felt unsupported. Dismissed. Was it our age? Was it my age? Was it that he had been feeling a bit bored and wanted a ruck? Was it that he felt insecure in some way and I had made it worse? No way of knowing until he came home . . .

I sat down and twiddled my fingers. I remembered the feel of that alien naked skin in Venice, the heat of the room, the scent of the lilies of the valley – and it made this seem even colder and cooler. I asked myself if I regretted not giving in. I thought I probably did, really, as I thought it would mean very little and would be something to bring out from a secret place of memories occasionally, as the hip joints grew stiffer . . . Ah, my dear, once upon a time . . . I smiled at the thought and then jumped at the rattle of the cups as my mother reappeared. She put the tray down on the low table and settled herself on the sofa opposite.

'Help yourself to biscuits,' she said, and leaned back against her dull old sofa and looked at me over the rim of her cup. I'd never liked that thin, floral china and I really disliked it now. Also, the biscuits were all-butter Osbornes, plain as you like, the selling point of which always made me want to say, Butter? Butter? Where?

'Well, I just wanted to apologise for being so pious with you the other day. That stuff about truth. And to thank you for trying to help. That's all. I suppose it was all done without thinking things through.'

'Well, that's you all over,' she said.

But I just sipped my coffee. I was not here to be provoked. In this, the decor of the room was helpful.

'And I'm going to make it up to Robert when he comes home.'

'If he comes home,' she said darkly. I realised that my mother, my only mother, was enjoying this. Or, at least, not minding it very much.

'All I wanted was to try to do something that felt right. To be able to say that I don't ask of others something that I can't give myself.'

'You do that all the time,' said my mother.

'What?'

'Ask of others things that you don't do yourself.'

'I don't.'

'You do.'

'What?'

'We all do it, Nina. It's called being human. Don't do what I do, do what I say. You're a dab hand at it.'

She'd gone slightly pink. Pink with emotion. 'You've been my daughter for nearly half a century . . .' I flinched. That was below the belt. What a way of describing a mature woman like me. But still I did not rise. She waited, maybe for me to object. I set my mouth. 'For a good many years at any rate, and you've never stopped doing it. You're always so bound up in being superhuman and showing everyone else up – I don't know how Robert bears it. Buddhism? Remember that? And the Japanese garden of tranquillity – when Tassie ate so many pebbles she rattled on the way to hospital? I mean, you've never rested, you've never just lived quietly and kept your thoughts to yourself like most of us do. Even your so-called work with that – Brian man – is heedless of others' feelings. Remember when you made Laurence bury that blackbird?'

This was getting ridiculous.

'No I haven't a clue –'

'Oh, cast your mind back. Poor Lollie – a sensitive boy – and you made him do the whole funeral rites. You said we all had to confront death sometime. You put the dead thing in his hands. I couldn't get him to come out of his cupboard for a week.'

'Well –'

'He was nine, Nina.'

'I really don't remember.'

'And your dad said that boys had to toughen up if they were going to be as tough as girls. He always took your side.'

'Not always – I remember when –'

'We always baled you out when you got hold of some tomfool idea and it looks like you'll be going on doing it. You've got everything most women would give their eye teeth for – but no. Not you. Let's just tinker with this bit of the perfectly smooth-running engine, shall we, and see what happens?'

'That's not what I do. It's about principle, it's about being true to your self – in this case it is simply and solely about Truth, without which the world would be –'

But the pink of my mother's indignant cheeks had deepened. There are high horses and there are even higher horses, and my mother had climbed onto the highest she could find.

'Oh, the world, the world. And what about your family? What about their world? My world? And Robert has put up with so much over the years. You've even got Tassie on the point of coming home because she's worried about *you*. And Johnno *would* come home if Tassie could locate him. When you should be the one worrying about *them*. And here am I – blast – no – *bugger* it – still worrying about *you*. Forty-odd years of people telling me how intelligent you are, how lively. Lively? They don't know the half. Always a bee in your bonnet and someone else picks up the pieces. Years and years of it. And Robert is still there, and he's still loyal, and he's still *alive* . . . And your father's been dead for all these years and you just snap your fingers as if nothing matters beyond you. And what have you been doing now? You've been having a lovely time in Venice with a queer.'

And there I was thinking I was an interesting and honourable person. I was genuinely shocked. Instead I found that, to my homophobic mother at least, I was just a flagrant abuser of a live husband. And a nuisance. Had Robert felt like that, too? And was that why this had happened – the proverbial straw? He'd had enough? I just stared at my mother's pinker cheeks and hard, bright eyes.

Now, I should exonerate her a little here, lest the admirable political correctness brigade take up the baton. She feels she can be so indelicate about Brando's sexuality and her terminology where he is concerned because of the following instance. When I first introduced them at a party at our house, not long after we were married, Brando put his arm around my waist and gave it a squeeze with his hand, that made me squeak. My mother looked from his hand to his face and then to me with a mixture of shock and anxiousness. Brando stepped in with his usual forthrightness, bowed and said, 'Oh, Mrs Carpenter, please don't worry about your daughter's virtue on my account for I am a rampant pansy.' Which finished her off completely where he was concerned, forever. So she took it as her future right to continue the pattern. If it doesn't exonerate her, it at least explains her behaviour. She'd been given permission.

Back to the pink cheeks and the assertion that my lovely husband had perhaps had enough of me and my ways. I partly believed it. And so, as of old, I hung my head and mumbled an apology. Never mind Robert. What I suddenly realised, to my shame, was that she missed my father, she still loved my father, and that far from being an old lady who was happy with her china cups, she was a widow who would never, quite, be happy again. Here I was turning my back on my husband when she'd lost hers forever. I could mumble an apology with impunity. I was sorry she was so hurt and angry, I was sorry that I had overlooked how much she still missed my father and it didn't matter that the reason for her anger had absolutely nothing to do with me and truth. But at least the feeling sorry was genuine. I realised that I had scarcely given a thought to my mother's being a blood-pumping woman with desires. 'I am so sorry,' I said again. And I really was. So far, so far I had not broken my bond. I smiled, a little wanly I think, and then it was over.

The box of necessary apologies was closed. She accepted it briskly, got up, brisk and straight, and went to the sideboard. Out came a bottle of whisky – I didn't even know she had a bottle of whisky – and she poured some into her cup of coffee. 'Being truthful, Nina, is not all it's cracked up to be,' she said. 'After your father died I wished, a thousand times, that I had been less truthful with him. And I think you'll feel the same way if you don't do something about Robert very soon.' She took a slug of her coffee. 'No – not all it's cracked up to be at all.'

'I'm beginning to realise that.' I reached for the bottle. For in those few minutes my mother had said more to me than in a lifetime.

'No,' said my mother, removing the bottle. 'Do get a grip, Nina. You're driving.'

Sixteen

Sing small:* to cease from boasting.

Albert Hyamson's *Dictionary of English Phrases*, 1922

IN THE CAR and wearing my shift of penance I checked my phone. Several missed messages from Brando (of course) but nothing from Robert. Just as well. If I had spoken to him at that moment I would have cried my heart *and* lungs out and probably begged him to come home. I drove home slowly, particularly slowly past the doctor's surgery. I had that deep down sick feeling that no medicine can cure. It is called shame. Beyond the windscreen people were coming and going, off for a night out, off for a night in, doing ordinary things, telling lies cheerfully and with impunity, living. And I had set myself above it all. As if. 'Facing the enforced journey,' said Bede, 'no man can be more prudent than he has good call to be.' The father of English history always had a word for it. The shame deepened. Nina Porter as Joan of Arc? I don't think so. Literature was supposed to give you lessons in life. One of the things I liked most about *Paradise Lost* was that it allowed me a heart-warming sense of *Schadenfreude*. Satan's tumble from overweening hubris was a reminder of how it could be. One which, thirty years later, I seemed to have forgotten. *Milton, thou shouldst be living at this hour . . . England hath need of thee . . .* He was

*'Sing small' is another phrase which carelessness in pronunciation has changed from the original. The phrase should be 'sink small', to be lowered in the estimation of one's fellows.

a sick man but he kept on writing what he knew to be right. He was a great man and England did indeed have need of him, but I thought rather miserably that it could probably very well do without me. Of course I couldn't change the way of the world. Not without turning my world and other people's worlds upside down. Truth is cruel. Truth is unkind. Truth is – only pure and good when it is tempered by judgement. The judgement of Milton and his likes, not mine, oh humble weed.

Self-mortification is dangerously close to self-indulgence. You can get quite smug about recognising how dreadful you are and I think I probably did on that journey home. I had certainly never driven more courteously nor been more radiantly aware of the world and the life that was going on all around me. Ordinary, simple folk, getting on with things, glad for the good, sad for the bad – and not to be judged by the likes of mere me. In fact, so courteously did I drive that once or twice the driver behind me hooted with impatience. Don't keep stopping at crossings or waiting for hovering pedestrians and the like, lady, some of us have a life to live . . . After the third or fourth bit of road rudeness some of the humility and mortification fell away. Remembering my mother's amazing and never-before-experienced use of the swearing B-word, I began to feel that itch again – and then I did something I'd never done before either. At the fifth display of bad behaviour, I gave a bus driver who tooted me at a zebra crossing the finger. Yes. And as I turned out of the traffic and into our road I thought that was probably one of the more truthful things I had perpetrated in the last few days. And I felt all the better for it. My mother had nearly won, just not quite, and there was a bit of angora stitched into the hair shirt I wore.

*

The phone call with Tassie was not helped by my getting the time difference wrong. And waking her from what was clearly a deep and happy slumber. The psychological point at which secret police make their house calls for maximum effect. Her first words were 'Has somebody died?' She sounded so slurry that I asked her, with maternal light-heartedness, if she was a bit drunk. This was not met by daughterly light-heartedness. Her repeatable words were spoken coldly, and sternly. 'Have you spoken to Dad yet?' To which I thought, but did not say, Mind your own business.

When did the sociocultural change take place with our children? When did we, the parents, with all our experience, stop being the boundary-setters for our offspring and stand back watching them set their own boundaries? And not only their boundaries. Ours. And then sit back while allowing them to go on imputing that we were dangerous if let out of the box too often? I would never, ever, have dared speak to my mother in the way Tassie spoke to me. The very idea of being interrogated about my adult, marital behaviour – 'Have you spoken to Dad yet?' – delivered in a voice as interrogatory as a schoolmistress enquiring about revision – showed how far this change had progressed. How feeble we had become as parents. No wonder, I thought with shame, that we bringers into the world of children get hammered by the pundits, no wonder. We'll drive our offspring hither and thither and cut their calorie intake to safe levels with aching hearts, but we won't stand up to them. I was about to say to Tass, in quiet, and humble tones, that I hadn't spoken to Robert, that I was truly, deeply sorry for causing such misery, and to metaphorically crawl to Walsingham, when she spoke again, in a voice that made

189

me think of impatient fingernails tapping on wood –
'Well?' she said. 'Have you, Mum?'

Now marriages are not enhanced by having children. Let
us get this straight. If we are speaking the truth, then
children change marriages, change its participants, bring
love, bring a glimpse of heaven in the slightest little gesture,
bring that all-important link with the future of the planet,
bring deep joy at the reproducing of one's genes – but they
do not bring enhancement to marriage. Marriage, at its
best, is between two people in love who can't get enough of
each other both in and out of bed and who find a trip to the
supermarket together thrilling. In short, in marriage, which
is strictly a two-hander, the only time you find that you are
not getting enough of each other is because you are asleep –
asleep – by the way – for as long as you need. Indeed,
children are wired to come between the partners in a
marriage, or at least to make themselves the most important
items in existence. They are wired to survive and that is how
they do it. It is their smile that twists the heart of the parent,
their cries that torture the nerves of the parent, their
intensity of living in the present (my nappy – *now*; my rusks
and milk *now*; my naptime *now*, etc.). Hitherto, before said
child appeared, each of the partners viewed the other as
possessing everything they needed in their emotional lives to
live well. After children arrive this is cast aside as the new
infant – with lungs and requirements of an unremitting
nature – divides and rules. They are not sent to enhance but
to use marriage for their own ends. To grow up as best as
they possibly can. Let us be quite clear on that. And what I
was dealing with here was not Tassie's interests in parental
strife – to which I would grant validity so far as she was
concerned but deny her the right to impose herself – but a
schism that had occurred in my marriage and which

belonged to me and my marital partner. My marriage. Our marriage. His and mine. And our lovely, beloved, bossy daughter could just butt out.

'Let's leave your dad out of it, Tass. Everything is going to be fine between him and me. And if it isn't, then you'll be the first to know. Right now this is marriage business. It may become family business later. But for the moment – leave it. Now, how are you getting on?'

If ever a maternal tone was designed to show that the mater was serious in not wishing to pursue a subject, it was mine. I sounded firm, convinced and sane. If ever an attempt to tell the truth produced some interesting and useful offshoots, it was this: I was retrieving the marital ground from the clutches of my offspring. As adults (and we parents will always be The Adults until we are suddenly seen to be dribbling and suffering from dementia when our – God help us – children become The Adults over us) we should take the confident high ground more often. This is what I knew, this was the truth that hit me back. Truth for Truth. I was proud of myself for speaking out and sorry I had not done so sooner. 'No, Tassie. This is not your business. Yet.'

Tassie said, 'Mum?' in that guarded way denoting she thought I had probably gone off my rocker. But I was no longer afraid. 'Now leave it, Tassie,' I said. 'Leave it to your dad and me. It's our muddle and we'll sort it out.'

That was it. I was pleased with the use of the word muddle, a comforting word, and felt that with its use I really was back in charge and no longer afraid. The sword of truth or the shield of verity protected me. Afraid? *Afraid of what?* What is it that these nice, middle-class, look-down-their-noses children are likely to do? Knife us in the guts? Burn down our houses? No, no. They might – just – make the love and sacrifice unworthwhile. They might do it publicly. If we go against their wishes they may take to drugs, which would be our fault. Or drink. Or stop eating. They might leave us to lonely old age and spit on our parental efforts and tell the world. They could disown us and stop us seeing our grandchildren – and then it will all have been in vain. I shivered, even then and in my rebellious mood, at the prospect. Tassie was puffing like a grampus down the phone. 'Mum, this is bad. You and Dad have never separated before.'

'He's on a working holiday, darling. Not in a bachelor flat.'

'You've never been apart like this.'

'How do you know that?'

Silence. And then an altogether less confident tone: 'Have you?'

'No. But we came close a few times. It's marriage, Tass, that's what people do in marriage – they argue and then they make up. But it's not your business. It's ours.'

'Dad wouldn't see it that way.'

'Yes he would.'

Oh God, I suddenly thought, how enviable are those oft-vilified parents who are known, with true British diplomacy, as lower class. They may be in the same self-created, oppressed boat as the supposedly more responsible middle classes, but – because feckless and given to obesity (as opposed to we the middle classes who are secret drinkers and constantly dieting on mixed leaves) – they tend to give up earlier on attempting to rein in and appease their offspring. A clip round the ear and if that doesn't do it – well – so what? That's their funeral. *I've spent sixteen years bringing him/her up and if he/she doesn't like it, then he/she can just piss off.* Frankly the lower classes strike me as a good deal more sensible and intelligent in this matter than the Lidl Châteauneuf-du-Pape brigade. Love is not love that gives in to the first demand. Love is not love that condones infant assertion over adult good sense. Watch those lions, see how they behave once their sweet little cuddly cubs get big. I couldn't help thinking that if Robert and I had merely opened a bag of cheese-and-onion taquitos and a can of lager when charged with bad behaviour by our children we might have been a lot happier. And so, actually, might they . . .

How feeble I was. Could I ever forget that useless moment when I said to Johnno, 'Now, Johnno, – if you don't tidy up your room Father Christmas won't come . . .' And Johnno didn't and Father Christmas did. After that it was downhill and racing rapidly towards asking Tassie, at the age of eight and a half, 'Now – what would you like for your supper?' And she, wisely spotting an opening, had taken it as her right to choose her food from that moment on, instead of what it should have been – a one-off piece of gentle humouring. Oh yes, they are programmed. From that day forth she selected her meals. And I, bleating like a hopeless sheep, obliged. Johnno also lumbered into the gap. Some nights I cooked three different dishes – one for Tass, one for Johnno, and one for us. This was followed swiftly by Tassie choosing her clothes, followed by Johnno choosing his clothes (including the trainers for which a mortgage was required) and, eventually, everything else in life that gave me authority they removed and I, in that unnameable fear, concurred. Walking Tassie to school I couldn't help feeling that *she* took *my* hand when it came time to cross the main road. And my innate fear that, should I not give in, she would begin that fearsome process of disowning me and telling the world of my iniquities, became entrenched. Yes – it had been downhill, and racing, all the way with both of them. Though Johnno was more inclined to put his headphones on and walk away when anything he did not want to do was asked of him. When he reached six foot two at the tender age of fourteen, all was lost – unless I stood on a chair.

With Tassie, the microcosm of having a poached egg on toast when all about her were eating fish became the macrocosm of her believing it was her right to make her parents toe the behavioural line. I could tell, now, down that crackly old telephone line, that my dismissal of her role as marriage guidance counsellor and peacenik shocked her. Why, she could not have sounded more astonished if I had asked her if she was remembering to change her underwear at acceptable intervals and had she washed behind her ears.

'Mum, that's not fair. It isn't going to be fine – not from the way Dad sounded when he spoke to me –'

'You've spoken to him since Ven – since I talked to you? I asked you to wait, Tass. Why couldn't you, just for once, do what I asked and no questions?' Part of me was thinking that she'd managed to get through to him while he continued to ignore me. A thought that provoked a little bubble of panic.

'He rang me, Mum,' she said in a voice of exasperating weariness.

'Oh. Why?'

'Same as you. To tell me not to worry and that it's all going to be fine. But it didn't sound as if he believed it. You really need to do something, Mum. So? What are you going to do? You are my parents and – well – I expect to be kept in the loop.'

It might have been all right if she had not used that phrase. In my day loops were little plastic squiggles that prevented pregnancy. Or something that Biggles did in his little aeroplane. Fortunately I reined in my first desire which was to enlighten her about the IUD. Usually I ignored our children's irritating use of current catchphrases but not now.

'Ridiculous phrase, in the loop, Tassie. Let's leave the subject alone, shall we? And don't get all dramatic and say you're going to catch the first plane home. There really isn't any point. I promise you'll be told if there is anything serious we think you should know. But there won't be. Your dad and I will be fine. Trust me, Tassie, I'm his wife.'

'And I'm his – your – daughter. Doesn't that count?'

'Not half as much. Now, what I really want to know is how you are.'

Even as I said the word I realised that there is something impenetrably solid about *wife* when it is said with utter conviction. The same with the word *husband*. So much more definite than partner. It implies unity, oneness, legal and emotional binding, two cleaved as one. At its best it is something that no one can break and no one can squeeze between. At its worst both the terms can be used as expressions of dismay. In this case they were expressions of unity. Poor Tassie. I almost felt sorry for her. The puffing increased.

'I'll see if I can get hold of Johnno. At least I can talk to him about it . . .'

'He'll grunt, Tass. You know that.'

'No he won't. Not with something like this.'

'Like what?'

'You and Dad. You.'

'All you need to know is that I love the old sod. And sometimes you get cross with the person you love. That's it, that's all, that's everything. And the old sod, for all my sins, loves me. And that is the truth, plain and simple. In fact, we are both behaving like silly so-and-sos and are best ignored.'

And then, thank the heavens, Tassie laughed. If she has one abiding quality that is entirely hers, it is that she can laugh at herself. Not very often but sometimes she can. Johnno is more like Robert. They both rearrange their lips over their teeth and look down, as if embarrassed and are not, actually, in the room. Something to do with saving the masculine face, perhaps? And primal.

'OK,' she said. 'If you're sure. When you call him an old sod it feels better.'

So that's the trick of reassurance. I might try silly bastard next time. That is, I thought painfully, if there *is* a next time. I might have sounded confident to Tassie – that, after all, is another role for the parent – but I didn't feel it, I didn't feel it at all. The Venetian bordello and the Venetian incident had shaken me. Life could turn on a sixpence. You only have to say Yes instead of No and that's it.

We talked for a while about what she was doing, seeing, eating and drinking – and then, as we were saying goodbye, she added, but now in a little girl's voice which, of course, wrung my heart, as it was intended to do, 'Will you ring me once Dad gets home and will you promise not to lie about what's going on?'

'I promise.'

I was beginning to find truth-telling had unexpected rewards, like applying at last the holy grail of feminism and being assertive. It was a little late for me to discover that it actually worked but . . . I put down the phone and felt as if someone had cut all my strings. Two and a half days to go and Robert would be back. Tassie was crossed off the list which felt such a relief that I thought about going back to bed. But no – I had places to go, battles to win, the next of which would roll Marathon, the Sack of Rome and Waterloo all into one. I had to try to put things right with Toni. Pure cowardice told me I couldn't do anything because she was in Scotland. Scotland was not Timbuktu. Scotland was part of the British Isles (no matter how hard it fought not to be) and there were things called trains, were there not, if one did not relish the idea of driving all that way.

If not the sword of truth then surely I could wear its breastplate? Aletheia, goddess of truth and daugher of Zeus, appealed to by Pindar most touchingly, '*Aletheia, who art the beginning of great virtue, keep my good-faith from stumbling against rough falsehood . . .*' Five thousand years ago and Truth was perceived as feminine. Given that most of our politicians are male, and given that they are perceived to be the biggest category of liar on the planet, go figure.

Seventeen

Upas: a baleful, destructive, or deadly power or influence;
from a fabulous tree with properties so poisonous as to
destroy all animal and vegetable life . . . around.

Sir James Murray's *New English Dictionary*, 1926

I TOOK THE train to Edinburgh. It had to be done and I just
couldn't wait. A surprised and warmly friendly Arturo told
me where Toni was staying. His innocent friendliness made
the situation all the more painful. As I made my way to the
station I toughened my determination. Whether or not she
was staying at the Monument Hotel – which is what she
had told Arturo – or whether she was staying in a
Travelodge on the A7 with Bob the Logistics – I had to talk
to her. Now. I knew she was definitely in Edinburgh, or
nearbye, because the dialling code for the number Arturo
gave me fitted the area. Toni never relied on her mobile in
case she couldn't get a signal. She thought of everything and
was irreproachable in that regard – possible illness,
accident, etc., made it an absolute. Once up there I would
go to the Monument Hotel and find her, and if she wasn't
booked in there, then I'd have to ring. Otherwise – to cite
the Pythons – my chief weapon would be surprise – minus,
sadly, those other requirements of fear, ruthless efficiency
and an almost fanatical devotion to the Pope.

Long train journeys can be evocative and with luck the
sensation encourages your ponderings mile after mile.
Sylvia Plath called it 'the incomparable rhythmic language

of the wheels, clacking out nursery rhymes, summing up the moments of the mind like the chant of a broken record . . .' Even though rails no longer clack, the thought of Plath remained. Something to do with the way Toni might look – made ill and brittle with the precariousness of love maybe. And the enclosed world of the rolling carriage. Plath was a great one for milking the strangeness and illusions of any experience, including train journeys, and giving her fellow-travellers dark and mysterious personae. I looked about me at my travelling companions – an elderly couple doing the crossword – engrossed and hunkered up together – two young boys holding something electronic, clicking away with their fingers and laughing horribly at whatever they conjured up. On and on, all the way down the carriage, ordinary lives, normal people, reading newspapers, drinking coffee, eyes closed, mouths open, telling lies when they felt it was necessary, telling the truth if they could. Unconcerned. And I – I had no idea what I was going to say when I got to journey's end. April green and clear blue skies raced by – another hour or so and it would be dark. Less to look at, more to think about. Sinister, almost, these close but impenetrable minds giving away nothing of what they were planning, thinking, hoping. No wonder Plath found trains and travellers evocative, like her three fat Frenchwomen knitting on a train at night with their blind, complacent faces and making what she called their webs of fate while the telegraph poles and the dark pointed pine trees rattled by . . . But Plath had always had that dark side. Toni used to be all light and laughter and fun. I had with me Mary McCarthy's book on Venice, but hadn't opened it. I could always go home. I began to wonder what the next station would be . . .

And then, fortunately, Brando rang. He was very excited.

'Your Italian has shown me all kinds of instruments and diagrams in the museum here. Oh my, Nina, they tell of despicable things. You wouldn't get away with it now. Well – not unless you paid a *fortune*.'

'Enchanting,' I said, but the irony was lost on him. 'Stop delighting in the proclivities of straights.' One or two eyes appeared over their newspapers opposite me.

'Perfect for the illustrations. We shall have an entire chapter devoted to ways to extract truth from the unwilling, including sexual favours. You'll like that. We can point out that if some of these little items were applied to our politicians nowadays it would make things a whole lot more transparent.'

'Well, politicians have certainly always fallen at the first hurdle of what you call sexual favours,' I said quietly. Not quietly enough, for even the two crossword puzzlers stopped their concentrating and gave me a startled look.

'I knew Venice would provide,' he said happily. 'Come back at once. I need you to interpret. Your Italian talks too fast for me.'

'He is not my Italian and he speaks excellent English.'

'Well,' he said, in his pompous voice, 'it's not good enough for the ah – nuance.'

'Brando – why say that? It's almost perfect.'

'Oh, I see – you're determined to squeeze the truth out of me?'

'I doubt it,' I laughed. 'But go on. Try.'

'All right,' he said, in a much smaller voice. 'If you must know, I miss you.'

I was astonished. 'What?'

'I shall not say it again.'

'Oh go on.'

'Once and once only. Now, will you come over?'

'Brando, I really can't. I'm on the train for Edinburgh. I'm going to see Toni.'

'But you'd much rather be here with me?'

I could answer that with absolute squeaky pure truth. 'Oh God, yes – I'd much rather be there with you. Much.'

'I suppose,' he said, 'it's the fault of having children. You stop being self-indulgent. Pity. The Italian and I are going to lunch on Torcello tomorrow, the Cipriani – pomegranate blossom and all . . .' He said this last wheedlingly.

'Sexy things, pomegranates. I'd be careful if I were you.'

'Not with that one, my dear. He's not TBH. Nowhere near it.'

TBH was our code. It stood for To Be Had. Brando's way of saying a straight man might surprise himself if Brando tried really hard . . . Well, in days gone by.

'You never know with those passionate Italians. You might find that pomegranates do it for him.'

He laughed. 'No – but he showed me some copies of papers with the pomegranate symbol all over them. Part of a cache of sixteenth-century spy-network stuff – about Catherine of Aragon.'

'What about her?'

'Details – to the very hour almost – of her menstrual cycle and beddings with Henry. The Italian says they wanted to know when she was likely to conceive. Or when she didn't. Useful politics.'

'Good God,' I said, so loudly that a few heads turned. 'Was nothing sacred?'

The turned heads looked on with interest.

'To the Venetians? I shouldn't think so. But at least they were honest about it. I'm quite sure it's similar for royals today. Think of Diana. I expect her wedding date was considered very carefully. Sure you can't get over for tomorrow?'

'Sure.'

'I'll give the Italian your love, shall I?'

'Brando – I miss you, too,' I said.

And he was gone. The carriage sank back into its torpor and I stared at the passing world. Deathbed regrets? A sultry room in Venice and the scent of lily of the valley? Perhaps. We stopped at a station, I remained in my seat and we sped on.

I still had no idea what I was going to say when I got there. As the April green and the gentle landscape made way for the craggier, broader sweep of the true north. Darkness came a-creeping and cowardly feelings joined it. I could just get off at Waverley, and turn around and go home. After all, I could get another train back easily. I could go back to Venice. Do my job. Brando needed me and I enjoyed what I did. I'd done my time as a diligent student, a good honest worker, a committed and capable mother, and now I could do what I pleased and indulge my friend, the dilettante. Back in Venice. I could. No. Yes. No. I couldn't do that. I'd never be able to face myself again. Oh yes you would, said the demon on my shoulder. But I banished it. I must see Toni, I must apologise for what I said – yet somehow not retract it. Remain truthful. How to make that balance? Perhaps Toni had a right to her fate just like the rest of us – and whether it was a moral one (judged by me) or not, it was hers. Words would come when I saw her. It was best not to pre-plan. I'd just give her a firm, friendly, warm apology for hurting her and a cool, calm pacific statement saying that I would never overstep the mark again. And that would be that. We would be grown-up, civilised women, dealing with what are now so fondly called *issues*. And then we would share a pot of tea or something stronger and all would be well and all manner of things would be well. Not quite. The big one to come was with Robert.

I stepped into a taxi, looked to neither right nor left as we sped along, and arrived at the hotel wondering whether it was calm serenity that I felt, or simply frozen fear. If my voice was anything to go by it was the latter. The words came out in a high croak when I asked at reception for Mrs Benedetto. And I was not altogether impressed with the warm relief on hearing that Mrs Benedetto was out at present. I sat in one of the overstuffed chairs amid the extravagantly ugly flower-arranged foyer – where a lorgnette and a floral *embonpoint* would not have looked out of place – and tried the Mary McCarthy book again. Perfect. I need not move for hours. Perhaps, I thought, Mrs Benedetto is out for the night. Relief wrapped me even more warmly. Yes, that was it. She and Bob the Logistics were out on the tiles . . . I was saved.

I was just reading around the interesting question of why a state so venal and cruel as Venice – which, among other little quirks, had a penchant for blinding its doges over a hot brazier of coals (my, they could certainly teach us a thing or two about painful truth) – could also be thought of as La Serenissima and so often referred to as beautiful as a dream or a fairy tale . . . and thinking that a fairy-tale setting did not, necessarily, mean *good* fairy tales, fairy tales often being full of the darkest and cruellest aspects of inhumanity and evil – when the rotating doors of the hotel rotated, and in came Toni.

I saw her before she saw me. But only fractionally. Then we connected. She stood by the doors as they circled slowly behind her, and stared. Her eyes were wide as a startled marmoset's – but they were not dark-circled and there was real colour in her cheeks. She wore a smart black trouser suit (oh those non-existent hips), very high heels (only she, only she) and a crisp, white shirt. She looked very businesslike with her even smarter black business bag slung over her shoulder and a neat-looking case for a laptop in her delicate little hand. And if it were not for the way her perfectly roseate mouth hung open, you could be forgiven for thinking you had just stepped out of a boardroom drama.

I stood up. Mary McCarthy slid to the floor. We both looked down at it and then back at each other. I thought: firm, friendly, warm, cool, calm, pacific – and prepared to be all these. Then I looked into those marmoset eyes again – and promptly burst into tears. I'd never heard of the Olympic sport of synchronised crying, but we invented it. Just at the exact moment when I opened my mouth for the first howl, the smart and businesslike Mrs Benedetto hurled herself across the divide, yelling my name, and also bursting into tears. The management looked on in amazement as we fell on each other's necks and clung to each other and sobbed and laughed. Toni said, as if it were being ripped out of her, 'Oh God, you were so right. So *right* . . . I couldn't wait to get back to London and tell you.'

And then, very cautiously, up crept a passing member of staff and, bending low, she picked up the McCarthy book most gingerly and placed it on the table in front of us. It lay open at the page that contained the salutary words: 'I envy you writing about Venice,' says the newcomer. 'I pity you,' says the old hand . . .' I reached down and closed the book. Everything contained a paradox. Of course it did.

*

How could I possibly have thought we would settle for a pot of tea? Something considerably stronger was needed to blunt the effect of those floral arrangements and, as I noticed now, the slightly embossed wallpaper in snuffbox yellow. I didn't know you could buy dark red blooms that looked like blood-soaked spears on the wheels of chariots. So the gin and tonics were ordered. Fingers were wiped under eyes, smudging mascara and streaking foundation. Buttons on jackets and coats were undone and bodies relaxed. We faced each other in those remarkably uncomfortable chairs and, after crying, we had a good laugh. I said I wanted to apologise, Toni held up her mascara-streaked hand and said it was not to be thought of and that it – my stern talking-to – had done her an amazing favour. That was when I undid the last of my jacket buttons and leaned back, sighing. She looked bright-eyed and bushy-tailed and – yes – happy. I began to feel the teensiest bit afraid. This was not exactly how I expected her to look if she had turned her world upside down and either dumped the chump or decided to tell her husband.

'So – Edinburgh?' I managed to ask eventually once we'd done all the cooing and doving and undoubtedly convinced the still pop-eyed management that we batted for the other side. 'Why here?'

'I could ask you the same question,' she said playfully.

'Well, I came to see you and to put things right.'

And she was off again. More mascara trails. 'Everything is all right. Thank you, thank you.' And I nearly went nearly off again too, but the drinks arrived and saved me. 'Do you mean you came all this way just to see me?' she said, managing to bring everything to bear in the sentence while getting a solid mouthful of the drink inside her.

'Yes.'

'Oh, Nina – that is just wonderful of you.'

'Yes,' I said. 'But why are you up here? And you look great, by the way.'

She touched the side of her nose in a gesture of conspiratorial inclusion. Mockingly, I hoped. 'I'm on a course. A business-management course. Isn't that wonderful?'

You never – quite – know your friends. I wanted to laugh at the joke but I could see that it was no such thing. So I did the only other possibility and raised my glass. 'To business-management courses,' I said. And downed about half of it, which felt considerably better.

She then raised her glass, in all seriousness, and nodded. 'Absolutely. Here's to it.'

Very cautiously I asked her why a business-management course, to which she said, 'Well, you were absolutely right. Bob and I needed to take the reins if we were ever going to be together – and I needed to be as good as his wife – no – *better* than his wife – at the business side of things in order to be his true partner in everything.'

I could not think of a single thing to say. Not one. So I just stared at her in what I hoped looked like open admiration. And then I did think of something. A lifeline. 'Does Bob know you're here?'

'Nope,' she said, happily.

'Does Bob know about the business-management course?'

'Nope,' she said, even more happily.

I found myself nodding at the floor and saying, 'Good, good,' and feeling very near to tears again.

'I want to surprise him.'

You'll do that all right, I thought.

'And I was going to ask you – when I got back – what you think about the timeline?'

'Timeline?'

She rolled her eyes as if to say, Oh what a silly billy for not knowing businesspeak.

'Timeline, Nina. Timeline means do I tell Bob first, or do I tell Arturo? I can't make up my mind. Instinct tells me go for the one that will give negative results first –'

'That's reasonable,' I mumbled. I had a feeling that there wouldn't be very much to choose between the two anyway. But no. I straightened up, looked my friend firmly in the eye and said that I thought she should first tell Bob.

'Why?'

Oh God. Why? Come on, Nina, think, *think*.

'Because he'll need to be warned before you tell Arturo in case Arturo does something crazy.'

'Arturo wouldn't do anything like that.'

'You don't know what he might do. You've never left him before. And even if he didn't try to shoot Bob, he might ring Bob's wife, or go round there and tell all – and what would Bob say then, if he didn't know?'

A sly look came over Toni's little kitten face and her dainty mouth pursed with amusement. 'Well,' she said, 'that might not be such a bad thing. His wife? Might it?' And she raised her little hand with impressive imperiousness and summoned the waiter to order more drinks.

'Well . . .' I said, as if contemplating a seriously tricky dilemma, which it wasn't because I was absolutely sure I knew what the outcome would be, and dreaded it – should I tell her what I was certain of? Not necessarily. Not if she hadn't asked me to pronounce on it. But I could steer her. '. . . You know, Arturo is Italian, and they are jealous lovers . . .'

'Hrmph,' she said.

'You don't know what fires burn beneath that slightly chubby chest.'

'I think I do. None.'

My friend had gone extremely hard all of a sudden. Fortunately the drinks arrived and with the bit of business that entailed I was able to pull my thoughts together again. 'It just wouldn't be fair on Bob. He ought to know before anyone else.'

'Why?'

Well, yes, come on, God – *why?*

'It's a monumental decision. It's your future together. He should be completely in the picture before you tell Arturo. Trust me. I speak the truth.' And I did. There was no doubt in my mind that Bob should be the first to hear about business management and the new dawn of togetherness. 'And I think, to be fair to him, you should wait until you're face-to-face.' The last thing this situation needed was for Toni to break out – two gin and tonics down – and ring him with the news. There's something about telephones and being able to dissemble in a conversation that you can't do when you are eyeball-to-eyeball. I could imagine that Bob the Logistics was a very smooth talker – and when he was confronted with reality – well – Toni had to be there to see his evasiveness for herself.

When she nodded and said that I was absolutely right I felt a wonderful wave of smugness. Eat your heart out, I thought to myself, as I pictured Bob's face when he finally had to confront reality, eat your rotten heart out. We freshened up in her room and decided to use the restaurant in the hotel. Toni had a double bed and with a little adjustment from the management, it was agreed I would stay with her. Naturally this confirmed the sapphic tendency and there was a certain pinkening of the receptionist's gills which was enjoyable. I was looking forward to being with Toni while she was so happy. One more night, I thought, suddenly miserable, of her looking like this – so positive and beautiful again – and then . . . At least she would be back in London when the proverbial hit the rotating thing yet again, at least she would be able to go home, at least Arturo would be there, at least, finally, she would know. And I'd be exonerated from troublemaking. This I thought, feeling very positive.

Downstairs again we ordered one more drink and waited while they got our table ready. Toni suddenly stood up and said, eyes alight with joy, 'I know *exactly* how to do it. Won't be a mo'. I'm just going back to the room to get something.' And she tottered over to the lift. Up she went. To return a few minutes later with her laptop. 'A videoconference. I can do it on my laptop. I'll contact him now. He'll still be at the office. Never goes home until he has to.' She looked so happy. I found myself cursing the invention of the wheel.

'I thought he was away.'

'Oh no, he's back.'

'Let's eat first,' I said.

'No – he might have gone home by then. And I've got another two days of this course to go. I'll do it now.'

And so she did.

Do I draw a veil over what transpired? Or do I describe in minute detail the dreadful moment when Bob's face appeared on the screen and he said, in his seductive voice, 'Hi, darling. Checking up on me? To what do I owe the pleasure?'

And she told him.

I watched with fascinated disgust as his face constricted into a rictus of horror. Very plain to see. Undeniable, in fact. His eyes went hard and he licked his lips like any cornered criminal. And no real attempt, no apparent will, to recover and pretend. Did she see it at first? Who knows? Her smile (I was sitting side-on to her) was still in place as he said, 'Now wait a minute, sweetie. Hold on –' And she put up her delicate little hand and said, ever so firmly, 'Don't even think about worrying. It's all going to be fine. *I'll* take on the business stuff. That's the surprise in all this. My course tutor says I'm first-rate. We won't need your wife any more.'

'Really?' he said, and now there was a touch of contempt in the rictus. 'First-rate at what?'

'Running a business. That's what I've been learning about. This is it, darling,' she said, bounding onwards until I was near to screaming. 'This is the moment. I'm going to leave Arturo and you are going to leave your unkind wife, and we are going to be happy together at last. We'll be a partnership.'

Toni's voice was louder than usual, much as we tend to talk loudly into our mobiles, I suppose. All around us in the foyer were eyes filled with curiosity. Not only at what seemed, impossibly, to be happening – a lovely woman talking animatedly to a screen which appeared to be replying (you could fairly feel the *embonpoints* shiver) but also what was being said. All motion seemed to cease. Couples and friends, who had been about to set off into the night, stopped, pretending they had a picture to look at, or something to say to each other. We were at the centre of a drama. The reception staff were also staring, taxi drivers who had called to collect their fares stood motionless by the desk, hotel staff hovered on the periphery – anyone coming through the doors felt a chill of inactivity and looked about them nervously.

'Let's wait until you get home,' said smooth-talking Bob. 'I don't think this is the time or the moment for such a big decision. OK, darling?'

I waited for Toni to back off. But her roseate spectacles had clearly slid down her nose. She saw. In that terrible, blinding moment of inner certainty, she knew. Bob's *OK, darling?* gave it away completely. Never had man sounded so false, I thought. Never had darling sounded more like an insult.

'You don't want me,' she said, 'Do you?'

'Now you're being silly.'

'You never wanted me, really, did you?'

'Of course I want you, just not – '

'Will you tell your wife tonight?'

'Now, Toni – you know it's not –'

It was over.

There are pyrrhic victories and there are pyrrhic victories. Suffice it to say that I caught the late train back to London. And so did Toni. But we sat in separate compartments. 'If you had kept your fucking ideas about truth out of my business,' she said once the screen went blank, 'I'd have still been happy. Thanks a bunch. Very sisterly of you.' I couldn't even say I was sorry, because I wasn't. Once you undertake to tell the truth even the most platitudinous conventions are lost. Instead I just sat there. All I could think of to say was that I was sorry I was right, and obviously lead balloons came to mind. So Toni got up, picked up her laptop, and swept off up to her room. We met again on the platform but no words were exchanged.

Back to the rhythm of the train and unbridled ponderings. The old adage of shoot the messenger was alive and well. And its most famous perpetrator, Tiberius, had a point. Thus do we convince ourselves of whatever we need to get ourselves through. I'm sure he felt a great deal better when a messenger arrived at Villa Jovis to tell him of some foul new development back at the centre of his Empire, or that a conspiracy was afoot in Rome, or that tracts about his behaviour were appalling his subjects, throwing said messenger onto the rocks below. Whatever the truth of what he learned, at least he'd enjoyed a moment of hitting back. I expect it did his twisted little heart masses of good to see that body bump its way down into the foaming waters below. It all goes back to love. If they hadn't made Tiberius give up his beloved Vipsania for Augustus' daughter Julia, he might never have ended up living such a foul and disgusting life atop Capri. I might not have ended up on the rocks, but I had removed Toni's great love and from now on I was dead to her. So much for truth.

When we reached London I saw my friend in the distance trundling her bag behind her, head held high, fury in every step. I wondered how long it would take for that bravado to sink into the stooped back and sunken head of misery. I just hoped Arturo and the children were too bleary-eyed to notice. There was going to be an almighty splash otherwise. As for me, well, I arrived back at the silent, dark house as morning was just hinting at her emergence from sleep – and in that colourless, cold crepuscular light I felt chilled and old and very stupid but at least I felt certain that Robert would return. I would go to the airport and wait for his flight and hope. It was all I could do.

No messages of note. Nothing from Robert. Sad. Nothing from Tassie. Good. Nothing from Toni. Bad. Nothing from my mother. Unsurprising. And another call from Brando. If he used the house phone, which he regarded as the office phone, then he was clearly in serious working mode. Or I was supposed to be. He was telling me to look out all the information I could find on those cages, particularly where they were hung. I already knew about them but my one-step-aheadness that usually pleased me now left me flat. Mary McCarthy was graphic on the subject. The cage, or *cheba*, was the Venetian idea of a hanging basket – only rather than pansies and trailing verbena it contained, usually, a miscreant monk or priest who'd been caught doing something immoral or criminal (the one being the other in fifteenth-century Venice). Torture was not part of the punishment – Brando would be sorry to hear this – but hanging there for anything up to a year and being fed on only bread and water was. Though I even had my doubts about this. Someone, surely, would sneak up to the cage at some point and push a bit of meat or cheese or fruit between the bars? A friend, a mother, or a wife . . .

I rang him. He sounded pleased to hear from me. 'Fascinating, isn't it?' he said.

Brando had been shown one of the original hooks, high up near the Rialto – courtesy of the Italian – and he wanted to know some other likely locations. 'We could plot a walk through the city describing where each was hung and the kind of crimes committed. That'd be original.'

'And horrible,' I said.

'Yes, but people like to be scared once in a while.' And shocked. It makes their own settled lives so much more delightful.

He was right. Lovely it was to look over the edge, into the pit, and then scurry off home to hot Bovril and *The Archers*.

'And you'll like this – mostly they were hung up there not for telling lies, but for telling the truth.'

'Such as?'

'You mustn't trade with that merchant for he is a murderer.'

'Inconvenient. The Venetians wanted to go on trading with anybody, murderer or not? Is that your point?'

'Exactly. Not unlike the wonderful world of commerce and empire today. If the merchant was a good contributor to Venetian business, he never committed a crime . . . Good, eh?'

'Very good,' I said flatly.

'It's a cruel old world, the world of capitalism.' He paused, delighted with himself.

'Yes,' I said.

'Oh come on, Nina, we used to have such fun.'

'And we will again,' I said bleakly. 'But not right now.'

He added, quite gently, that he hoped things bucked up and that I was to let him know . . . He was only being partly selfish and that really was too much. Not only had he confessed to actually missing me, now he was being *kind*. Down came the tears.

'Could you please stop being kind to me?' I said.

'Certainly.'

'It's making it worse.'

But he had rung off.

One of our urban foxes was making its piteous last call for love as the morning crept on. It seemed to express everything I felt. If this was the moral high ground, then, frankly, you could keep it.

Eighteen

Chessiker: an unpleasant surprise.

R. L. Abbott's *Manuscript Collection of Nottingham Words*, 1905

WHAT DO YOU wear to meet your husband when you don't actually own a set of sackcloth and ashes? You go through your dull wardrobe, is what you do. And you try not to make an issue out of what to wear because part of you tells yourself that you have been married for years and years and that it doesn't matter that much: if he loves you he loves you, Dior and pearls or jeans and sweatshirt. But the other part of you – the irrational part – and you know it's irrational because it is accompanied by words from an irredeemably awful song about keeping young and beautiful spinning around in your head: 'You'll always have your way / If he likes you in a negligee . . .' – thinks differently. In a parallel life it would make you weep with laughter, the thought of turning up at Heathrow Airport in a diaphanous, floaty thing, but you are far too concerned with what to wear to find anything funny at all. Bad. Very bad. I held on to Brando's words 'I miss you' for their friendship. Life felt like a giant chessboard at the moment, pieces moving forward and back and the one taking the place of the other – Toni back with the pawns, Brando up with the knights, my mother behind with the bishops, Tassie ahead with the queen, the Italian checked rather than mated, and Robert, well, obviously, he must be the king. I, of course, was the board.

It was the white linen again – after all, look what it had done for me in Venice. And I then – carefully and slowly – began putting on make-up. That most basic of deceits, the painted face. It was nine thirty in the morning and I was applying mascara. Unheard of. I rang Brando before I left just to say I was sorry for being such a misery and letting him down, but if I expected more of the same soothing warmth, I was disappointed. This time it was too early for him and I got a few unrepeatable words followed by the suggestion that I call back at a sensible time. That was more like it. Or better still, he added, get on a plane and get straight back here where there is work to be done.

'Brando,' I said, 'I'm going to the airport to meet Robert. This is make or break for my marriage. Your book will wait. This won't.'

'That kind of attitude,' he said, sleepily, 'is why women do not rule the planet and we men do.'

When Brando starts referring to himself as one of 'we men' you know he is very cross.

'Go on then, run to hubbie. But remember – you've got a fan here if ever you want one.'

I softened. 'Why, thank you.'

'Not me, you klutz, the Italian. If it doesn't work out with Robert you can cut your losses and –'

'Yes, thanks.'

I put the phone down fast. It was as if just by hearing those words I had committed the deed. And despite the irrationality of it, all I thought was that if I felt so guilty Robert might take one look at me and guess. The white linen, I hoped, had a virginal quality to counter this. The jeans might remind him of our innocent youth.

The plane was slightly early so by the time I'd parked the passengers were starting to come through. No time to do what I felt like doing which was to pass out with anxiety. Everybody in that long stream of trolley-pushing travellers was smiling and waving or looking around with benign expressions for a familiar face. And they looked sun-tanned and healthy. It was a happy band. And then, suddenly, there was Robert, pushing a trolley and wearing his old familiar sloppy denim jacket and the blue shirt I'd bought him before he left. He was not smiling. Nor was he looking around benignly. Nor, really, was he looking particularly healthy. And his suntan, which was definitely there, had more of a jaundiced look about it. My heart felt heavy at the sight. On the other hand, how galling it would have been had he come leaping through the barrier with ravening good cheer on account of having had such a good time.

He was pushing the trolley in front of him as if he were on tracks. The rest of the group were scattered around, Hugo and Lorna, Polly and Susannah and a couple of others behind them. Hugo and Lorna looked perfectly normal, if a little more subdued than the rest of the passengers. They still clutched their Burberrys though I didn't think they looked quite so ironed and crisp some-how. Indeed, the whole of the group looked slightly flat. Maybe that was how we always looked when we returned from these jaunts. Those trips were usually tiring affairs. That was probably it for they were certainly moving slightly floppily, as if they were still half-asleep. Or maybe Florida had softened them up. Cut a few strings.

I smiled and gave a tentative little wave as they came closer. Lorna remained considerably less bright and bouncy than usual as she gave me a little wave, a strange half-smile, and they walked on. Odd – and rather chilling. No one seemed to have much to say. Robert still wasn't looking very hard for me. Maybe he thought I wouldn't be there to meet him. Or maybe he didn't want to be met. Only one way to find out. He reached the end of the barrier and he still hadn't seen me. His eyes were fixed and rather hooded. This did not bode well. So I went over to him as he came through the barrier, and I touched his arm. He looked round. I said, stupidly, 'Did you have a nice time.' And he said, rather flatly, 'Thanks for coming.' To which I said, 'That's OK.' And we set off for the car park with no further words. There was an invisible barrier between us – I didn't touch his arm again, or hold his hand, or any of the things I might normally have done. Nor did I ask about Florida. Instead I trotted a pace or two behind like a good, obedient wife until he had to stop and ask which way we should go. He looked haggard in the glare of the airport lights, and in pain. My heart hurt just looking at him. He also had bags under his eyes. I wondered if he had been having – miserable, miserable thought – late and abandoned nights.

At the car I asked if the flight had been OK and he said that it had. 'They do you well on a Virgin,' he said. In the old days I would have laughed at the innuendo. Not now. 'Thanks for picking me up,' he said again, and immediately seemed to fall into a doze. 'Oh,' I said, 'I didn't say hello to the others.' He gave a little half-smile with his closed lips but did not open his eyes. 'They'll live,' he said. And we drove off.

*

It began to rain as we arrived at the house. If I was looking for omens then this was one. It had been sunny and warm while he was away and the light evenings had that usual early-spring sense of good, warm days to come. Now it was back to cold, dull dampness. Robert lugged his case out of the boot, I zapped the lock of the car, took a very deep breath and marched up to the front door. In we went. Robert did not even look up at the house. He kept his head down and walked up the path without looking left or right.

Once indoors my husband, whom I thought I knew like myself, left his case in the hall and did a most extraordinary thing: he went into the sitting room and *turned up the thermostat*. I did not dare to crow as I would once have done. By now I was a little frightened. Then he slumped down on to the sofa and closed his eyes again. He really was a strange colour. Perhaps the Florida sun was different? I went into the kitchen and did the utterly British thing of turning on the kettle. Rain lashed against the back door, wind bent the trees in an agony of cruelty and the gas boiler burst into life. I had never, in all the years I lived with him, known Robert turn up the central heating. Never.

'Coffee?' I called. 'Or tea?' But when I went back into the sitting room, he was half upright and sound asleep. I slid onto the space beside him and snuggled into his crumpled body. It smelled of shampoo, aircraft, his own unique scent – and – oddly – faintly of alcohol. With the radiators warming up and steam on the windows and our comfortable closeness, I, too, fell asleep. And as I began to lose consciousness I had a cold, hard stabbing thought that all this unusual behaviour, his pallor, his monosyllabic responses, could mean only one thing. I was still *persona non grata* – time and separation had not smoothed away any of it. I looked at his nice, familiar sleeping face and wondered how often in the future, if at all, I would be invited to look upon it at such close quarters. And had anyone else?

The telephone roused us both. I opened my eyes and jumped up, startled out of the deepest of sleeps. Robert looked about him and blinked. Then he focused on me as I headed towards the noise. 'Leave it,' he said. 'If it's urgent they'll leave a message.' He rubbed his eyes and took a sip of the water I'd put next to him. The room was like an overheated greenhouse. 'Come and sit down.' He patted the space beside his but I said that first I would bring us some tea – I was thirsty and so must he be. In fact I was buying myself time. We were like strangers with a code of delicate behaviour between us and I was wondering where my husband – my marriage – had gone. I passed the answerphone which clicked towards message but then went silent. As the number only registered as unavailable I knew it was Brando. At least he had shown some tact. Then – hilarious moment – I turned down the thermostat as I passed it and from behind me Robert said, 'Well – that *is* a first.' The sound of his laughter was so unexpected and so welcome that I took heart, just a little, even though there was a definite edge to it.

When I returned with tray, mugs and teapot, he was sitting up and emptying his pockets of all the palaver that goes with travel. This was a characteristic of his and I liked the fact that he seemed to be behaving more normally now. It was now the afternoon and we had slept for nearly three hours – extraordinary. I handed him his tea. He had a line down his face from the sofa's piping. I touched it. 'You've got a furrow,' I said. He ran his fingers over the crease. He still looked tired, his eyes were pinkish and he was certainly no advert for the benefits of Florida. My only mental picture of Florida was rows of men and women of retirement age sitting in reclining chairs facing the sun, wearing oddly shaped straw hats and with paper shields over their noses. I think it was Miami and I think it came from a movie.

'So – how was Florida?' I asked, a little too heartily.

'Big and hot and humid,' he said. 'Quite wearing really. All right if you want to laze about on the beach or travel in air-conditioned limos but if you just want to walk to places or do some kind of sport it's – exacting. I liked it though.'

'Culture zero?'

He looked offended. 'Actually, no. We were at Lauderdale beach – just up from Fort Lauderdale – mainly art deco and with a full-scale imported twelfth-century Cistercian abbey church all of its very own.'

'You're kidding?' I felt so happy. If he'd been tramping around architectural sites and whatnot, he hadn't been clamped to the casino and the waiting arms of a blonde.

'Randolph Hearst brought it over – lock, stock – piece by piece – and then lost the numbering for the bits . . .' He began to laugh – same edge to it, I noticed. 'So when they finally reconstructed it about thirty years later they had a heap of the stones left over . . . Still – it looks good – if a little out of kilter with all the rest. Just not quite – true.' He gave me a look. 'Miami, by the by, is beautiful in a modern way – they know how to build high and build elegantly. Such is capitalism.' He said this last a little wistfully. I let it go. The dead hand of international financial collapse was fairly low on the list of current interests.

'Did you go to a casino?'

'Loads,' he said.

'Did you win?'

'Broke even.'

'Gamblers always say that. And what else?'

'Surfing. Eating a lot. Getting out what you call my antlers with Hugo and the rest. You know the sort of thing.'

'So you had a good time. I'm glad. Am I forgiven?'

He got up, holding his mug in a tightly clenched fist. He put his hand to his head which looked worryingly dramatic. The line of the sofa piping still there. 'For what?' he said.

'For not coming with you.'

He put his mug down on the small table and sat down again quickly, as if his knees had buckled. This was bad. He dropped backwards against the sofa cushions and then – most curiously – he laughed. Only this time it was a proper laugh. He still held his forehead but with his free hand he squeezed my knee and said, 'Forgiven? I think it's me who should be apologising to you. I should at least have rung.' He held his head again. 'Christ,' he said, 'but I don't half feel ill.'

'Is it the food? On the plane? Or have you caught something?' I was really anxious by now. His colour was definitely not right.

'I don't think so,' he said. 'It's much more likely to be –' He looked down at his feet, 'It's much more likely – oh God –' He winced again. 'It's definitely a hangover.'

A hangover? Robert? He was never a big drinker. He couldn't take too much and hated the aftermath of feeling ill. Two or three glasses of wine with a meal was his absolute limit and usually far less.

'It was tequila sunrises' fault,' he said.

My turn to laugh. 'Nice girl, not too bright. What did she do. Hold your nose and force you to drink?'

He dropped his head into his hands again and groaned.

Perhaps the blonde at the casino *was* called Tequila Sunrises?

'Oh God,' he said, 'I'm so glad to be home . . . I think I'll go and have a bath.'

And for the time being I had to be happy with that.

Later – when he'd bathed and shaved and put on fresh clothes and I'd unpacked his case – good wives unpack their husbands' cases – but I'd never been a good wife – I'd never done it in my life until now and now I knew why good wives unpacked their husbands' cases – it was so they could look for any clues of an untoward nature – Tequila's underwear or something unspeakable purchased at the chemist's of which I found none – well – he suggested we went out for an early supper. Just round the corner at Douro's. Portuguese – so much less common than Spanish went the family joke. At least I was spared the Italian which did a fine line in Venetian cuisine. I was beginning to think that I had more to hide than my pale, jaundiced husband.

I didn't know whether it was ominous or not, to be going out. I'd thought we'd stay in and I'd be an even better little wife and knock up a little something and salad – but Douro's it was. Douro's is quite dark, quite intimate and – at that time of the evening – quite empty. We'd never actually been to Portugal but we knew the menus pretty intimately – whenever one of our neighbours came back from their holiday they'd invite us and others round for an *authentic Portuguese meal* – which was invariably *feijoada* (bean stew), *acorda* (bread stew), or something flavoured with piri-piri. What we liked best were the sardines and the tuna dishes and that is what we usually ate at Douro's – only this time Robert ordered *cozido*, which is like cassoulet or *pot-au-feu*, saying that he needed something substantial.

He declined wine and ordered water instead. I did not decline wine. I thought I might need a little drop to get me through whatever it was he was going to explain. Let me tell you there is something shuddery about your husband of longevity saying he thinks he owes you an apology when he just might have been locked in the arms of a leggy blonde.

Bread was brought, with olives and my wine; his water arrived. Afonso, who brought it, enquired after our health and then departed, and we settled back in our chairs.

'So –' I said, 'Miami is beautiful? Really?'

'Parts of it are. I think you'd have liked some of it. Of course it's brash as well and a bit over the top and I suppose with the money crunch the lights will be going out there, too – but some of it – much of it – is great. The art deco stuff is amazing, there's a museum with a collection of Meissen you'd love, parks and waterways all over the place – we stayed near a place called the Venice of America – pretty little canals – all very picturesque – and not as trashy as you might think.'

I wasn't thinking trashy, I was avoiding thinking Venice, and instead thinking normal, this is all normal. 'Yes – well – I'm sorry I didn't go with you. I let you down and it was a pointless bit of pretentiousness, selfish and –'

But he was smiling at me in a kind of wonderment. 'You have no idea,' he said. 'None at all.'

This was true. At that precise moment I felt ill-prepared for anything.

'Well, bloody what then?' I said, quite aggressively.

'How much we *all* hated it. Not just me. Every single one of us.'

'Don't be silly. You didn't speak to me *once*. Just that message. If you're just trying to make me feel better then –'

'Not at all.'

'Then why did you all go?'

'Precisely. This is what we ended up asking ourselves. Why?'

I drank deep of the Vinho Verde. 'All these years? Or only because it was Florida?'

'There was nothing wrong with Florida – I told you,' he said, a little testily – sure sign he was still suffering – and he started moving the cutlery and wine glasses around on the table, as if he were arranging his thoughts. Finally he looked up from the acutely important decision about where to place the olive-oil bottle. 'So – we'd have been fine there if we hadn't all been competing with each other and worrying about Hugo's bloody points scheme and last one in's a dork and all that. And never mentioning that capitalism, the engine of our world, this world, was in major collapse. It wasn't great doing all that mad stuff when we were in our thirties – but now –'

'You can't claim the privileges of age and retain the playthings of childhood?'

'Exactly.'

'Dr Johnson.'

'He's right. It's a death wish. I've never seen so many fixed grimaces as we all tried to look as if our screaming muscles were fine, just fine. It would have been laughable if it hadn't been so sad. And I include myself in that . . . And the trouble was I suddenly saw it all through your eyes. I knew you were right. I should have phoned you and told you –'

'More to the point you should have phoned me *and* my mother –'

'Oh God, I know,' he said, and held his head again.

An anxious Afonso came over – sensing that Robert was suffering in some way – and asked if we wanted anything.

Robert patted his arm and smiled wanly. 'Not unless you can administer a quick rub-down with horse liniment.' Afonso shrugged and looked at me.

'We're fine,' I said. 'Unless . . .?' Robert shook his head. He still looked quite green. There was a strong smell of hot oil and garlic in the place, which might have accounted for it. Afonso backed away still looking perplexed.

Robert leaned back in his chair. 'It was Lorna who started it. On the last night. We were all sitting round the pool, lovely evening, drinks et cetera. Hugo had congratulated us all on everything, particularly James who'd sprained his ankle in the rowing competition – so he's in for a promotion then – and good old James gives a big smile and says, Not at all – to which Lorna suddenly said, because she remembered your ear, that she wondered how you were getting on without us all and whether you were coping OK and how miserable for you. And something clicked in me, thinking of you sitting around the house, all on your own, or maybe working with Brando, or in the garden pottering, seeing Toni for a pasta or curled up on the sofa watching something daft – any of those normal, ordinary things.'

My eyes did not waver. I thought about the day I got into a fight with a nun, the Campari evening, the Waverley night – and still my eyes did not waver. Just like a stopped clock is right twice a day, I thought, so somewhere in the world there is someone who considers stuff like that normal.

'I knew that you'd be fine and that I missed you and wished I was – well – just with you. You were on your own in our lovely house in its lovely neighbourhood while our lovely children were far away and out of our hair at last – all paid for by what I do day to day, not the kind of poncy, corporate rubbish I was doing. It was all so bloody bogus.

So I had another tequila sunrise or two and said it all. I just stood up and said that I wasn't going to do anything like this ever again, that I didn't see the point, that I hadn't enjoyed all the competitive stuff, that James was a twerp, that I didn't think it really proved anything, that you had spotted it first and that given the state of the world it was all bollocks.' This last was delivered with maximum intent and Afonso, who had been sidling up again, scuttled away. I gave him a little reassuring smile, more or less implying that my husband was having a turn. And resumed listening. It was hard to take it all in.

Robert was moving the cruet again. 'Then I said that I'd much rather be at home with my wife, or relaxing on the beach with her if I had to be here, or doing the whole tourist bit – you know, floating around on the Venice of America and poking around in the art galleries – seeing the place instead of wrecking myself for the next month pretending I was fit as a fucking stud.'

'Is there any other kind?'

'Huh?' He looked at me blankly, in no mood to be stopped by what I thought was quite a witty aside.

'Do you think you could lower your voice when it comes to the profanities? Afonso is breaking out in a sweat over there. Sorry to interrupt.'

He nodded and spoke more quietly. 'And I told them exactly why you hadn't come – that it was nothing to do with your ear –' He paused and some of the old Robert emerged as he asked sympathetically, 'How is your poor ear, by the way?'

'Functioning perfectly. Get on with it.'

'You hadn't come because you were far too sensible to pretend to like the whole thing and that I was going to be as honest as you in future – and that was that. No more Team

Building for me. Thanks. Or at least not that kind. And I had another drink – and another.'

'Blimey,' I said, impressed. 'What did Hugo say? Did he sack you there and then? And poor James and his injury. And Lorna? Did she throw her drink over you?'

He smiled. 'None of that,' he said. 'Because Lorna suddenly said, "Well, well – *at bloody last*," and ordered another couple of pitchers of drink, and then Polly piped up and said something about it all being a stupid charade and then James said that he thought so too, his ankle being an indicator of the kind of madness it all was – and before you knew it, everyone was laughing, drinking and saying it was all very stupid and how could we ever have been persuaded otherwise. A microcosm of the corporate world, Lorna said.'

'And Hugo?'

'Well, he stood there in his immaculate dinner-suited get-up – those end-of-the-pier-show clothes – looking like a pastiche out of a piss-taking movie – with the sky behind him full of stars and a big, white moon beaming down so that you expected him to say something along the lines of "The name's Bond" – and then he laughed, too.'

'He did?'

'He did.'

It was my turn to rearrange the condiments.

'And then the drinks arrived and we drank them. I went to my room and got a bit of sleep but I don't really remember very much detail after that. Except that on the plane back Hugo kept slapping me on the back and saying that I was quite right, that these bonding trips were a thing of the past, obviously, and this would be the last. That he took the point, took the point. God knows how we got on the plane with all that booze sloshing about – they probably thought that because we were business class we'd be elegant drunks. We just had to shut Hugo up until we were in the plane. He kept trying to make a speech until Lorna did that dog-warning voice of hers. I think he was slightly annoyed – embarrassed probably – but more, much more, he was relieved. So there you are. I told them, Truth Will Out. And I'm sorry, so sorry.' I was about to be humbly gracious when he added with a chuckle, 'Then we had a right old argument about where the saying comes from and that you'd know. I said it was probably the Bible.'

'It's Shakespeare,' I said.

'Which play?'

I could feel myself going pink. '*The Merchant of Venice*.'

'Oh, Venice,' he said, amused. 'Might have known.'

'Launcelot says it as part of his debate between corruption and the angel of conscience. "But at the length truth will out" – or something like that. More water? How was the stew?' But it didn't work.

'Polly thought it was Shakespeare but she couldn't place the play. Dear old Venice. You'd really like the Florida version. Maybe we should compare them one day.'

I rushed on before the truth overwhelmed me. 'He's also the one who says, "It's a wise father that knows his own child." Launcelot.'

He raised his glass of water to me. 'Are you trying to tell me something?'

'It's what I'm paid to know,' I said quickly. 'It's why Brando employs me. He even thought that Shylock was the –'

He looked at me in the same amused way he used to look at me when I first knew him. 'Was the what?'

'Doesn't matter.'

'So, am I forgiven?'

'You're a prat,' I said. 'There's been hell to pay.'

'I'll talk to your mother first thing tomorrow. And Tassie. I promised to call her. She made sure of that.'

'I'll bet she did.'

'And Johnno? I don't suppose . . .?'

I shook my head. At least that made us smile again.

'I kept thinking of you being here, being normal. I think I was jealous. I did think about coming back early.'

Good grief. Perhaps I did have a guardian angel. 'You're tired,' I said very quickly, and put up my hand to touch his face. He looked puzzled and then held my fingers and looked at them. 'What happened here?' he said. He was holding the hand that went into the lion's mouth; it still hurt and I winced. He examined the faded bruises and my damaged ring.

'It got stuck in a hole,' I said.

'It's a helluva mess. How?' He looked at me seriously.

'Nothing important. Just me thinking I could do something that I couldn't.' Still he looked at me. 'Forget it,' I said, 'for now.'

He shrugged, kissed the bruises and then examined the ring. 'We can probably get it fixed. Hurt much?' I watched his familiar fingers as they gently traced its shape, the purse of his lips as he did so. Any minute now and I'd be crying yet again.

'Not now it doesn't. Let's just eat up and go.'

When we arrived home I shovelled him up the stairs, tucked him into our bed and went back down thinking that lies had a nice, soft, protective quality and feeling more relief than I did after giving birth to both babies. In a way some battles had been won. I now understood my mother better, gave her some credit for being frail and human as well as bossy and opinionated, and I resolved to be kinder to her. I had given my daughter her boundaries, or rather my boundaries, and I would have given them to Johnno if I could locate him. It was about time. And I had been tumbled down the rocks by my best friend and lost her – but honourably; it didn't help much, the honourable bit, but at least I could hold my head up. Yet there was one great big fly in this smug little ointment pot. Venice. The Italian. What was I going to do about that little bit of deception? Forced errors in tennis, forced lies in politics; I revived my creeping sympathy for politicians.

Downstairs, in the light of one lamp, I listened to the clock ticking towards midnight and my husband's faintest of snores. Truth, it seemed to me, is sometimes best kept to yourself until you can make it worthwhile. Like those Venetians in their hanging baskets who exercised Truth without Power and made it into a futile thing. They were hardly a good advert for its happy joys. Maybe I felt better for my efforts but nobody else did. Not even Robert despite being free forever from those appalling Bonding Breaks. Whoever invented us as human beings gave us the power of judgement. Where truth is concerned, we should use it. Robert may have thought he had learned that truth is best, but my lesson had been quite the reverse.

For now I just wanted to get into bed beside my pale, tired, possibly still-pissed husband, and fall asleep with my head on his chest and wake up to find it was all just a dream.

Nineteen

Swacker: something huge; figuratively, A Big Lie.

Reverend Robert Forby's *Vocabulary of East Anglia*, 1830

IT TOOK ROBERT about twenty-four hours to get over his little problem with imminent liver failure. And then suddenly, like a small child after vomiting, he was completely better. It was Sunday. Outside our windows the sun shone anew and the few showers that April bestowed hardly made a mark. Everything was well in our world after all and we had made it through a dangerous journey. I'd been harnessed before too much damage could take place, and out in the garden, as I set the coffee down on the table and the birds trilled loud and the leaves rustled in their fresh greenness, well – it was near perfection.

The upstairs window sash opened and Robert, with the telephone to his ear, leaned out. 'Tass sends her love,' he said.

'Oh, I'll speak to her.' I ran towards the back door but Robert called again. 'No – she's on short rations with the phone and I can't call her back. Anyway, it doesn't matter, she'll be home next Saturday.'

'And Johnno?'

'The week after.'

'Oh good.'

'If he can find his ticket.'

'Normality returns,' I said.

'And now,' he said in a triumphant voice, 'I've arranged to take a few days off . . .' He tapped the side of his nose. I didn't think anything of it and began clipping at the mightily overgrown wisteria which should have been done in March. I was getting on top of things again, and I was happy – both children coming home, Robert here, no blondes in the casino, so he said, and the memory of that sultry hotel room buried and forgotten. Life was good. Clip, clip, clip, I went, innocent as you like.

Ten minutes later Robert bounded out of the kitchen into the garden like a boy of seventeen. He put his hands on my shoulders, kissed me on both cheeks and said, 'I'll do your mother later.'

'Yes, you might need to build up to that.' Clip, clip, clip.

'And you and I, dear wife, are going away. We're going to have a few days to ourselves before the travellers return.'

'Lovely,' I said, my mind still on the wanton greenery. Clip, clip, clip, I went. 'Where?'

'Venice,' he said, happily.

Clip, clip, clop.

'Venice, Florida?' I asked, smooth as I could. 'It'll be a bit of a rush.'

'No, we can do that another time – when we've got longer. No, this is Venice in *Italy*. Reprise the romance. It's years since we were there. I couldn't stop thinking about the real thing when I was in the Florida version. It reminded me of all sorts of things.'

I put the clippers down in case of an accident.

I went through everything I could. Pointed out that the children's rooms needed a clean – to which he – understandably given my – to put it kindly – impromptu approach to housework – looked deeply sceptical. To my suggestion that there might be an airline strike so that we

233

wouldn't be back for their arrival he said, very sensibly, that if there were an airline strike it would probably affect them, too, and they would also be late back. And I didn't have the heart to say, 'Not if it's only in Italy.' I ran my mind over the suggestion that my mother might get ill – but since she was as robust as a Second World War jeep (same vintage) this was pointless. I tried saying that Brando would need me, but Robert said he'd give him a ring, the old romantic. *Brando?* I found myself squeaking for the third time that week. On no account was Robert to speak to Brando.

'No – I'll do that.' And so I gave in.

'Do not, under any circumstances,' I later whispered down the phone to Brando, 'say anything to Robert about my coming to see you in Venice. Not ever.'

'Why?'

I told him.

Brando laughed. Oh, it was tremendous fun. He always said that old queens were good at spotting a weak spot and going for the jugular first. From a lifetime of practice in his case. But this time, not if I got to his jugular first. 'Well, why didn't you say that I was out here already?'

'Because I couldn't think straight. And it's a bit late to suddenly remember now.'

'That's true,' he said, and laughed even more enjoyably. The Brandos of this world. Such fun to be had with the rest of us. It probably keeps them alive.

'I'm warning you,' I said, 'please . . .'

'Well, what do we do when we meet in the piazza?'

'We look surprised.'

'I'm not very good at that,' he said.

'Brando, you know you can act anything.'

'And I thought you were speaking only truth?'

Oh, it was cruel, cruel.

234

'You are perfectly bloody good at it if you want to be. Now you're just turning the screw and behaving like a true harpy.'

'Thank you,' he said. 'A true one. Good. I take that as a compliment. Must have caught it from you. So – if we meet in the piazza you want me to blacken my soul by lying while you remain pearly white?'

'Will you please, please promise me that you will be surprised if we meet?'

'Well, I will, of course I will. But what if our Italian friend spots you? He's bound to be out and about.'

'What Italian friend?' I said coldly.

'Where are you staying?'

'Oh, I don't know. Robert's doing the booking.'

'Well, good luck,' he said, nose-punchingly amused. 'You'll need it.'

You see, it is no good saying that husbands, men in general, fall into the category of short-memoried unromantics. Men are the romantics and women the pragmatists. Women are quite good at playing the romantic role, but underneath they are merely the manoeuvrers of the male's romantic leanings towards things they want. It's called steering with a loose rein. This was corroborated when Robert said, with such joy I could have wept, that he had booked us into La Calcina. 'Scene of our earlier lusty triumphs,' he said happily. His look was questioning so I said, 'Oh, lovely.' Which I didn't think constituted deceit. Not really. But Aletheia was out there and mocking me. And I also realised, though I didn't want to, that this was the biggest test. This was the real test. This was when the truth was going to hurt like hell and yet it had to be told. Did it?

'You look a bit worried,' said Robert cheerfully. 'Hmm?'

'Difficult to work out what to pack. Given the time of year.'

'Oh, it'll be cool, being only April,' he said. 'You'll need a jumper or two.' I so nearly said that it was, actually, very warm there for the time of year and instead had to miserably watch him packing his North Face stuff and could say nothing, nothing.

It was bad enough arriving at the mouth of the lagoon and having to look awonder and agog as if I hadn't been there for years, but as we left the vaporetto and headed for the hotel I was seriously concerned. Even Robert, with all his triumphant bonhomie, looked anxiously at me.

'Are you OK?'

'Just a little –'

'I know,' he said, fortunately continuing the habit of lifetime and assuming he could read all my thoughts. 'It's all coming back. Where are those two young things now?' He looked about him as if remembering. I kept my eyes down – just in case the Italian appeared – and agreed that it certainly was all coming back to me.

And as we wheeled our cases over the rough stones, up and down little bridges and around the thronging tourists, my pleased-as-double-punch husband took my hand with his free one and squeezed it and said, 'You know, this is where all our ills began.'

That stopped me in my tracks. 'Meaning?'

'Well – it's a little-known fact, but this city is where banking credit first began in the West.' He looked at me, very pleased.

'Really? Amazing,' I said.

'Yes. Marco Polo brought it back here from China. The first credit in the West began in this beautiful place. Without the Venetians we'd never have thought of chequebooks. Astonishing, really.'

'Astonishing.'

'And if you think about it, it puts what's happening now in the right sort of perspective.'

'It certainly does,' I said, trying to avoid the image of a set of very white, smiling teeth.

'None of this would be here.' He extended his arm to indicate the canal, Redentore, Salute, the palaces lining the way. 'All of this came from banking and borrowing. So what survives here shows that we will survive there.'

I nodded and looked newly enlightened. 'It's all just lovely,' I said. 'Lovely.'

We trundled our cases up and down for a while and as we came near to the hotel, he stopped, looked about and said, 'Amazing that it's all still going on, just the same. It's like we've never been away. Isn't it?'

'Yes. Just the same. It certainly is.'

'And warmer than I expected.'

'She's a changeable lady,' I said. 'You never know what to expect.'

'True.'

When we got to La Calcina I waited for the first of many denials I might be forced to make – but the woman who ran it was Venetian to her chandelier drops. She never wavered as we checked in, she never indicated that I had only just checked out, and her smile of greeting stayed quite believably fixed as Robert said that we'd not been back for too many years to count – and that the place was wonderfully just the same – even the hotel – wasn't it, darling?

Darling muttered that it certainly was as we made it to our room. And then I remembered perfidious politicians. In this case Herr Hitler. He it was who said, and proved, *The bigger the lie the likelier it is to be believed*. How about: *The bigger the truth the likelier it is to sound false*? As Robert opened the windows to our balcony and stepped out and the hot, familiar breeze came floating around me as I lay on the bed, I said, 'It's the place for fantasies, Venice.'

Robert, leaning on the rail, looking down at the water and the craft going by, nodded. 'Yes. It's got a certain dreamlike quality.'

I slid down even further and lay there looking, I hoped, captivatingly abandoned. 'The last time I was here,' I said dreamily, 'I was visited by the incarnation of Casanova. He tried to seduce me but I didn't give in. I waited for you . . .'

Robert turned and smiled and shook his head. 'Daft thing,' he said. I opened my arms to him. 'That was good of you,' he said as he lay down beside me. 'To wait for me. Thanks.'

'Don't mention it,' I said as we began to undress each other.

Please.

Acknowledgements

Venice Observed, Mary McCarthy, Heinemann, 1961
Venice, Jan Morris, Faber & Faber, 1993
A Venetian Bestiary, Jan Morris, Faber & Faber, 2007
A History of Venice, John Julius Norwich, Vintage Books,
    1989
Gray Standen for her invaluable help with the Italian bits.

State of the Union

Douglas Kennedy

Hannah Buchan thinks herself ordinary. She is not the revolutionary child that her painter mother and famous radical father had hoped for. Raised in the creative chaos of 1960s America, Hannah vows to reject her parents' liberal lifestyle, and settles instead for typical family life in a nondescript corner of Maine.

But normality isn't quite what Hannah imagined it would to be, and try as she might to fight it, the urge to rebel against the things that hem her in grows ever stronger. Eventually, a series of encounters puts Hannah in an exhilarating but dangerous position – one in which she never thought she would find herself.

For decades, this one transgression in an otherwise faultless life lies buried deep in the past, all but forgotten – until a turn of fate brings it crashing back into the limelight. As her secret emerges, Hannah's life goes into freefall and she is left struggling against the force of the past.

State of the Union is a stunning and grippingly honest story about life, love and family, set against the backdrop of two different but strikingly similar eras.

'The story is sit-up-until-3am readable, the wide-ranging cast of highly individual characters is beautifully handled.' *Sunday Times*

'Kennedy is a complete genius when it comes to understanding the minds of stylish but troubled women. What's more, he does so enthrallingly and movingly.' *Daily Mirror*

arrow books

ALSO AVAILABLE IN ARROW

The Pursuit of Happiness

Douglas Kennedy

New York, 1945 – Sara Smythe, a young, beautiful and intelligent woman, ready to make her own way in the big city attends her brother's Thanksgiving Eve party. As the party gets into full swing, in walks Jack Malone, a US Army journalist back from a defeated Germany and a man unlike any Sara has ever met before – one who is destined to change Sara's future for ever.

But finding love isn't the same as finding happiness – as Sara and Jack soon find out. In post-war America chance meetings aren't always as they seem, and people's choices can often have profound repercussions. Sara and Jack find they are subject to forces beyond their control and that their destinies are formed by more than just circumstance. In this world of intrigue and emotional conflict, Sara must fight to survive – against Jack, as much as for him.

A mesmerising tale of longing and betrayal, *The Pursuit of Happiness* is a great tragic love story; a tale of divided loyalties, decisive moral choices, and the random workings of destiny.

'Kennedy cannot help but write grippingly, and he weaves threads of love and betrayal into a thrillingly masterful ending'
Observer

arrow books

ALSO AVAILABLE IN ARROW

The Truth About Melody Browne

Lisa Jewell

From the *Sunday Times* bestselling author of *Ralph's Party*.

When she was nine years old, Melody Browne's house burned down, taking every toy, every photograph, every item of clothing with it. But more than that – Melody Browne can remember nothing before her ninth birthday. Now in her early thirties, Melody lives in London with her seventeen-year-old son. She's made a good life for herself and her son and she likes it that way.

Until one night whilst attending a hypnotist show with her first date in years she faints – and when she comes round she starts to remember. Slowly, day by day, Melody begins to piece together the real story of her childhood. But with every mystery she solves another one materialises, with every question she answers another appears. And Melody begins to wonder if she'll ever know the truth about her past . . .

Praise for *The Truth About Melody Browne*

'A touching, insightful and gripping story which I simply couldn't put down.' Sophie Kinsella

'Stunning.' *heat* 5 stars

'Classic storytelling' *Elle*

arrow books

FIREFLY SUMMER

Maeve Binchy

Kate and John Ryan are happy in Mountfern, a peaceful and friendly village, and, for their four young children, an unchanging backdrop to a golden childhood. The summers are long and hot, and the twins Michael and Dara, and their siblings Eddie and Declan have, in the ivy-clad ruins of Fernscourt, the once-grand house on the bank of the river burned down during the Troubles, a place to play like no other.

Then Patrick O'Neill, an Irish American with a great deal of money in his pocket, buys the ruins of Fernscourt. No-one in Mountfern could have guessed what Patrick's dream would mean for their small village, and it's not until the very end of this tale of love won and lost that Patrick O'Neill himself will understand the irony and significance of his grand dream for Fernscourt . . .

'Warm, humorous, sad and happy. Reading it is a joy'
Irish Independent

'An adept storyteller with a sharp eye for social nuances and a pleasing affection for her characters'
Sunday Times

'Warm, witty and with a deep understanding of what makes us tick, it's little wonder that Maeve Binchy's bewitching stories have become world beaters'
OK Magazine

arrow books

ECHOES

Maeve Binchy

Growing up in a seaside town, Clare O'Brien and David Power shout their hearts' desires into the echo cave, praying that their destiny will lead them far away from Castlebay, the small town in which they live.

Years later, in Dublin, their paths cross again – David, following in his father's footsteps, is studying medicine, and Clare has won a scholarship to University College.

But eventually Castlebay draws them back – and it is against a backdrop of empty grey skies, sea-spray and wind that this drama of ambition, betrayal and love finally reaches its turbulent conclusion . . .

'A powerful story of love and jealously'
Sunday Telegraph

'Compuslive reading . . . Ms Binchy has the true storyteller's knack'
Observer

'Binchy's novels are never less than entertaining. They are, without exception, repositories of common sense and good humour . . . chronicled with tenderness and wit'
Sunday Times

arrow books